The Domino Masters of Demerara

Khalil Rahman Ali

HANSIB

First published in 2015
by Hansib Publications Limited

P.O. Box 226, Hertford, Hertfordshire, SG14 3WY
United Kingdom

info@hansibpublications.com
www.hansibpublications.com

ISBN 978-1-910553-07-7

A CIP catalogue record for this book
is available from the British Library

Production by Hansib Publications Limited
Printed and bound in Great Britain

To my wonderful wife Manjeet, our beautiful daughter Sonya, and all of our relations and friends. To all the readers of my work. To all fellow Guyanese.

To beautiful Guyana, the land of many waters, with One People, One Nation, and One Destiny.

To all peoples of the world who have had to leave their homelands to seek betterment elsewhere.

Preface

The board game of Dominoes is immensely popular in Guyana, the Caribbean, the Americas, and amongst ex-patriots living in the United Kingdom, United States of America, and Canada. It is normally played by three or four people in a very fast way, with much enthusiasm, and aggression. There are club, district wide, national, and international competitions which evoke significant rivalries amongst the players, teams, and supporters.

The Domino Masters of Demerara is about one such rivalry involving players of three villages on the West Coast of Demerara, Guyana, South America. The three teams had reached a point where they had to play a final and deciding game of the local competition, which was left unfinished, due to an electrical power failure.

It was the 6th of August 1985, and Guyana was still in the throes of a challenging economic downturn, continuing migration to the USA, Canada, the UK, and other islands of the Caribbean, inter-racial tension, and political instability.

Despite this difficult situation faced by the Guyanese people of African, Indian, Chinese, Portuguese, and Amerindian heritage, they used their fighting spirit, humour, hospitality, and survival instincts in their efforts to overcome their problems.

The final game of Dominoes is played out over an unusually long period, which allows Michael "Histry Maan" Brown, the self-appointed coach of the Anna Catherina ACES team, sufficient time to use his knowledge of Guyana's historical and other events, to influence the tactics and moves made by Vishnu "Double Six" Prashad, the Captain of the ACES.

The Domino Masters of Demerara sheds light on how the villagers view their situation, share a desire for greater tolerance, unity, and support for each other, and, a belief in the vision of a Guyana of One People, One Nation, and One Destiny.

Will Michael, Vishnu, and their friends succeed in their quest for victory as the Dominoes champions? Were they only just interested in the game? Was there some other purpose?

Contents

I.

Double Six

"Double Six!" shouted Vishnu Prashad, the captain of the Anna Catherina Dominoes Team called "The ACES", as he slammed the first domino onto the sturdy wooden table. The seven dominoes remaining from the pack of twenty eight, shuddered from the vibration, but remained face down.

Vishnu's two other opponents in the final game of a very closely contested championship match of Dominoes between teams from the three neighbouring villages of Leonora, Anna Catherina, and Cornelia Ida, on the West Coast of Demerara, Guyana, South America, stared at him with deep suspicion. They knew that Vishnu, whose nickname or "call name" was "Double Six", had an uncanny knack of picking out this, the highest value domino, regardless of who shuffled the pack with all the numbers facing down.

The referee for the contest had tried to conceal all the dominoes by moving them around with the palms of his hands as swiftly as he could. But once Vishnu's sharp brown eyes had locked onto his favourite domino, no amount of cover or artistry in the shuffle could deter his gaze. Then, as the referee allowed the three players to choose their seven dominoes each, Vishnu knew exactly where to locate the Double Six.

He sat upright on the well-carved wooden chair made from the local mahogany wood, and with the stealth and swiftness of the jaguar's attacking instinct, he pounced on his prize. He then quickly gathered up the six other dominoes he needed for his set.

Vishnu "Double Six" Prashad was of Indian heritage, dark brown in complexion, very slim, and about five feet and nine inches tall. He was wearing a light blue short-sleeved cotton shirt which was tucked into a pair of khaki trousers held together by a narrow black leather belt. He loved wearing white yachting shoes which he always kept in tip top condition. Normally, he appeared a few years younger than his age of forty five. But as captain, he always seemed to frown a lot as he took his responsibility very seriously. He had earned this recognition through several years of greater success than failure at Dominoes. He was also an accomplished card player, and claimed to be a good student of any games or sports he played, always willing to listen, and to learn from others.

Afzal "Mule" Amin, the captain of the Leonora team called "The LIONS", was also of Indian descent, and an imposing figure of about six feet tall, with large hands. He tried to draw his seven dominoes from the area that Vishnu targeted, but failed to intercept or block his opponent's reach for the Double Six.

Afzal was forty six years old, and wore a red tee shirt which seemed to be under great pressure from his powerful, and muscular upper chest. The sleeveless tee shirt allowed his large and well-defined biceps to be displayed for all to see, and admire. He wore a pair of blue denim shorts to emphasise, and show off his bulky thighs and calves. He prided himself as being one of the strongest men across the whole of the twenty miles wide West Coast of Demerara.

He would often walk with a deliberate swagger, pushing out his large chest, and smiling at all his admiring onlookers on either side of the wide tarmacked main road that passed through all the villages. Young men and children would often walk up to him, admire his muscle-bound frame, and try to pose like their hero, even though most of them were scrawny, or, in some cases, very overweight. Afzal preferred to wear smart, modern, designer label sneakers specially obtained from his relations in the United States of America.

The audience of about sixty very excited and partisan supporters of the three teams, stood in awe as they also knew of Vishnu's trick. They had been warned by the referee, who was an African Guyanese gentleman from Hague village which was next to Cornelia Ida, and which was not connected with the finalists, to remain silent throughout the most important game that would decide the champion team, and village, for the entire region of the West Coast of Demerara.

This deciding game was specially re-convened from the official finals day of the preceding Sunday which had over-run, and had to be stopped due to darkness caused by a disruptive, and irritating power cut. The village hall which was located in Anna Catherina, and owned by Arthur Ching, a member and vice captain of the ACES team, did not have a reserve electric generator, and thus the tournament was left undecided.

Arthur Ching was a forty years old Chinese businessman, and about five feet and ten inches tall. His height and weight caused him to stand out amongst other Chinese in the district. He was an affable man who was very popular amongst the villagers, and always wore a gentle smile, which caused his small eyes to almost shut. He loved to wear very brightly coloured short-sleeved cotton shirts, khaki shorts, and loose-fitting brown leather sandals.

Peter "Smokey" Ramdin, of mixed African and Indian heritage, was the third competitor, and captain of the Cornelia Ida team called the "COBRAS". He was about forty five years old, dark brown, slim, and about five feet and six inches tall. He was also a very friendly man who was extremely popular in all the villages. His very toothsome smile would always light up any room.

The blackout had created great tension amongst the supporters of each team over the following two days to Tuesday, the 6th of August, 1985. The final showdown was the main point of conversations and argument within any gathering of two or more residents of the three villages. Small bets were waged as to which of the three captains would finally prevail in the deciding game.

At one such gathering, in the beer garden called "The Happening", located in the middle of the one mile wide village of Anna Catherina, and directly opposite the imposing wooden Monarch Cinema, Michael "Histry Maan" Brown, the forty-nine years old African Guyanese sugar factory worker, and self-appointed advisor and member of the ACES, held court with all the five other members of the team.

Michael "Histry Maan" Brown was not a formally educated man, but had developed a keen interest in all matters concerning the history of his beloved Guyana. He was about six feet tall, slim and sinewy, and with a gaunt look which he accentuated to emphasise how seriously he took his knowledge, and his assumed authority. He wore a pair of ill-fitting spectacles just over the tip of his straight long nose. He was very proud to present the image of someone who was professorial, and thus demanded unquestionable respect and attention.

Michael had called the meeting to discuss tactics for the final game which became the most critical that the ACES team had ever encountered in their history. The meeting place was normally very busy with customers stopping by to have a few of the local beers or strong spirits along with their snacks or full meals, before either going across the road to see a movie at the grand old cinema, or, continuing on their journey. It was Monday afternoon, just after lunchtime, and the start of the one o'clock movie slot. It was also blisteringly hot, and heat waves could be seen just above the black shining tarmac of the main road. There was a very slight hint of dry air which was not enough to reduce the impact of the humidity, as the tide of the Atlantic Ocean which was only about four hundred yards away, was out.

Traffic on the main road was quite busy with hire cars, lorries, donkey or horse-drawn carts, motor bikes, and bicycles, moving in both directions. There was a three feet wide dusty pathway at each side of the tarmac with just about enough room for pedestrians to avoid being hit by vehicles, or falling into the generally untidy drains. Occasionally, cattle, horses, donkeys, sheep, goats, and stray dogs would wander onto the road, causing frantic manoeuvres by drivers or cyclists to avoid hitting them. People took their lives into their hands as they tried to walk or run across the road from one side to the next, and often, if this was not well executed, drivers would brake hard, and blow their horns two or three times to get their message across. Many of the annoyed drivers would also shout insults at such pedestrians.

In the midst of this busy roadway, some boys of about ten to twelve years old set about a game of marbles by a clearing alongside one of the kerbs. Pedestrians tried their best to avoid walking over the three holes which were about six feet apart, and which were used as the target for rolling their marbles into, as the game progressed. The loser of the game was expected to stoop over one of the holes, and the winner would flick their small steel marbles onto their bare knuckles, causing grievous pain on the victims.

Michael placed himself at the head of the wooden table, adjusted his old spectacles, and peered over the rim, trying to catch the eyes of Vishnu, and then the others.

He said, "Gentlemen, before we discuss the final game, I think that we have to understand why we did not win the championship well before we reached this situation."

Arthur Ching, known fondly as "Speedy", leaned slowly forward, and said, "I think that we lost our way when you Michael, the "Histry Maan", lost both of your games to Peter Ramdin. He lived up to his name "Smokey" when he blew you, and the Leonora player off the table."

Michael was visibly shaken by the retort, and tried to compose himself. He picked up his open bottle of Banks Beer, lifted his spectacles to rest just above his forehead, and took a drink.

He licked his lips, and said, "Ah, I love this beer when it is very cold. Arthur, we know you as "Speedy", not because of your speed of thought, your sharpness of wit, or your decisiveness of play, but because of your slumbering nature. You were the one who was spending too much time trying to convince everyone that you were cleverly reading the play like a true Chinese Grand Master of Dominoes. But you were our biggest loser on the day!"

Arthur reached out, and took a piece of fried chicken from the platter that they shared. He dipped it into the saucer containing the hottest pepper sauce, which was an eye-watering blend of *scotch bonnet* and *wiri-wiri* peppers. He took too much sauce, and as soon as he bit into the succulent meat he had to gulp down some ice cold water to ease the blistering sensation in his mouth, and on his lips. His fair cheeks became reddened almost immediately.

He choked, and said as he opened his blood red eyes, "Michael, you always have a nice way of using words to insult your friends. God help us all when you decide to attack your enemies. But the truth is that you think you are so clever, can quote history, and yet you are not very good at playing this game. You did not win all of your games, and that is a historical fact. Another historical fact is that my Chinese ancestors were the ones who invented Dominoes way back in the twelfth century. I bet that you did not know about this bit of history!"

Carlos "Reds" D'Souza poured a shot of the golden XM Rum into his personal glass tumbler, and rocked back as he drank it straight without mixing it with water or soda.

He said, "Oh man! The taste of the true gold of our beautiful Guyana! I am so proud of my Portuguese ancestors from Funchal in the glorious island of Madeira, for discovering the secret of such rum. Gentlemen, we should have all had a couple of shots of this true energy-giver before we played in the championship. That is what I did, and that is why I won all of my games. I repeat, all of my games!"

Carlos, although of Portuguese extraction, had a dark red complexion on his moustachioed face, a thick neck, and, hairy arms and hands. He was about forty-four years old, of stocky build, and the shortest of his teammates. He was called "Reds" by everyone who knew him in the district, and would always take delight in reminding people of his fair European heritage, by unbuttoning his cotton shirt to expose his pale chest, and pointing to it saying, "I am not a red man, I am white!"

Carlos took another shot of his favourite tipple. John "Black Buck" Charles smiled, and reached for his pouch containing a small bottle referred to as a *flattie*. He discretely uncorked it, and drank a mouthful in one gulp.

He said, "Well my friends, this "*Bush Rum*" is by far the best thing we have in Guyana. One shot of this can put anyone of you to sleep."

Arthur smiled, and asked, "Is that why you nearly fell asleep in the middle of that game we had to win to level up the tournament?"

John said, "Aha! You all think that I am a stupid Half-Amerindian, but I know my limit with alcohol, unlike you people. You talk too much, you drink too much, and when it comes to winning, you do not know what to do. I won that last game when I noticed that my two opponents were trying too hard to put too much pressure on each other. I waited patiently. I watched every move, and stood still and calm. Then, as soon as the opportunity came, I closed both ends of the game, and won it with my favourite "Double Blank" domino."

Michael said, "There you are! We all need to be patient, and not to rush into things. We must observe the situation closely. Look at what our opponents are up to. Then, strike decisively. This is true for all Guyanese people. We want everything here and now, and if possible, for free. But we must work hard, take our time, and then make the right move."

Arthur said, "Here we go again. Our Histry Maan is giving us a lecture only after copying what he just heard from John."

Nazir "Snake Eyes" Khan broke his unusual silence, and said, "Leave the Histry Maan alone. He is only trying to help us to think about what Double Six has to do in that final game. We need to make Double Six feel strong, fit, and ready mentally for tomorrow. And one thing he should not do is to drink any alcohol. In fact, we should be playing some practice games with him now, to help him sharpen up, try out his tactics, and then let him go home to have a good rest."

He calmly raised his glass of *mauby*, and asked his friends at the table to "Raise your glasses to victory!"

They all shouted "Cheers to victory for the ACES!"

Nazir, at thirty five years old, was the youngest of the ACES team. He was of Indian heritage, of light brown complexion, five feet seven inches tall, slightly overweight, and with eyes that were unusually green. He was fond of wearing green shirts, blue jeans, and white sneakers.

He stared at Vishnu, and said, "Now captain Vishnu, what do you have to say?"

Vishnu picked up a piece of deep fried *banga mary* fish that was on a plate beside the platter of fried chicken. He slowly chewed the fish as the others looked towards him in silence.

He swallowed his mouthful, wiped his closed mouth with his right hand, and said, "You see my friends, just how lucky we are in Guyana? Here we are on a Monday afternoon, discussing a game of Dominoes as if this is the most important thing in our lives. We should all be at work trying to earn our living, and thus help our poor country to come out of the difficult situation we have."

Michael interrupted Vishnu, and said, "Double Six, you are right. But we have to sort out this final game first, and then when we win we will have all the time in the world to discuss Guyana's economy and politics. But since you raised the subject, I have to say that this beautiful country of ours has had nearly twenty years of disaster after disaster. We continue to suffer with shortages of everything. Things like *channa*, *daal*, sardines, apples, grapes, cooking oil, flour..."

Just then the fluorescent lights in the cosy bar went out, and John said, "Electricity! The only things we are never short of are power and water cuts!"

They all broke out into laughter as the manager and owner of "The Happening", reached over to switch on his emergency generator to quickly re-instate the electric lights.

Michael said, "There, you see how we Guyanese can change anything if we want to, at the touch of a switch!" He looked behind and around him, leaned forward, and winked at his team members.

Vishnu said, "Yes, everything, except this government."

Nazir said, "We do not have to change the government. You know our saying "The stricter the government, the wiser the population". This is how we have been surviving all the restrictions since the late 1960s, and the start of the "Buy Local" policies."

Arthur said, "Yes, our President has been right to try to make us all use what we have here in Guyana, and to stop depending on so many expensive goods from overseas. I agree that the policies caused a lot of businesses to suffer, and people just left the country, and ran away from the problems."

Michael fixed his spectacles over the tip of his nose, and said, "I agree with Arthur. Yes, our President has the right ideas, but unfortunately we Guyanese do not like to be dictated to. Since the banning of goods took place, we have managed to find new ways to replace most of the things we could not get anymore. But I never agreed with the alternatives for some of the most delicious foods we all grew up with. You can never replace *channa* and *daal* with green peas and black-eyed beans."

Carlos said, "We know how smart Guyanese people are. As one group of business people suffered, another emerged. Do you remember how we all suddenly became hucksters and hustlers travelling to the Courantyne, to Surinam, and even islands like Trinidad and Barbados, to do trading? Most of us would never have left this country to go anywhere else but England or America. We have become much stronger because we had to get off our asses, and do something."

Nazir shifted uneasily, and said, "Yes, and some people ended up in jail for smuggling contraband goods!"

John said, "Correct! We know just where you picked up the name "Snake Eyes". It was when you came back from the first six months jail sentence you served back in 1970."

Vishnu said, "Whatever we say, and whichever government is in charge, we just cannot hope to build this country on small enterprises alone. We need much more investment in building strong foundations like transport, schools, hospitals, roads, and always have reliable supplies of clean water and power."

Michael said, "I agree with all of this, but the one ingredient that is missing here, is our unity. We as Guyanese people have to stop bickering, bad-mouthing, and blaming one side and the other. We must try to build the kind of unity and spirit we have here in our Dominoes team. We are the ACES because we are all Domino Masters, and can work together towards a great victory!"

John said, "True again my friends. But someone has to remind our politicians about such a simple fact. Will they ever listen to us?"

Vishnu took another piece of the delicious fried fish, and dipped it into the pepper sauce. He calmly ate it, and smiled at Arthur. He said,

"You see gentlemen, I can quite easily handle any challenge. The more this pepper is hot, the more I love it. I know just how I will handle that game tomorrow. I will be cool under pressure. All I need is for you all to place greater confidence in me as your captain, and everything will work out right for us as a team, a village, and, who knows, as a country!"

Michael leaned forward, and whispered to Vishnu, "All I want you to do tomorrow is to deliberately slow down the game, listen to my conversations between every move, and play accordingly. There is no need for tomorrow's game to be played in the usual fast way, as it is the final and most important game of the championship."

They all applauded, and proceeded to have their drinks, and the remainder of the snacks.

When Vishnu eased back in his chair at the game after landing the Double Six, he avoided the stares of Afzal sitting to his left, and Peter, sitting on his right. The next play, moving in a clockwise direction, was to be made by Afzal, then Peter, and back to Vishnu.

Afzal flexed his bulky chest and arms as if he was preparing to control the mules belonging to the Leonora Sugar Estate. His job of minding the six mules was unique, and began when they were retired, and replaced by tractors, to pull the punts with the cut sugarcane from the fields, along the canals, to the weighing site of the factory.

Every year, when there was the local sports day at the Leonora Park Cricket Ground, a special race track was cut out at the unused land beyond the northern end of the cricket field. The mule race was a special treat for the spectators, and Afzal's mastery in controlling the six large animals, was a spectacle in its own right. The mules responded to every command by their keeper, and were soon ready for the race. This began with the official starter firing his pistol raised high above his head. The starter then made a frantic dash to get well out of the way of the galloping giants, much to the delight of the spectators. Other events on the day were the "Greasy Pole" climb, and the "Catch the Greasy Pig" race.

The greasy pole was a metal pipe of about twenty feet long and four inches in diameter. It was covered in black grease and placed over the trench that flowed on the right hand side of the cricket ground. The competitors had to climb along the pole, and grab a prize which was firmly tied at the end of it, and dangling high above the slow moving murky water of the trench. The crowd was well entertained as each competitor tried their utmost to crawl along the pole. They quickly lost their tenuous grip, and plunged into the trench. Eventually, as further attempts were made, and much of the grease also slid off the pole, one determined climber would succeed in reaching the end. The winner would grab the prize, and much to the delight of the hundreds of spectators, dive into the trench whilst holding the prize aloft.

The greasy pig race consisted of a continuously squealing specimen which was covered liberally with black grease. The pig would be given a fifty yards start to run for its freedom. The chasers made their mad dash to try to catch the pig with their bare hands, and failed time and again. The pig would scamper amongst the spectators in its frenzied effort to escape the clutches of the diving chasers. This caused much mayhem amongst the spectators as they tried to avoid being soiled by the animal. The eventual winner would successfully catch, and hold aloft the screaming pig as the prize.

Peter glanced at Afzal, and then fixed a gaze at Vishnu who bowed his head, and avoided eye contact with his rivals. The players were not allowed to speak to each other, and the spectators were encouraged by the referee, to remain as silent as possible.

Michael turned to Arthur who was standing next to him, and he whispered to his friend. "The Double Six is the best domino to draw in the game, simply because it has to be played before any other, and also, this means that Vishnu has already gotten rid of one of his seven dominoes. Besides, the number sixty-six is very significant in our history. On the 26th of May in the year 1966, we became an Independent Nation. It was the birth of Guyana. We were not British Guiana anymore. We were free!"

Some of the spectators overheard Michael's whispering, and stared at him in a way to urge him to be quiet. He ignored them, and continued to provide Arthur with more of his historical knowledge.

He said, "You see, our President was then the Premier, and then he became the Prime Minister on that fateful day."

Arthur brushed Michael aside, and said, "I know all about this. What has this got to do with this game of Dominoes? Please keep quiet, and watch our own leader and master of Dominoes at work."

The referee turned around momentarily, and felt pleased that Arthur had helped him to retain silence amongst the spectators. He quickly re-focused on the game, and awaited Afzal's play.

Carlos winked at Michael, and whispered, "So, we became independent from our British masters, only to go on to fight amongst ourselves?"

Michael smiled, and said, "This battlefield is full of brothers, close relations and friends from our three villages. Sometimes I agonise about why we must do such battles against each other. What benefit can we gain from humbling others?"

Nazir said, "Yes, let us prepare to watch our leader do battle, and not spare his opponents. I only wish to celebrate an ACES victory. I do not care about the losers."

* * *

Ramesh Prashad, the nineteen year old only son and child of Vishnu and Parvati, glanced at his wristwatch, scanned the room briefly, and after staring at his father, quietly slipped out onto the roadside. He mounted his 250cc Kawasaki motorcycle, and roared off eastwards in the direction of Cornelia Ida.

Michael looked at Vishnu, and caught him smiling with some pride. He said, "My friends, there goes our ACES captain's dashing chip off the old block! Young Ramesh was born in May 1966, and is a greater gift to Vishnu and Parvati than our country's Independence!"

Nazir smiled, and said, "That young man must have many more important things to do, than to stand around here to witness this game."

Carlos nodded, and said, "Hmm, I wonder what he is up to now."

2.

All tied up

Afzal "Mule" Amin looked up slowly, casting a stern gaze on Vishnu "Double Six" Prashad, and Peter "Smokey" Ramdin, in an effort to intimidate his opponents. Then he looked at the five dominoes he had carefully organised in his left hand, with the remaining two held together by the fingertips of his right hand. It was common for players to gather up the dominoes which were with the most suites from sixes, fives, fours, threes, twos, through to ones or aces, and zeros or blanks. Normally, the majority of like numbers were held in one hand.

The set of dominoes used for this final game, was owned by Arthur. It was a special collector's item, and each domino was made of ivory coloured bone, with a brass strip running across the middle of the underside. The thin brass strip allowed the dominoes to be shuffled vigorously without causing the painted numbers to be erased. The back of each domino had a similar design of the maker's emblem. The referee had taken great care to examine each domino to ensure that it was in a perfect, unmarked condition, and was not tampered with in any way.

Afzal carefully selected the Six Blank from his left hand set, and placed it quietly and confidently against the Double Six. Vishnu and Peter looked at Afzal's left hand which concealed his majority dominoes, and this set them thinking about how many Sixes or Blanks he held.

Michael "Histry Maan" Brown could not resist offering comment on the play. He turned to Carlos "Reds" D'Souza, and whispered, "Now, the Mule is showing that he has many Sixes in his hand, and maybe, more Blanks."

Carlos shook his head, and said, "No. I think that he does not have many Sixes, and is trying to bluff Peter."

Michael then whispered. "Well, whatever the tactics, the Six Blank brings back very fond memories for me, and my lovely wife, Doreen.

It was in 1960, when we were all in our early twenties, and we used to go to the brown sandy beach by the seawall in the village, to do some wrestling, and other exercises."

Carlos kissed his teeth, and said, "Histry Maan, you were useless at both wrestling and running. I remember that on one Sunday afternoon at our local beach, you decided to show off your new flowery underpants to some young ladies who were strolling along on top of the seawall, and minding their own business. When you were limbering up you looked like a skeleton being worked by a puppeteer!"

Arthur "Speedy" Ching giggled, and said, "Yes, you loved to show off. And when the girls started to laugh at you in those very strange underpants, you decided to go for a long run on the sand. You ran off too fast, and in a very short time, you collapsed as if you had a heart attack."

Carlos could not restrain himself from laughing, and said, "By the time we all caught up with you, it quickly dawned on us that you were in really grave trouble. You were lying on your back with your big eyes wide open, and frothing at the mouth."

Michael said quietly, "But my Doreen Smith came to me, and kissed me full on the mouth. It was like being in heaven!"

Arthur said, "No way! You were on your way to hell, and that poor girl who happened to be a trained nurse, gave you the kiss of life treatment, and managed to revive you. She even had to pull up your flowery shorts which had slipped down from your waist, and exposed your private parts. You were not a sight for sore eyes! And, you were too confused to remember anything."

The referee turned to the three ACES team-mates, and reminded them to observe silence during the tense game. He looked at Peter who was in deep thought contemplating his first move, using as much time as possible for this final battle of the captains. It was clear that the pace of the game was being deliberately slowed down by the players as opposed to the normally very frantic, rapid, and excitable play with each opponent slamming down their domino to emphasise how strong their move was.

Michael continued to use the long gaps in play, to have his say, "You both know that my Doreen could not resist chasing after me from the moment she kissed me on that beach. We met again in this same hall at the Saturday Night Dances we used to have here."

Carlos smiled, and said, "Here you go again. It was you who was chasing that poor girl. You were always ignored by all the girls on the dance floor, because you had the most stupid looking dance moves which made most of us just laugh. None of the girls, including Doreen, wanted to be seen dancing with you. Worse still, you used to mime the words of the songs as your body, your legs, and arms were moving as if they were completely out of rhythm and control."

Michael said, "Yes, but who had the last laugh? True love has nothing to do with what you wear, and how you move. It is about the mind. I know that I stopped going to school, and took up my apprentice work at the Sugar Factory. But although I do not have qualifications, I know about the facts of life. I charmed her with my knowledge, and she finally fell for me."

The audience began to express their impatience with Peter Ramdin's slow play, and the fans of the ACES and LIONS started to offer advice, and to chide him to make his move. The referee called for silence.

Arthur said, "Michael, if Peter wants to spend time to concentrate on his next move, let him do so. He also knows just how important this final game is for all the people of Cornelia Ida. The same applies to our Vishnu, and, the captain of Leonora"

Nazir turned to Michael and Arthur, and said, "You are both talking nonsense. This is a simple game. Any fool can just find a domino to match what is on the table in front of him. If he cannot do so, then he has to do a "*rap*". The more these three think about the game, the more they will make mistakes. I wish that they just play as quickly as possible, and get to the end. We all have better things to do than to stand around here, and witness this performance."

John said, "No wonder young Ramesh could not wait to get away from this place."

Carlos said, "Now, now gentlemen! This is not just any old game. It is a matter of great importance for all the people in these three villages. We love the competition. We love the passion, the rivalry, and the spirit of our willingness to fight!"

Michael said, "Yes, I do not mind the rivalry, but as long as we remain respectful to each other at the end of the game, then it would have meant something. As the English would say, "It's not the winning that counts; it's the way we play the game"."

John said, "No wonder the English can never win at anything!"

Peter "Smokey" Ramdin was noted for his slow approach to Dominoes, as well as at *Cricket*. He was in his mid-forties, and during his earlier cricketing years, he was a classical right-handed *batsman* who modelled himself upon the great, legendary master batsman from Port Mourant, Berbice, Guyana, by the name of Rohan Kanhai.

The difference between Peter and his hero was that he was much more defensive, occupying the *batting crease* almost selfishly, taking his time to slowly accumulate his *runs*. Rohan Kanhai was an exciting batsman who *scored* very quickly. Despite this clear difference in approach, Peter's team-mates from the Cornelia Ida Cricket team, appreciated his consistency, and his knack of *scoring* the bulk of the team's runs. He became known as "Smokey" on account of his mixed-race, and he was extremely popular in his village and across the West Coast of Demerara, not only for his Cricket, but for his stylish Indian dancing, and beautiful singing of *Hindi* songs from the Indian films, despite not knowing the Hindi language.

Peter loved to talk about Cricket, and was like his fellow countrymen, quite passionate about the game. He studied the records, read countless Cricket books, and listened to the Radio commentaries on the game. He could recount almost every key moment in the famous Cricket *Test Match* between the West Indies and Australia which took place at the Wooloongabba "The Gabba", in Brisbane, Australia, from the 9th to the 14th of December 1960.

The West Indies Cricket team was made up of the best players principally from Guyana, and the Caribbean Islands of Barbados, Jamaica and Trinidad and Tobago. This was the first of five *Test Matches* between the two teams. The match became most memorable because it was the first ever *tied* Test Match in the history of Cricket at that time, and gave the West Indies and its peoples new respect, and recognition. The remaining Test Matches were played before large, enthusiastic, and excitable crowds which applauded the brilliance shown by the players of both teams.

Peter would call the younger Cornelia Ida cricketers together at the end of their practice sessions, and tell them about how to keep calm when under pressure, listen to the instructions from their captain both on and off the field, and always try to give of their best in every situation of every game.

At one such session, he told the youngsters, "On the final day, the 14th of December, 1960, Australia was well on their way to victory, needing only a few more *runs* to do so. Our great West Indies team was captained by the Late Sir Frank Worrell of Barbados. He was the first ever African cricketer to captain the West Indies in a *Test Series*. Just before the final *delivery* of the final *over* of the match, Worrell is said to have told the great and legendary *fast bowler*, Wesley Hall from Barbados, "Whatever you do, do not *bowl* a *no-ball*!" The *scores* were level, and the Test Match all tied up. All the last two Australian *batsmen* had to do was to run for a *single* as soon as the *ball* was *bowled*. Hall, who had bowled his heart out all afternoon, mustered up his last reserves of energy, remembered his captain's instructions, and ran up to bowl the final delivery, from well behind the *bowling crease*."

Peter paused as he tried to build up more suspense for the climax of his story. Then one bright young man raised the index finger of his right hand as if to signal "*out*" by an *umpire*. He said, "And then Joe Solomon from Berbice, Guyana, swooped down like an eagle, picked up the ball, and hit the *stumps* with a swift and deadly accurate throw. The batsman was *run out*, and that became the first ever tied Test Match!"

The other youngsters cheered approvingly, but Peter was very annoyed at the young man's over-enthusiasm, and rude intervention.

He said, "Right! Now, remember that every delivery, every run, every *catch*, and every action must count in this great game of Cricket. And, do not give up when you are cornered. Always do your best. And, young man, you must keep learning about the game, but never interrupt anyone when they are speaking."

Peter then turned to the group, and said, "You must always remember to carry yourselves with dignity, both on and off the field, like the great Worrell. He was a truly inspiring leader, with great poise, and was always respectful of others. You must all learn from such masters. By the grace of God, one day anyone one of you may be called up to lead your country or the West Indies, and you must practice these things from now. Do not be rude, and always show respect to others. Now, go home and think about this."

The guilty young man paused, and said, "I am sorry Smokey."

Peter put his right hand up to stop the young man. He said, "Who the hell are you calling Smokey? You and all of your friends here are not yet wearing long pants, and you are not old enough to call me by this name. From now onwards, you will all address me as Mr Ramdin. Do you all understand me?"

The young *cricketers* bowed their heads with respect. But the persistent young man continued to make his point.

He said, "Mr Ramdin sir, I am truly sorry for calling you Smokey, and I will not do this again."

Peter said, "That is good. Now, what do you wish to add?"

The young man said, "Sir, my friends and I respect all of the old players you mentioned, and we all look up to them. But we have some even greater players who have taken the West Indies to the top of the cricketing world."

Peter smiled, and encouraged the young man to continue.

The young man said, "Sir, we are great fans and followers of Clive Lloyd, our Guyanese hero, and all the greats of today. Gordon Greenidge and Desmond Haynes from Barbados, the best ever pair of *opening batsmen* for the West Indies. Vivian Richards, the master blaster. Alvin Kallicharan, who hammered the great Australian fast bowler, Denis Lillee, at the Oval in London."

Another young man intervened with, "Don't forget Larry Gomes from Trinidad, who later took Kallicharan's place."

Yet another young man added, "And, the *fast bowling* machine which battered everyone in front of them. Andy Roberts, Malcolm Marshall, Colin Croft, Joel Garner, and Michael Holding."

Peter could not resist the urge to join in the naming of the great West Indian cricketers, and shouted, "Jeffrey Dujon, the *wicket keeper*!"

The youngsters cheered happily, and continued to name other players of that wonderful period of West Indian Cricket, as they took their leave of Peter, who just shook his head, and smiled with pride at his charges.

Back at the Domino game, Michael shouted at Peter, "Come on now, and stop day dreaming! We do not have all day to wait for your play. If you do not have a Six or a Blank, just rap loudly, and let our champion put more pressure on the Mule."

The referee turned sharply to Michael, and said, "Look Michael, if you comment like that again, I will have to ask you to leave the hall. Please everyone, be quiet!"

Undeterred by the warning, Michael whispered, "When we think too much, it can bring confusion, and loss of reason. This in turn can bring complete ruin. Just look at our Vishnu, who is in control, calm, poised, and always ready to transcend to the next level."

Nazir sneered, and muttered, "Vishnu is so damn calm, and it looks like he is in some kind of trance. Like a *yogi* in meditation. He'd better stay awake."

Carlos said, "No Nazir, Vishnu is all tied up in concentration. He will not be able to drift off like a yogi."

* * *

When Ramesh finally arrived at his destination in Cornelia Ida, which was only one mile away east of the hall in Anna Catherina, he pulled on the brakes of his motorcycle sharply. The rear wheel skidded on the dusty kerb, and he skilfully avoided a fall. He looked up at the first floor window of the recently re-painted two storey wooden bungalow.

Sati, his seventeen years old sweetheart, rushed breathlessly to the opened window, and when she caught sight of her Ramesh, her heart pounded with great anticipation.

She quickly dashed to the main double door at the top of the stairway leading down to the concreted ground level and pathway towards the six feet high metal framed main gate. Ramesh dismounted his motorcycle, and after carefully parking it on its own stand, he headed for the gate which was secured shut by a large padlock and chains.

Sati ran to the gate, and reached out to touch Ramesh's hands when a voice was heard. "Sati, come back inside right now! You were warned not to leave the house!"

Sati stopped briefly, and shouted back, "Yes Maa! I am only collecting something from someone at the front gate!"

Ramesh grabbed at Sati's hands so hard that she winced in pain. But she did not resist his touch, and he pulled her towards him.

He said, "Sati, why have they locked you in? Why can't we see each other? What is happening?"

She closed her large almond eyes, and whispered, "Go away. I will tell you later. Go!"

She then turned, carefully climbed back up the stairways, and slammed the door on the first floor firmly behind her.

3.

Mind over rations

Peter "Smokey" Ramdin finally decided on his first move, and picked out the Four Blank domino. He looked into Vishnu's and Afzal's eyes, and vigorously slammed it down onto the table. This caused all the dominoes to vibrate for a moment, but without resulting in any of the seven obscured ones to be revealed.

The referee stared at Peter with a strong gaze to signal his disapproval at the extreme aggression shown by the player. If any of the seven dominoes in the obscured pack was overturned thus showing the number or numbers, then the game would have had to be abandoned as void, and would then have to be re-started afresh.

It was now Vishnu's turn to play, and as he studied his options in responding to the Six and Four at the open ends, he looked up, and saw Michael whispering to Carlos.

"Carlos, the Four Blank reminds me of the very bitter World War Two years, and how this affected our parents and grandparents living in the early 1940s in this country."

Carlos said, "I heard that the war started in 1939."

Michael said, "Yes. But it carried on up to 1945. I was only nine years old when it ended, and I can still remember how everyone was jumping up and down with such joy. I still cannot understand this, especially since we in Guyana were not actually fighting with anyone!"

Carlos said, "Here you go again. You are supposed to be the man with all the knowledge about history. We as a country were still being ruled by Great Britain, and when war broke out, everyone or every country under British rule in the British Empire, was also at war with the Germans, who were then joined by the Italians, and, the Japanese."

Michael raised his voice slightly, and said, "I agree. So, in around 1943 and 1944, my father went off to help build the Atkinson Airfield. This was used by the Americans to re-fuel their warplanes, before they flew off towards North Africa. Besides, this was a way for the

British to help secure their Colonies, and also, to make sure that we were all on their side, fighting, and supporting the Motherland."

Arthur said, "So it was a case of us being dependent on the Motherland, and her in turn, dependent on us for support. I do not think that our Chinese people in Guyana cared too much about the war, other than when the Japanese got involved. I think that the Chinese began to take much more notice, as Japan was a sworn enemy of China."

John said, "Now, that is a surprise for me. I thought that you all came from the same culture and race, and therefore there should not be any hatred amongst your peoples."

Michael said, "No John, Japanese and Chinese people are like chalk and cheese. They are very suspicious of each other. I heard that Chinese people here in Guyana do not buy Japanese cars. John, I wonder what would have happened to your Amerindian peoples if say, the Germans had won the war?"

John said quietly, "Nothing much. Our peoples have suffered at the hands of all types of invaders into this country. You should know what the Spanish, the Dutch, and the English did to destroy hundreds of thousands, if not millions, of our peoples here and in the Caribbean Islands. They called us savages, and that gave them the God-given right to slaughter innocent defenceless people, then tell us to become Christian, and to believe in that same God."

Carlos said, "John, I have heard a lot about the various tribes of the Amerindian peoples of Guyana, or, I should say, Kaywana, which means the land of many waters."

John said, "Yes, we have many tribes here in Guyana, in Venezuela, and Brazil, and of course, other countries in the whole of South America."

Michael said proudly, "I can even name the most important tribes in Guyana. We have the Akawoi, the Arawak, the Warrow and the Wai-Wai. I read that many of our Amerindian peoples had fled from Venezuela where the Spanish colonists had put pressure on them to settle down, and, from Brazil, where the Portuguese colonists tried to do the same thing. I believe that our Government in Guyana is right to allow the people to live as they choose, and to try to support them with the things they really need."

John said, "You are right. My peoples need their rights to their land, good education services, good healthcare, and fair representation."

Carlos said, "I cannot apologise for what the Spanish, Portuguese and even the English and Dutch did to Amerindian peoples through the last few hundred years."

Nazir said, "Listening to you all made me think that we should stop calling John "Black Buck", and calling Amerindian people, "Buck" people. We should be showing John and his people much more respect, and understand that these people are the original Guyanese. I am proud of all our races and cultures we have here."

Michael placed his right hand on Nazir's left shoulder, and said, "I agree with you my brother. You are Indian, Carlos is Portuguese, Arthur is Chinese, and I am African, so I do not see why we should not call John, Amerindian. We must all be proud of our roots and heritage, and this is what makes Guyana stronger."

Nazir said, "Man, I heard that my ancestors, the Pathans of North West India, were brave people who stood up to all kinds of invaders, and fought them with all their might. But coming back to the question as to what would have happened if the Germans won the war, I think that the Amerindians would have stayed where they are, and just try to adapt to the new rulers. All of us would have had to do the same, and today we would have been speaking German, and driving more Volkswagens."

Carlos said, "We would be singing *calypsos* in broken German! I cannot bear to think of this!"

Michael laughed, and said, "Yah! We would have to listen to the Mighty Adolf Hitler instead of the Mighty Sparrow from Trinidad!"

The referee turned to Michael yet again, and said, "Please gentlemen, no more talking during this game. It is distracting the players. They need to concentrate without your conversations in the background."

Michael said, "Ref, I agree! But how are you going to stop the noise of the cars, lorries, and tractors passing on the road just outside of this hall? Our champions, the Domino Masters of Demerara, are well used to playing in these noisy surroundings. That is why they are champions. They have strong minds, and can concentrate better than most players."

John said, "And they are all very clever men. They know how to read the play, what tactics to use, and how to win. So, as long as they do not speak, then everything will be fine. We will keep our discussions as quiet as possible. Otherwise, it will be very boring for us all, to just stand here, and wait forever for each player to make his move."

Just then, everyone's attention on the game was interrupted by the harsh screeching of vehicle brakes, a deafening thud of metal crashing into metal, and the sound of metallic motor vehicle hub caps rolling noisily along the tarmac road, and finally settling into silence. Most of the spectators rushed out of the hall to the scene of the carnage. A few of them pulled people who were trapped in the two cars, and laid them out on the grass verge alongside the road. Both drivers seemed to take the brunt of the head-on crash, and they appeared to be lifeless. Within a few minutes, a police car pulled up at the scene, and the officers took control of the incident. The two drivers and their passengers were all taken away to be treated at the large Public Hospital in Georgetown, the Capital City of Guyana.

When the mess was cleared up, and the spectators returned to the game, Michael resumed his conversation. He said, "There you are ref! That was yet another case of bad driving, and maybe even bald tyres and poor brakes causing mayhem on our roads. Thank God that nobody was killed by those fools driving those death traps at such speeds!"

Arthur said, "We have to do something about getting proper motor vehicle spare parts, new tyres, and more speed control on the roads. These things are as scarce as food in those war years you were telling us about Michael."

Michael said, "Yes, back in those war years, there was a great food shortage, and people in the colonies had to suffer the same kind of rationing as the British people."

Nazir said, "How the hell could this happen when we had so much food all around us? My father told me that we used to make the best of everything that we grew in Guyana."

Michael said, "Yes, we have always been able to produce more food than our population needs, and that is why we export our sugar, rice, and even ground provisions abroad. But the rationing during the war was about shortages of butter, cooking oil, and other things we used to import from overseas."

Nazir said, "I heard, and saw in the movies, about how the Germans used their submarines to torpedo the merchant ships that used to bring goods to this country, or take supplies to England. They were hoping that if they cut off such supplies, the British and their supporters would be weakened in many ways, including their spirit."

Michael said, "Just as it is in Dominoes. You cut off certain numbers during the game, and you undermine your opponents. Then, when they are suffering, you deliver your Aces."

Carlos said, "Michael, I do not understand this. Does this mean that our own government, by restricting some of our favourite foods, are really trying to help us, or trying to weaken us?"

Vishnu smiled, and resumed looking more closely at the dominoes in his hands.

Michael said, "Carlos, you have to use certain tactics differently in different situations. War is physically and mentally brutal, and destructive. But this war on our national debt, and our over-dependence on foreign goods is more about our survival. It is an economic war to achieve better progress in the future."

John laughed, and said, "What future? This has been going on for far too long, and the people are sick of these stupid restrictions. Only God can help us out of this damn mess!"

Nazir said, "At least we are not starving, and we get most of the things we need from our relatives living in America, Canada and England. Thank God for their barrels and crates of everything from car parts to canned foods."

Michael looked at Vishnu, and then his friends. He said in a hushed voice, "Yes, we must continue to use our commonsense, feed our bodies and minds, and then when our intellect is sharpened, we will always become stronger. We can resist any force, and when we use our faith in God, we become even more powerful. When we seek this God within us, we can become indestructible. We can remove any obstacle."

Carlos said, "Michael that is a very powerful thing to say. It must have come from the lips of great Generals preparing their troops to go into battle. But you might be going over the top here. This is only a game of Dominoes, and this kind of speech is just too much for us."

John said, "Michael is not as stupid as he looks. He is talking about us all making sacrifices, using our intelligence, and working for the good of ourselves, and others who need help."

Nazir said, "Al hamd ul Allah! In Islam, we are expected to perform a sacrifice known as *qurbani* for the benefit of ourselves and Allah. Other poor and needy people may get some help from the sacrifice, but the real benefit is in doing it for the Lord, as a mark of our true belief, and devotion to Him."

Michael said, "Amen my friend, Amen! This is the kind of sacrifice that Vishnu, our great leader and champion, is performing right now. He knows how to use his intelligence to make the right move. It's a case of one for all, and all for one!"

Vishnu smiled at Michael, and prepared to make his second move.

* * *

Ramesh was very perplexed by Sati's behaviour, but decided to accede to her wishes for him to leave. He then mounted his motorcycle, and started to ride off when he barely noticed someone running towards him. He swerved to avoid hitting the man, but lost control of the vehicle. He was sent crashing to the ground, and slowly managed to get up.

The man stepped forward, and angrily grabbed Ramesh by his neck.

Ramesh's right elbow was bleeding from a gash he sustained in the fall, and despite the pain, he wrestled with the man. They both fell heavily onto the dusty kerb, and as the struggle continued, they rolled down the slight incline, into the muddy drain. As they exchanged punches, Ramesh realised who was fighting with him. It was Raana, the young neighbour of Sati's.

A small group of people from the neighbourhood gathered around the two men, and soon they were parted.

Raana shouted, "I told you to keep away from Sati! She is mine, and if you don't stop molesting her, I swear I will kill you!"

Ramesh said, "Sati will never go with you! If you want to kill me, do so right now! Or else, I will be waiting for you!"

Ramesh dusted himself down as best he could, and rode off, leaving the crowd to pacify Raana.

4.

Illusion and reality

Vishnu played his Four Ace, and thus presented Afzal with a Six at one end, and an Ace at the other. Someone living in a large house situated directly alongside the main road, and opposite the hall, turned up the volume of their radio. The dulcet tone of a very popular music programme presenter could be more clearly heard, as he introduced an old but much loved Hindi song by Mohamed Rafi, one of the greatest playback singers of India.

Everyone, of all backgrounds, knew of Mohamed Rafi and the other Indian singers. Peter Ramdin was a particularly ardent fan of both the male and female singers, such as the legendary Lata Mangeshkar, and her sister, Asha Bhosle. His preference for the latter was linked to the fantastic dance numbers that were normally accompanied by the traditional Indian classical and modern dance moves of the beautiful actresses in the Hindi movies.

Peter's own dance moves were copied over several years of watching hundreds of the three hour long Indian movies which always contained music and dance, even when the story was entirely an all-action thriller.

The Indian Film Industry, known affectionately as "Bollywood" through being mainly based in the Indian City of Bombay, was a source of hundreds of movies every year, far out-stripping the English language films from Hollywood in the USA, or those from the UK. People of Indian heritage, living everywhere in and outside of India, were fed with a phenomenal amount of music and dance in a media which kept them well connected with their culture, religions, art, and of course, their country.

The Hindi films which were distributed to Guyana, and other parts of the Caribbean, contained English sub-titles so that everyone who read English, could easily follow the stories, and the meaning of the songs. Many of the older generation of Indian people were still able to follow the Hindi dialogues of the actors, despite having originated from the Northern States of India where Bhojpuri, Punjabi, and Bengali were spoken, or from Madras in the South, where Tamil was spoken. This generation of Indian Guyanese were able to mix their Hindi with broken English to create a local dialect which was different from the Creole dialect which originated from the Africans.

The very creative use of the Indian dialect featured in the local Indian *Chatney* songs made popular by the famous Sundar Popo of Trinidad, and, the Creole dialect was the basis of the lyrics for the *Calypso* songs made famous by the Mighty Sparrow, also of Trinidad.

Peter, although of mixed Indian and African heritage, had a natural gift for imitating the songs of his favourite male singers such as Mohamed Rafi, Manna Dey, Hemant Kumar, Mukesh, Kishore Kumar, Mahendra Kapoor, and also the earliest singing stars such as K L Saigal, K C Dey, and C H Atma. He learnt the dance songs of Lata Mangeshkar and Asha Bhosle by heart, and sang along as he performed the Indian dances, particularly at Indian weddings.

People from all the surrounding villages would gather around the wedding houses just to see Peter out-perform all others on the normally well cleared dance areas specially set aside under the large tents, or, under the houses with open areas at the ground level.

He moved with all the grace and timing of the formally trained Indian actresses such as Waheeda Rehman, Vijayantimala, and Asha Parekh, for the classical and semi-classical songs, and the vibrancy of the immensely popular Helen who performed more modern western style cabaret dances. The Indian girls and women at the weddings simply could not compete with Peter, and they would gradually drift off the dance area as the master took centre stage.

He was never formally trained as an Indian singer or dancer, and yet he acquired immense popularity across the West Coast and West Bank of Demerara. The hosts at the weddings which Peter decided to attend, whether or not he was officially invited, felt happy that he was there to entertain free of charge. He certainly livened up the celebrations, particularly after the extremely long Hindu marriage ceremonies. However, the hosts also realised that they would have to prepare more food and drink than they needed for the official invitees. Peter's followers were mostly uninvited to the weddings, but did not fail to join the guests for a meal before they moved on. Most of them were the least interested in who were being married.

Afzal looked up, and saw Peter smiling and miming to the song from the radio. Some of the COBRA supporters began to sing along with the song, and Afzal began to frown. The referee intervened once again, and asked the audience to remain as quiet as possible. This had no real impact, because as soon as they stopped singing, the sound from the radio could be more clearly heard by the players.

Afzal knew that he must concentrate harder on the game, and that both Peter's and Vishnu's supporters were keen to disrupt his flow, as much as possible.

Michael, never one to miss an opportunity to disrupt an opponent, turned to Nazir, and said, "I love that Rafi song. In fact, I am also a great fan of Indian movies. I love watching all of the great Dilip Kumar and Raj Kapoor films. They are truly great actors who are the equal of any Western movie star. I love the way they speak and move. And, they could sing just as well as Mohamed Rafi and Mukesh."

Nazir said, "I know that everyone in our villages love to go to the Indian movies, particularly here at the great Monarch Cinema, the Roxy in Leonora, and the Earlo in Uitvlugt. Only Cornelia Ida, Hague, Windsor Forest and the other villages in the east, do not have their own cinema. Mind you, there was a cinema called Astoria in Hague, but I understand that it was destroyed by fire in the 1950s."

Michael nodded, and said, "Yes, Mr Rayman Ali, our very popular and successful businessman in Anna Catherina took the powerful generator from the Astoria Cinema, and used it to supply his own store, house, and some rented accommodation at the back of his yard, with electricity, for a few hours every night. This was well before we began to receive the government electricity supply."

Nazir said, "Actually, Mr Rayman Ali's father-in-law by the name of Dost Mohamed from Leonora, owned the Duchess Cinema before it was bought by Mr Robert Sookraj, who named it the Earlo after his only son's name. Mr Robert Sookraj and Mr Rayman Ali were very close friends."

Arthur said, "Man that Robert Sookraj was a great businessman who ended up owning most of the cinemas in Guyana, before he then sold them off."

Michael said, "You know that we do have a great tradition of great business people from all parts of Guyana. Mr Rayman Ali's father was Haji Abdool Kadir who built that grocery, and general store from scratch. He had a very large family as did Mr Dost Mohamed. Mr Rayman Ali's wife was Sahidan Mohamed who was very much loved by her customers and everyone used to call her "Auntie Baba". One of her brothers was Mr Yusuf Mohamed, better known as Jack. He was a great pioneer who brought hundreds of the American Juke Boxes that were in all the popular joints. He also brought us Popcorn and Ice Cream machines. These things helped to liven up all the villages wherever Mr Jack installed them."

Nazir said, "Michael, It is very sad to see so many of those great people leave Guyana to go to America, Canada and England. But I have to point out one small bit of detail just for your information. Your favourite Indian stars do not actually sing in the films. They mime the songs, just as Peter is doing. He is now pretending to be the suave Dilip Kumar, acting in the old Hindi film called Leader."

Michael smiled, and said, "The only difference is that Peter is dark and ugly, and we will soon see whether or not he is a true leader."

Nazir giggled, and said, "Michael, if you think that Peter is ugly, I don't know what we can make of your looks."

Carlos said, "Just look at the Mule. He always fancied himself as one of those legendary Hollywood Western movie stars. In fact, when he was much younger in the 1960s, he would watch those movies with John Wayne, Robert Mitchum, Rory Calhoun, Alan Ladd, and so on. Then, as we all left the cinema, he used to try to walk like his heroes, and worse still, try to talk like them."

Arthur, who also loved the Western films, said, "Yes, it was not only Afzal who did this. You were all trying to be like your heroes. You were even worse when it was Christmas time, when you wore your stupid cowboy outfits, and fake guns in holsters. The early Christmas Day movies were always sold out, with hundreds of noisy young John Waynes and Gary Coopers firing your pistols. You even aimed your toy guns at the screen, and shot at the bad guys, or the Red Indians."

John said, "Yes, the Red Indians. None of you cared about the Indians in those Western movies. None of you realised that this was yet another form of propaganda put out by the Americans, about how the Indians were savages, and uncivilised. They showed us how their great Cowboy heroes defeated the Indians, slaughtered hundreds of thousands of them, and stole their land. This is no different to what happened to my peoples, all over North and South America. I hated those Western movies with Indians in them."

Michael said, "John, my brother, I agree with you. But we used to treat those movies as only entertainment. The cowboys also hunted down and killed or arrested the white guys they called "Outlaws"."

Arthur said, "Well, I loved those movies because they were simple to follow. But I never pretended to act like John Wayne or any of the others. I am more interested to see the Chinese and Japanese martial arts films!"

Arthur took up a pose as if he was about to play some Kung Fu or Karate.

Nazir stood back, and said, "Steady on Arthur! Be careful now with those lethal hands of yours! You could not imitate the Cowboys because there were no Chinese heroes in those Westerns. Chinese people were portrayed as unimportant, and would be seen running around doing errands, and other things. The only Western heroes were white Irish Americans."

Michael said, "No, the true heroes of America were us Africans. America's wealth was not only built up by the Cowboys herding cattle alone, but by millions of African slaves toiling in the cotton fields, and so on. Our African ancestors were also brought here in Guyana and the other colonies, and when slavery ended the Indians from India came to work on the sugar plantations, not long after 1834."

Carlos said, "Michael, you always seem to miss out some crucial facts in your history. My Portuguese ancestors were brought here as contract labourers, before the East Indians and the Chinese. Madeira, which is an Island in the Atlantic Ocean, and some hundreds of miles off the coast of Portugal, was once the world's greatest sugar producer. In fact, even Christopher Columbus used to be a trader in sugar, travelling to and from Lisbon in Portugal, and Funchal in Madeira. I read that he got married to a young lady in Madeira, and later on he set sail as an explorer. Of course, we know that he and others founded America and the new world in 1492."

Michael said, "Carlos, this is the first time I have heard you say so much about your ancestors. Please tell us some more."

Carlos coughed slightly to clear his throat, and said, "Well, Madeira is a beautiful Island, and I hope to go there someday. I hear that it is very hilly and mountainous, and in those days it was very fertile, with a nice sort of a sub-tropical feel. Sugarcane was the most important agricultural activity, and the Madeirans were very good farmers. Maybe that is why the Sugar Plantation owners in Guyana felt that Madeirans would be best suited to work here."

John said, "All of this makes sense to me. But I do not understand why the Portuguese from Madeira could not handle the sugar plantation work here in Guyana."

Carlos said, "Well, the heat here in Guyana, and the working conditions were very hostile to Portuguese, and they got away from the estates as quickly as they could. They preferred to open retail businesses and restaurants, and to work in banks, particularly in Georgetown."

John said, "Man, I hear that Madeira is now more famous for their wine!"

Michael said, "Hmm, this sweet thing called sugar led to both evil and good. The evil was through African slavery, and the good is about us all living in this new culture here in Guyana."

Nazir said, "I like that Michael. But sugar is not only the root of the good and the bad; it is also the cause of ugly! Just look around this room, and see how many of us have lost so many of our teeth, due to too much sugar."

Arthur smiled, and said, "That's a case of the Good, the Bad and the Ugly!"

He then took out a packet of parched and peeled peanuts from his right trouser pocket, and offered to share them with his friends. He munched at a handful, and said, "I do not blame Michael for not getting all the facts about our history. We were never taught such important things about our different peoples, our cultures, and our heritage and so on, in primary or secondary schools. All I remember in High School is the glorious British History, their Kings and Queens, their Explorers, Leaders, and Warriors."

Nazir said, "And, these Western and English movies have been the other means to brainwash us into believing that the heroes portrayed are the only ones to notice. Just look at how we have always enjoyed the James Bond movies. They show how only one Englishman could outsmart a most powerful enemy whose plans were always to destroy the West, and take over the world."

Michael interrupted Nazir, took some peanuts from Arthur's open packet, and said, "Look, James Bond was a classic example of how the English operated. He would allow himself to be captured alive by this powerful enemy, and whilst he was inside the massive operations, he would find the weakest point, destroy it, and then make his escape. This is how all the Colonial powers sneaked into countries like India and all over Africa, made friends with the stupid rulers, gave them some sweeteners, and gradually took over their countries. Then they set about exploiting the new wealth, before granting them independence."

Arthur said, "Well at least I can say that this is not the way of the Chinese. Our people are very quiet, hard-working, and friendly. We have never gone to other lands, and colonised them."

Nazir said, "Aha! But you Chinese people know how to quietly slip away from our sugarcane fields, open up your rum shops, restaurants, and grocery stores. You made sure that your children took as much education as possible, and kept well away from our local politics. Then, no one bothers you."

Michael said, "I wonder why Ian Fleming, the writer of the James Bond stories, identified Doctor No as the bad guy in his first book. Perhaps he was trying to tell the world to look out for the Chinese!"

Arthur took some more peanuts, and smiled as he said, "Us Chinese are not the bad guys. We love to live in peace with everyone, everywhere. And, we do not need to belong to any political party. In fact, one of our very own Raymond Arthur Chung from Windsor Forest village became our first President of this country on the 17th of March 1970, until the 6th of October 1980."

Michael said, "Arthur, I am very proud of the Chinese people, and how you all live with us in peace. You seem to be so liberated, and your minds are focussed on your work. But you all seem to be so selfish."

Nazir smiled, and said, "Nice one Michael!"

Arthur said, "I agree with most of what Michael just said, and I have to say that we have never been selfish. We always try to help our small community of Chinese, and, everyone else. We know that we have to rely on everyone as customers for our businesses. So, we can never afford to be selfish. We are much smarter than you think."

John said, "Arthur, just for the record, the Chinese did try to invade India in the 1960s."

Nazir said, "I remember hearing about the Chinese trying to invade India from the North, and they failed to take any part of the country. It did help the Indian people to become more united. Millions of people, including the famous actors and actresses, gave their jewellery and money to help their country. Also, I am very happy to say that despite the war, our Indian and Chinese people here in Guyana, did not fall out with each other."

Nazir reached across, shook Arthur's hands, and continued, "My friend, there are still no hard feelings between us, even though the better side won the war."

Arthur smiled, and offered some more peanuts to Nazir.

Michael adjusted his spectacles over his nose, and said, "My friends, this is a great example of mutual understanding, respect and tolerance. This is what we need a lot more of in Guyana. Our ancestors tried to build this over one hundred years ago, despite their differences. So, we need to learn a lot more about each other. And, not let anyone try to divide, and rule us."

Just then, Michael turned around when he heard a very familiar voice. It was unusual for women and girls to attend the Domino matches.

Doreen, Michael's wife, stood at the entrance with her arms akimbo, and wore an angry frown.

She said firmly, "Michael, I need you to come right now, and help me with the grocery shopping. And, stop all this stupid game and nonsense talk. Otherwise there will be no peace when you get home!"

Nazir chuckled, and could not resist offering Michael some advice. He said, "Never mind the Indians and Chinese fighting wars. This one being offered by Doreen will be most painful for you. Here you may be the great historian, and Domino tactician, but we all know who wears the trousers at your home."

The long pause in the game continued as everyone laughed at Michael's new predicament. Vishnu looked on at him with some real concern. Suddenly, Michael was forced to choose between the importance of the game, or, the severe consequences for disobeying the love of his life.

He said, "Doreen, my darling, please ask one of our five lazy children at home, to help you this time. Sweetheart, I am much needed here. So please, my pumpkin, just for this one last game, try to understand me."

Doreen stamped her right foot firmly on the wooden floor, and in a greater show of anger, she shouted, "Don't you sweetheart and pumpkin me! You stay here with all these good-for-nothing layabouts, and you can go home to them! I have had enough of you and this stupid game!"

Michael clasped his hands, and pleaded, "Please do understand my *dumpling*. One of our boys can easily help you just for this one time."

Doreen kissed her teeth, and stormed out of the hall. She could be heard cursing Michael until she cleared the building, and headed off onto the roadside.

Arthur looked at the sullen Michael, and said, "Man, never mind pumpkin and dumpling, you better prepare for some squash when you get home!"

Everyone laughed out loudly. Even the referee could not maintain his usual seriousness, and giggled as he gestured to Afzal, to continue with his next move.

Michael smiled, looked at Vishnu, and whispered, "I do hope that my choice of personal sacrifice by staying here will bring us all the benefit of victory for the ACES. It is much more important to appreciate our selfless sacrifices to be here in this battlefield. I prefer to take this action than that demanded of me by my divine life partner."

Nazir said, "Michael, when you get home, you will truly become history!"

* * *

It was only five months ago when Raana pleaded with Sati to meet him at their favourite secluded part of the high seawall in Cornelia Ida. He stooped down in one of the arched cave-like spaces beneath the concreted sea defence structure, and waited impatiently for Sati to arrive.

Raana and Sati, along with their other school friends, regularly used the spaces to play games after school, until just before darkness fell. Their affection for each other grew steadily over the years until they reached their teens. Their parents began to warn against meeting in those play areas, as they became more frequented by lovers, after sunset.

Raana then continued to court his childhood friend when they both visited the Monarch Cinema, or the Roxy Cinema. Sati would slip away from her girlfriends who were supposed to be acting as her chaperons. Then she would sneak beside Raana to watch the movies together.

Their romance blossomed into a very passionate affair, and soon the villagers began to talk about the two lovers. Sati's parents became very concerned, and she was soon prevented from meeting or seeing Raana.

This enforced separation was deeply hurtful to both, and Raana decided that they should meet to discuss what to do in the future.

As he kept his silent vigil inside the caved area of the seawall that he and Sati most favoured in the past, he could hear the frightening roar of the massive waves of the incoming Atlantic tide. The waves had gradually covered the brown sandy beach, and had begun to slam into the large fixed rocks jutting out of the seawall. This caused the water to form into cream-coloured foam as each wave rolled up to smash against the formidable fifteen feet high seawall, and then retreated before the next rush of increasingly larger waves.

The angry tide made further inroads until the water began to splash over the topmost rim of the seawall. This excess water washed over the six feet wide walkway, and fell over the edge of the cave below.

Raana began to feel more nervous about waiting any longer for Sati to arrive, fearing that the angry high tide would deter her from taking any risks with the inclement weather. A large dark rain cloud began to form directly overhead, and within a few minutes, it produced a heavy tropical downpour.

Then, as Raana was about to give up on his plan to meet Sati, he saw the slight figure of the love of his life, heading towards him. She was completely drenched, and Raana picked up the dry blanket he had placed on the concreted floor of the shelter, and wrapped it around his shivering, and tearful sweetheart.

He hugged her as tight as he could, and he whispered, "Sati, I love you so much. We have to be together, forever."

Sati broke free from the embrace, and said, "No Raana. We are not to meet again. I came to tell you that this is the last time I will see you."

Raana cried aloud, "No! This cannot be! If you go away, I will never live another day!"

Sati asked, "What are you talking about?"

5.

"Ruff" justice

Afzal brought everyone's attention back to the tense Domino match, and slammed down his Ace Three, leaving Peter to consider the two ends now showing a Six and a Three.

During one of the practice sessions of the ACES team, in a local rum shop, they took a short break from their heated and aggressive Domino playing, and decided to enjoy some local dishes. Arthur had purchased the food from the restaurant located next to the rum shop that was opposite the Monarch Cinema. The mini banquet consisted of curried fish, including *hassa, patwa, and* banga mary, some boiled rice, *daal purie roti*, and daal.

They all tucked into the mouthwatering food with great relish and enthusiasm. Then they quenched their thirst with their personal choice of drinks, including rum and coca cola, Banks Beer, mauby, cream soda, and water.

A few children had stopped by on their way home from the local St John's Anglican Primary School in Anna Catherina, to play an impromptu game of *hopscotch* on a games area they sketched out on the smooth concreted paving in front of the rum shop.

The paving covered the normally open three feet wide drains that were intended to take water overflows from the main road passing through the villages, and from the houses situated on both sides of the road. Some parts of the drains were kept immaculately clean with the waste water flowing smoothly, whilst other sections were overgrown with wild *tanya bush* which was difficult to eradicate, and tended to re-grow in a very short time after being cleared. The water became stagnant, and thus encouraged mosquitoes to flourish alongside other insects.

It was quite common to see local poultry, particularly ducks, feeding in the drains. The ducks loved to catch the tiny *cacabelly* fish which thrived in the murky unclean water.

Arthur invited the ACES team members present, to join him at the largest table in the rum shop, and pointed to the food spread out along the middle. They wasted no time, and began to enjoy their meal.

Vishnu said, "Well my friends, we must thank Arthur for providing us with such a great feast. Today, I am paying for all the drinks."

Everyone cheered loudly, including the other customers in the rum shop.

Vishnu said, "Gentlemen, I am not paying for everyone's drinks. I am paying for my great team-mates only."

Michael said, "But Vishnu, you are missing a great chance for us to get more fans to come to support us. Please buy them all a drink, and I am sure they will come to support the ACES at the grand final game."

Carlos said, "Look, I will buy everyone else their drinks, and Vishnu can buy ours."

Everyone in the rum shop shouted "Up the ACES! Up the ACES!"

The children also paused in their game, and spontaneously shouted "Up the ACES! Up the ACES!"

Michael said, "And who will get some soft drinks for the young fans outside?"

Nazir volunteered his offer, and said, "OK! I will buy them a drink each."

No sooner had the youngsters heard this offer, they shouted more vigorously, "Up the ACES! Up the ACES!"

This attracted a growing crowd of school children, and by the time Nazir's order was taken, the numbers rose from a few, to dozens. He quickly instructed the rum shop owner to stop serving any more drinks to the ever growing crowd.

John said, "Nowadays, this is typical of us Guyanese. We just pounce on any offer to grab anything going for free. I cannot recall us behaving like this when we were children."

Michael said, "That is true. We grew up with more discipline at home, in our churches, temples and mosques, at school, and even on the road. If anyone of us ever misbehaved, or swore, or did not greet an older person with respect, by the time we reached home, our parents would be waiting for us to dish out our punishment. In those days, we were taught to wait patiently for our turn to receive anything, and to be grateful. I think that since our so-called independence, and all the restrictions, we have become so dependent on handouts, that we have forgotten basic manners, and common respect."

Vishnu said, "Michael, you may be right, but I think that we began to behave differently towards each other ever since the early 1960s. I remember how people became wild during the Black Friday fire in Georgetown, looting and stealing from the general stores, and even from each other. Then came the horrible and most shameful months in our history; the racial violence between our African and Indian peoples."

John said, "That period was known as the Racial Disturbance. I don't know who came up with that term."

Michael said, "Yes my friend, 1963 and 1964 were nasty years, full of racial hatred, and unspeakable evil. This was all instigated by politicians claiming to represent us. We were all living at peace in our villages, until one act of cruelty by one upon another triggered a similar or more vicious response. I could never understand what drove our people down such an unforgiving path."

Arthur said, "I remember that as a Chinese person, I did not know how to react, because all of my school friends were Indian, African, and of course, the odd Portuguese. And, worse still, they all just suddenly stopped talking to me!"

Carlos said, "Man, we were all scared. Especially when we heard one man say that they were going to slaughter anyone with straight hair! I was even thinking that I should shave all the hair off my head!"

Michael said, "Yes, people on all sides behaved poorly towards each other. But whilst we reflect on how evil, and gruesome the killings, beatings, and the burning of property were, there were some moments of light relief."

Nazir said, "I remember the stories about those people acting as vigilantes to protect their own communities, especially during the night time. The vigilantes were self-appointed gangs, some of whom were just petty thieves, and jailbirds. They were masters of stealing poultry, and even the noisy pigs from anyone's yards, so that they could feast whilst on their watch. To me, this was only a poor excuse for thieves to steal other people's property, knowing full well that they would get away with this."

Vishnu said, "I heard the story of a very dark-skinned Indian man from Leonora's vigilante group. One night, he was ordered to go to a family's pig sty to steal a pig. He took off all his clothes except for his shorts, and daubed cooking oil all over his body. He crept into the pig sty, and as he moved slowly amongst the resting pigs, a young lady from the family who was on her way to the outdoor latrine at the bottom of the yard, saw some slight disturbance in the pig sty. Then when she pointed her torchlight into the dark sty, she saw two large eyes staring at her. She screamed and ran away as fast as she could, shouting "Daddy...Daddy...there is a strange black hog in the pig sty!""

Everyone in the rum shop burst out laughing heartily, and each began to take turns to relate similar stories about the time of the racial conflict.

Nazir said, "Oh yes! I remember one of our own local policemen who somehow managed to get into the Police Force without passing the entrance examination, and the minimum height requirement. He was short, overweight, dunce, and very one-sided. He took great pride in his uniform, and made sure that he was always seen in action, stopping cyclists to check on their brakes and lights."

Carlos said, "Yes, I think I know who you are talking about. He was one of my schoolmates, and I can confirm that he could not read or write properly all the way until he left school."

Nazir looked around the premises, and out onto the pavement, and said, "So, on one evening, just after sunset, he stood out in front of the Monarch Cinema, and stopped a young Indian man. He ordered the cyclist to get off the bicycle, and stand aside. In no time at all, a large crowd of us gathered around to witness the drama. The policeman I am talking about is known to us all as "Ruff" on account of the way he barked his orders. He told the young man that he will be charged for poor brakes, and no headlights. Then he took out his notebook and pencil to take details starting with the name and address. We all goaded Ruff to lock him up, to take away the bicycle, and to charge him."

Carlos butt into the story, and said, "My friend was the shortest guy in our class, but he had the longest name. I think it was something like Ramakrishnan Dhaniram Doodnath Maharaj. We all called him Ram."

Nazir continued, "So when Ram called out his full name loudly and very quickly, Ruff was completely taken aback, and appeared very edgy and nervous. He then asked Ram to repeat his name very slowly. Ram started by saying his first name slowly, and then followed up with the others as fast as he could. Everyone in the fast growing crowd laughed out loudly, and Ruff shouted at us to keep quiet or to go away. We all ignored him, and in fact the crowd became even greater as the people leaving the cinema also began to gather around. Even the cars, and other vehicles passing by, slowed down near the scene. Drivers who knew Ruff also shouted their advice to him to do the charge, and clear the crowds away from the main road."

Michael said, "That Ruff was always unfair to people he did not like very much. He is still playing the big cop even in his retirement, following people around, and snooping on everyone. He has been a real disgrace to the Police Force. I do try my best to avoid him these days."

Nazir said, "So Ruff just about wrote down the first letter R, and asked Ram to spell out his name slowly. But the crowd started spelling out the names in such a way that Ruff became even more confused, and very agitated. He gave up on taking Ram's name down on his notebook, and asked Ram for his address. Ram was now enjoying the incident, and he shouted out "Metenmeerzorg! Near Uitvlugt!" The crowd went wild with laughter as they all knew that Ruff would not have any chance of taking Ram's details, and thus execute the charge. We gave Ruff more advice to "Take him away!", "Lock him up!", "Seize his bicycle!" Then we all laughed louder as Ruff soon backed off, and let Ram walk away with his bicycle, and without a charge."

Vishnu said, as the laughter in the rum shop died down, "It was Ruff, in his great desire to impress his bosses at the Leonora Police Station, who would always claim to witness all the acts of violence, arson, and general lawlessness allegedly done by Indian people. Do you remember the incident when the Indian vigilantes were actually given permission by the Indian owner of a large rum shop next to a block of houses where many African people lived, to burn this down and thus cause all the neighbouring houses to burn as well? The useless gang of fools tried no less than nine times on nine separate nights, to set the rum shop alight, and every time they failed miserably."

Nazir said, "How the hell can anyone fail to set anywhere alight with so much alcohol around?"

Vishnu said, "Well, those so called heroes failed every time until finally, they managed to set the building ablaze. It was the greatest fire ever seen in our village, and even bigger than the fires in the sugarcane fields. It was also very noisy with the constant explosions of the bottles of rum and beer adding to the fury of the fire. By the time the single green British Army fire engine arrived, it was too late to stop the total destruction of the rum shop, and, the rapid spread of the fire to the houses occupied by the African tenants. They all ran out wailing and screaming. They pointed to people looking on, and began to accuse them of starting the fire."

Arthur said, "That fire took a very long time to come to an end, despite all the buildings being made entirely out of wood."

Michael said, "Man, Guyanese timber like greenheart and crabwood are the toughest, and best in the world."

John said, "So Vishnu, what happened? How did Ruff come into this?"

Vishnu continued, "Ruff, as usual, was one of the very first police officers on the scene causing more disruption by getting in the way of the British soldiers who were trying to cordon off the whole area, and were guarding the site, armed with their rifles pointing towards the growing crowd."

Carlos said, "I don't think that the British soldiers who came to Guyana to help stop the racial disturbance were trigger happy. They were very experienced men who were actually respected by both the African and Indian troublemakers."

Vishnu said, "Right, can you people let me get on with the story?"

Nazir said, "Vishnu, just get on with it man."

Vishnu nodded, and said, "So, Ruff decided to do something about the incident, and picked out one of the Indian onlookers at the scene. He took hold of the man's arms, and put on a pair of handcuffs. Then he marched him off to his jeep, and bundled him into the back, despite all the protests from the crowd. Ruff then revved up his jeep, and sped off to the Police Station."

Michael kissed his teeth, and said, "Ruff used to do this with people all the time. The man is a complete jackass."

Vishnu said, "So, at the trial of the Indian rice farmer who was charged with arson of the rum shop and the other buildings, the courtroom at Leonora was packed with his relatives and friends, and, those attending on behalf of the many others to be tried for all kinds of criminal activities. The farmer decided to defend himself, and when asked to explain why he was spotted by Ruff, running away from the scene of the fire, he presented his defence."

Arthur said, "A lot of people could not afford to hire lawyers to defend them, and ended up being convicted for all kinds of incidents. This really made Ruff a very successful policeman in the eyes of his bosses."

Vishnu continued, "And so the farmer started by saying that he had only just arrived at the scene, and just because he said something to Ruff, he was wrongfully picked upon, and charged with arson. He then said, "Your Honour, the Lord Jesus Christ had one cross to carry, and we all know how much he struggled every step of the way, even when people tried to help him. Look at me. I am a very sick man with two large swollen feet and legs caused by elephantiasis. Also, two swollen arms. That's four crosses! I even have two more crosses to bear!" The man pointed to his scrotum area, and the Magistrate said, "OK! I get the picture!" Then the farmer said, "So, if the great Lord Jesus Christ had only one cross to bear, and he could not even walk, how the hell can you expect me to run with six crosses?" The whole courtroom erupted with laughter. The Magistrate called the court to order, and instantly dismissed the case, much to the delight of everyone except Ruff."

Everyone in the rum shop broke out into laughter, and people started to chat amongst themselves as they recalled the story.

Michael said, "That is the kind of defence our Lord Jesus Christ should have used to save himself! But then, how would we all be saved if he was set free?"

Vishnu said, "There was also the incident where some of the Indian vigilantes had decided that they would take the law into their own hands, and try to assassinate Ruff."

Everyone in the rum shop stopped talking to listen to Vishnu's story.

He said, "One night, one of the would-be killers armed himself with a *pooknie gun* which was a clumsy attempt at making a pistol from a piece of copper piping. He managed to tempt Ruff out of his living room at his house, and aimed the gun at his helpless target, who froze in absolute terror. The marksman fired the gun by using a hammer to hit the end where a shotgun bullet was fitted. The gun exploded in the left hand of the gunman, and although Ruff was only about six feet away, he was not hit by any of the scattered pellets. Ruff pretended to be shot, held his hands to his chest, and screamed for God's mercy. He then fell back into his house. The gunman ran off, and later boasted to his vigilante friends that he got Ruff."

Everyone in the rum shop laughed at the story, then Vishnu put his right hand up, and said, "Wait, there is another story to tell you about another attempt to kill Ruff. This time, our brave vigilante heroes planned to build a bomb out of carbon, gunpowder from unused bullets, and a large Ovaltine tin can. They crept up to Ruff's house unnoticed, and planted their bomb under the ground floor of the building, and managed to get away without being seen or caught."

Michael said, "Oh yes! I heard about that bomb. Some workers found it many years later when they did some building works at Ruff's house."

Nazir said, "What happened to the bomb? It must have been dangerous to handle even after so many years!"

Vishnu said, "The bomb could never explode as the vigilantes had set it up with a wick made of string, and daubed with tar. So when they thought that they lit a fuse, this never happened. Ruff slept through that night, and very many more, completely unaware of the bomb. I think that the vigilantes just gave up on trying to kill him, and he is still here with us."

Michael looked directly into Vishnu's eyes, and said, "Explosive devices in the wrong hands will cause any mission to fail. Getting as close as possible to the target, and using a better handgun would have been more successful. Clearly the vigilantes were never properly prepared for their missions."

Nazir said, "Thank God those idiots failed, and the racial conflict ended. We must learn the lessons from those times, and must never allow our politicians to mislead us all to do such evil things to each other, ever again."

Michael said "Amen to that my brother! Amen to that!"

Carlos said, "I know that it is hard to forgive and forget. But I do believe that God intervened when after so many Indians were massacred at Wismar, and that boat packed with explosives was making its way to finish off the survivors at the harbour, was blown up into bits by someone who was careless with a lit cigarette. That was a case of instant retribution. I am sure that it helped to ease some of the pain and suffering of all concerned Guyanese. I suppose that we can forgive, but we should never forget."

Michael lifted his glass of rum, and said, "Let us raise a toast for our people. We need to stay together, and work for each other, and then this country will move upwards, and onwards."

Everyone in the room raised their glasses, and shouted "Here! Here!"

Michael continued, "We as Guyanese, and as ACES Domino players, have to keep our focus on the one vision of victory, and triumph over those who would like to see us lose our way. We must use all of our senses, and intelligence, and direct our energies towards goodness. Then we could really begin to taste true liberation."

Carlos said, "Let's drink to that. Vishnu, you have to lead us all into our championship battles by making us keep our focus on our game, not to panic or to be afraid of what our opponents may do, and play with confidence. We must win! We have to win!"

Everyone in the rum shop, and the younger fans who were listening into the conversations from their play area, shouted "Up the ACES! Up the ACES!"

Michael noticed the Ace Three that Afzal played with confidence, and returned to his usual commentary on the game.

He said, "You know that a lot of people get very suspicious about the number thirteen. It seems to represent some form of bad luck, and the quicker we avoid it, the better becomes our fortune. Unfortunately, in our local history, the 13th of June 1980 was one of the ultimate examples in bad luck."

Carlos said, "Michael, I think I know what you are referring to. It must be the day that one of our brightest scholars and politicians, the late Dr Walter Rodney, was killed by a bomb in his car."

John said, "Now, this story will go on for a long time, until someone investigates this thoroughly. This assassination story will run like the Kennedy conspiracy theories still being debated."

Nazir said, "We all know damn well who was behind the Rodney killing. We don't need any dumb ass to tell us what happened that day. I only hope that whoever did this, will pay heavily for it one day."

Vishnu looked up at Michael, and seemed to signal to him to stop the conversation.

Michael said, "Look my friends, I only wanted to show how for some people, the number thirteen can be very unlucky, but for others, it can actually bring luck!"

* * *

Sati and Raana sat quietly for a few minutes just peering out of their shelter. The excess water from the angry ocean continued to pour over the seawall, and combined with the relentless rainfall, to form a mini waterfall over the front of the concreted cave.

Raana took a small soda bottle out from his trouser pocket, and said, "Sati, if I cannot have you, and be with you, I will drink this poison."

She screamed, "No! Raana, you cannot do this! Please, I beg you!"

Sati tried, and failed to grab the bottle from Raana.

She continued to sob, and sank to her knees onto the bare concreted floor, clasping her face with both hands. The wet blanket slid off her shoulders, and fell to the ground beside her.

Raana knelt down beside Sati, and pleaded, "You can join me. Then we can be together, forever. And, no one will ever hurt us anymore. Please Sati, do this with me."

She said, "No Raana! We cannot do this! You said that Muslims should never kill themselves!"

Raana said, "I do not care whether I am Muslim or not. All I want is for the two of us to be together."

He put down the bottle, and took out a white handkerchief from the back pocket of his denim trousers, and attempted to wipe the tears streaming from Sati's eyes. She took the handkerchief, wiped her face with it, and gave it back to him.

Raana said, "So, what else can we do? My family also do not agree about the two of us. Where can we go from here?"

Sati said, "Raana, my family told me that you and I are too young. We should wait until we finish our schooling first."

Raana said, "I cannot wait any longer. We have to be together now."

Sati said, "Look, I have to go back home now, or else they will notice that I have left the house without anyone's permission."

Raana broke down in tears, and muttered, "If you leave me now, you will never see me again."

The raging storm eased up appreciably, and Sati slid away as soon as the rain stopped.

6.

Sugary spice of life

Peter looked closely at the end of the string of dominoes with the Six, and then at Vishnu, as he contemplated playing a domino there. He then further scrutinised the six dominoes he held, and played a Four Three at the other end, thus presenting a Six and a Four for Vishnu to think about.

Michael turned to Carlos, and said, "You know that in the great and beautiful game of Cricket, some batsmen such as our friend Peter here could hardly hit sixes. He was more of a classic *strokemaker* who relied on timing the ball very well, and placing it between the *fielders*. Many times he would *late cut* balls for *fours* past the *slips*. Afzal, on the other hand, believed in using his great strength and power, and would often smash great *sixes* out of the small Leonora Cricket Ground, and sometimes even further into the pond next to the St John's Anglican School directly opposite the Cricket Ground. He would often hit two or three sixes as soon as he went in to bat, and we all marvelled at this."

Carlos said, "But Afzal was always too impatient when he was batting, and instead of taking his time to build a big score over a long *innings*, he just loved to entertain the crowd, and would get out too quickly. He was, in his early years, just like the great Rohan Kanhai, who was the most entertaining right-handed batsman of the 1960s, and early 1970s. I loved to just look at the master as he would walk to the *crease* with his white shirt collar up, and with a neat white kerchief tied round his neck. Whenever he hit a four or a six the crowd at the great Bourda Ground in Georgetown, would rise up in sheer awe. Then, he would play a beautiful forward defensive stroke to the next ball, and the crowd would shout "Nooooo!"".

Michael smiled, and said, "That "No!" was to say to Kanhai to stay there, and not let the bowler tempt him to give his *wicket* away with a rash shot."

Arthur said, "Well, Afzal had a weakness against good *spin bowling,* and especially against *left arm spinners* who turned the ball away from the *right handed batsman.* Sometimes, such spinners could get the ball to come back into the batsman from the off, and either *clean bowl* him, or trap him *LBW.* The great Sir Garfield Sobers, who was the best all-round cricketer of all times, had this ability."

Michael said, "Oh yes! Sir Gary was the best ever! He could bowl left arm *fast medium* at a decent pace, then his left arm spin, and, of course, he was gifted with his fantastic left hand batting. He still holds at least two world records of hitting six sixes in one over, and the highest score of three hundred and sixty five not out in a Test inning. Anyone beating this man's records will have to be regarded as a true great of the game."

Nazir said, "Michael, nobody will argue with that. But the ball Arthur is talking about is called a *"chinaman".*"

Michael said, "That's right Nazir. It was not named after Arthur, our own Chinese friend here. It was named after a Chinese born cricketer by the name of Edgar Ellis Achong. I bet Arthur did not know this."

Arthur said, "Of course I know about Achong who was the first Chinese man to play Test Cricket, and who invented the chinaman ball! Otherwise, how could I explain it like I just did? In fact, this is similar to the right arm leg spinner's *googly*, with the ball turning back into the right handed batsman instead of turning away as a normal leg spinner."

Michael said, "Arthur that is very impressive for someone who was never good at playing Cricket. You have obviously picked up a lot of knowledge about the game. And yes, the beauty of the chinaman and the googly is that they are bowled with the same action, and the batsman always finds it very difficult to predict which way the ball will turn."

John said, "Cricket is such a marvellous game. It can be played by anyone, and even my Amerindian peoples play this in the settlements. They would set out a wicket in a clearing, and use the coconut branches to carve out bats, and bowl with rubber balls. We can still see the youngsters in our villages doing this, and they manage to organise games at the seaside on the fairly level brown sand when the tide goes out. You have to be a good batsman to score fours and sixes in the beach games, as there are normally more than ten fielders waiting to pounce on any hit by the batsman. Teams with as many as fifteen players instead of the normal eleven, can still end up scoring only a few runs in their full inning."

Nazir said, "Man, I love the beach *bumper ball* games, especially when Leonora plays against Anna Catherina or Cornelia Ida. The only thing that does not always go right on those Sunday mornings is when the players put Michael in charge of the large pot of *cook up rice*."

Michael said, "Hold on there Nazir. All I do is to put everything you people take to cook, and dump it into the pot almost filled with rice, peppers, onions, garlic, chicken pieces, chunks of beef, and other items. I cannot help when even before the pot is cooked fully, you start helping yourselves with more than your fair share. Some people naturally find themselves scraping the bottom for whatever is left."

Carlos said, "It was never nice to play a game all morning, and then find that almost all the food was eaten by some very greedy bastards."

Nazir said, "Carlos, the last time this happened to you was when you kept batting and not scoring any runs until the tide came in, and caused the game to be abandoned."

Carlos said, "Well, although we Portuguese have only produced a few really good cricketers, our first love is really for Football."

Michael said, "Yes, and yet Guyana has never done as well in Football as we have in Cricket."

Carlos said, "Michael, I hope that you are not trying to blame our Portuguese players for our poor Football."

Nazir said, "That is why many of us Guyanese love to follow the Brazil Football teams, and such legends as Pele and Garincha. Besides, they are the most winners of the Football World Cup, which England only won once, in 1966."

Michael said, "Oh, 1966 in England. You know that the Portugal players gave Brazil and Pele a very hard time there. Portugal had an African player called Eusebio, to rival Pele. But, it was England that emerged the winner in the final against their arch rival West Germany, by four goals to two."

The referee tried once more to restrict the conversations during the final Dominoes game in progress.

Michael ignored him, and said, "You really have to give credit to England for inventing so many sports and games. The British Army troops did introduce Football at Cornelia Ida, and soon there was a tournament between some teams on the West Coast, back in the 1960s. It was quite fearful for our youngsters to play Football against those strong and rugged British soldiers, many of whom wore their army boots instead of proper football ones. It was a no contest when a soldier charged towards a skinny lad in the Cornelia Ida team. But soon the boys learnt great skills from watching the Rank newsreels, and especially the games that Pele and his Santos teammates played in. In no time at all, everyone in the Cornelia Ida team wanted to be Pele."

Carlos said, "It was sad to see the British troops leave Guyana."

John said, "But before they left our Cornelia Ida Football team taught them a good lesson."

Nazir said, "Of course, you do know that when the troops played their final game against the champion Cornelia Ida team before they left for England, they were trashed by the home side by ten goals to nil!"

John said, "You may not believe this, but my late father loved Football, and because his surname was Charles, he named me John Charles after a famous footballer from Wales in the UK. My father did live in England during the 1950s where he started on a Law Course. But, like so many of our young students who went abroad to study, he felt very homesick, very cold in the winter months, and nearly became mad after suffering from acute depression. Luckily for him, he was rescued by a relative when he left his rented room which he shared with another student, and travelled across London to Trafalgar Square. He was found sleeping in the open after spending hours just looking at the hundreds of pigeons, and feeding them with breadcrumbs. Dozens of the pigeons would gather around him, with some sitting on his head, and he soon became a spectacle for visitors passing by. After he was saved, the family brought him back to Guyana."

Michael said, "John, I heard how good your father was. Because he felt that he failed to become a qualified lawyer in England, he could not face anyone in the village, so he spent a lot of time away in the bush, working in the gold mines as a *pork knocker*."

John continued, "Yes, that is how he met my Amerindian mother. He lived with her in her village, and after the elders of her tribe finally agreed to their marriage, he taught her English and other subjects. Do you know that she became so learned that she was one of the very first from her Arawak tribe to be given a job as a Primary School teacher? Me and my brother and sister were born in the settlement, and both of our parents taught us at home and at school. Then, when my mother contracted pneumonia, and was being brought out by boat to be admitted at the Best Hospital in Vreed en Hoop, she became much more ill, and just rested her head on my father's lap as me and my brother took over the paddling. Not long after, my father said to us that we must turn back. We did not understand, and tried to argue with him. But then he said that she had gone to her ancestors. We all burst out crying so loudly in the boat, and it just drifted slowly back to the jetty, as if it was being guided by some strange spirit."

Those who heard John's story were visibly shaken, and tried to console him as he dried some tears from his eyes.

Nazir touched John's shoulders, and said, "John, you are a wonderful person. I remember when you and your family came to this village, and everyone used to just stare at you and your brother and sister as you walked together to go to the local school. Some children taunted, and bullied you, calling you bad names, and throwing pebbles at you. That is when they gave you that terrible name "Black Buck"."

John said, "You all know how much I hated that name, and you are very good friends, because you speak to us all, and treat us with much more respect."

Michael said, "Nazir, Vishnu, Arthur and I became your best friends, and we tried to make you all feel happy, and we made sure that you played with us. We got to respect you even more when we all saw just how clever and good you were at school. It is a great shame that you did not go on to become lawyers or doctors."

John said, "Unfortunately for us, my father could not afford to keep us in school, or to even send us to High School in Georgetown. Besides, he could not bear to see us go away, even for one day."

Carlos said, "Never mind John, at least you, your brother, and your sister took to teaching, and I am sure that your father was very proud of you."

John said, "Yes, he must have suffered too much when he was in London, and then when he lost his one true love and life partner, he must have grieved silently right up to the time that he took his own life."

John wiped the silent tears streaming down both his dark shiny cheeks. Carlos and Michael reached out, and held his arms in an effort to comfort their friend.

Vishnu continued to study the six dominoes on the table, pointing with his right index finger at each number, and checking the remaining five dominoes he held in the palm of his left hand, taking great care to prevent anyone from peeping at them.

Another familiar Indian song began to play on the radio across the road, and once more the spectators began singing along with the popular hit.

The referee desisted from asking for silence, but he kept a close watch on the three players as he awaited Vishnu's third play.

Michael said, "Just look at Vishnu our leader, how he is concentrating on his game. It is as if he is in some form of meditation, thinking about whether he should attack or defend like a true ACE. You can see how he is trying to work out who is in possession of which domino."

The referee looked sternly at Michael, and said, "Please do not comment on the game. If you continue to ignore me, I will call this game off, and also ask you to leave the hall."

Michael nodded, and stopped speaking for a while. This time, all the ACES supporters also stopped whispering, and obeyed the referee's warning.

Carlos whispered, "It is so good to see some of our young people showing such politeness. I just hope that all the others can behave like these young ACES."

John said, "That is true, but right now, you and I are not showing them good examples by speaking when we were all told to keep quiet. Do you remember how we were made to obey our teachers in school?"

Nazir whispered, "Oh yes. I can still feel the marks on my ass, where our fearsome head teacher beat me with his *wild cane* so damn hard, I could not even cry!"

Carlos laughed, and pointing to Nazir's backside, said, "Nazir, you were always the one having to be sent to the head teacher for your special corporal punishments. Your class teacher just could not cope with your mischief in class, and, outside the classroom."

Nazir said, "Corporal punishment? Man I got Major General beatings!"

Michael said, "I even remember when Nazir broke into the head teacher's office, and took a razor blade to slightly cut into all of the canes so that when the lashings were to begin, and he tried to bend and flex his favourite wild canes, they would snap. But sadly for poor Nazir, the head teacher also accused him of the vandalism, and added more lashes to the original six he should have had."

Carlos smiled, and said, "Nazir, you even tried to use cardboard inside your trouser seat to act as a protector against the brutal lashings. But the head teacher knew of all such tricks, and made you remove your padding, and your trousers."

Nazir frowned, and said, "I used to be beaten by that bastard even though I was innocent. He just seemed to love caning my ass. But I did learn to behave, and this helped me very much when I was in jail. I made sure that I obeyed the really bad guys, otherwise their punishment was much more evil than a few lashes from a wild cane. You had to be very careful when they asked you to bend over in the shower room and pick up their bar of soap that they deliberately dropped near your feet. Man, there were a lot of prisoners who ended up walking out of prison in a very strange way."

Carlos said, "You mean that they all started to walk like John Wayne?"

Michael whispered, "Shh! Nazir and Carlos, please spare us, especially the youngsters, with such details. Mind you, the sentence you served did not include the famous cat-o-nine tails! Being whipped by that must be most gruesome."

Nazir said, "I can tell you that most victims would have preferred the cat-o-nine tails instead of buggery!"

Just then, everyone's attention was drawn to the most welcome and recognised voice of the man who made and sold *badaam lacha*. He called out loudly as he rang the bell on his bicycle's steering handle, "Come on and get your badaam lacha this side!"

The young ACES fans dashed out of the hall, and quickly surrounded the vendor as he parked his specially adapted carrier bicycle, with the still very hot product neatly packed in a large cartoon box fitted into the carrier tray over the smaller front wheel. Some of the older spectators, including Arthur, also joined the other customers from the village. In a very short time, all the stock of badaam lacha was sold out.

Arthur took some of the sweet, and shared it with his friends in the hall.

Michael said, "You know, we are so lucky in this country, to have and to enjoy so many varieties of sweets and cakes. This badaam lacha made out of sugar, along with other sweets such as *payra*, *gulgula*, *gulab jamoon*, *jalebi*, and *mithai*, all came from India."

John said, "And don't forget that us Amerindians founded the cassava which goes into the sweet *cassava cakes*."

Arthur said, "Yes, my wife makes beautiful and delicious cassava cakes, *Chinese cakes*, *salaara*, and, *cassava pone*."

Nazir, "Guys, you are making me feel so damn hungry! What about the *pine tarts*? They are my favourites. And, Vishnu's favourite is the *sugar cake* which we all used to make as children. No wonder so many of us Guyanese have lost most of our teeth!"

Michael said, "The great thing about our culture is in the variety we all love and enjoy. You know the saying "Variety is the spice of life"? Well, I say the variety is the sugary spice of life!"

Vishnu looked up briefly at Michael, licked his lips, smiled at his two opponents, and finally decided to make his move."

Michael led another chant, "Up the ACES! Up the ACES!"

* * *

Raana fell to his knees, and continued murmuring, "Please stay with me! Don't go! Don't leave me! Oh Sati!"

Sati could not hear Raana as she continued to walk purposefully away, without glancing back to check on Raana. He continued to sob loudly, and in just a few moments, he unscrewed the bottle, and drank all of its contents in one effort.

The effects of the poison began to envelop him as he slumped to the ground on his back. He coughed heavily, and soon lay still after vomiting, and frothing at the mouth.

A couple of young lovers heard the commotion, and paused to peer into the dark cave. They saw the still body of Raana, and after some hesitation, they stepped cautiously into the cave, and took a closer look.

When they saw the empty soda bottle beside the young man, the woman screamed, and pleaded with her companion to do something quickly.

The rain from the storm had completely stopped, and the darkening red sunset cast the only natural light over the area from the seawall to the nearest houses about two hundred yards away.

The woman agreed to run off for help whilst her companion stayed with Raana, trying to revive him. Within fifteen minutes, some able-bodied young men from the village arrived on the scene, and they lifted Raana by his arms and legs, and took him along the narrow pathway to a car that was parked at the end of the street leading to the main road.

Sati was completely unaware of Raana's action, and the rescue. She had quietly sneaked into her home without being noticed by her parents.

7.

Close to God

Vishnu smiled as he slammed down his Six One domino, and slid it to the end with the Six thus leaving Peter to consider his new challenge of a Four at one end, and an Ace or One, at the other.

The ACES fans smiled, and voiced their appreciation with words of congratulation and encouragement to Vishnu. The COBRA supporters showed more concern for Peter, and the LIONS' fans remained quite passive.

Michael turned to Carlos and John, and said, "You know, we are also truly blessed in our villages, and in this country, to have so much diversity."

Carlos frowned, and said, "Diversity? What does this mean? Man, I don't know why you love to use all these big words when little ones will do!"

Nazir said, "This reminds me of the story about the very dunce schoolboy who went home to complain to his father about how his teacher kept punishing him for his bad spelling in front of the whole classroom. The father was so upset by this that he stormed up to the teacher, and demanded to know why his son was being asked to spell big things like "cow"."

Michael butted in with, "And the father told the teacher to ask his son to spell little things like "mosquitoes"."

Carlos laughed, and said, "Now that was really diverse!"

John said, "No, I think that Michael is talking about the many races of people we have here, from African, Indian, Chinese, Portuguese, and Amerindian heritages. We all have our own religions, cultures, and attitudes."

Nazir said, "Diversity for me is shown right here in Anna Catherina. We have an *Islamic Mosque*, two *Hindu Mandirs*, a Catholic Church, a Seventh Day Adventist Church, a Methodist Church, and, an Anglican Church. Seven ways to find God! But then, we also have seven rum shops! It is really like good and bad living side by side!"

Carlos said, "Man, I never thought about this thing in this way. It is like God and the Devil living side by side amongst us!"

Arthur said, "Well, we Chinese call this *Yin* and *Yang*."

Nazir raised his eyebrows, and asked, "Who the hell are Yin and Yang? I have never heard of these people. Arthur, can you tell us more about these two Chinese guys?"

Arthur smiled, and said, "No Nazir, Yin and Yang are not the names of people. You see, in our ancient Chinese philosophy, Yin represents darkness, coldness, wetness, and other things which are seen as negative forces."

Nazir looked worried, and asked, "Does this mean that because I am dark, I am to be called a Yin?"

Arthur said, "No Nazir, Yin is nothing to do with colours or races of people. Yang is hot, dry, aggressive, and is associated with the sky, the sun, and so on."

John said, "But we have Yin and Yang operating all the time. One cannot do without the other. It is like a man and his wife."

Arthur said, "Part of what you said is closer to what Yin and Yang is. In life we have to have light and dark, hot and cold, fire and water, life and death and so on. One depends on the other to provide a balance for existence. I cannot agree that a man is Yin and a woman is Yang, or, the other way round."

Michael said, "But we can say that God is like Yang, and the Devil is like Yin."

Carlos said, "You see, Michael always comes around to what I am thinking. I just said that it is like God and the Devil living together."

John said, "No matter what you say, I still think that Yin and Yang are like man and wife."

Arthur said, "No John, it is not like that. Yin and Yang gives us stability, strength, success and so on. But if you have too much of one, then it can result in disaster."

Nazir rubbed his stomach, and said, "Man, the way I feel right now is like Yin and Yang having a hell of a fight in my stomach. This is making me even more hungry, and very angry, by the minute!"

Carlos said, "It is good to know about all these ideas from different cultures and communities. I read somewhere that when it all started there was one great mirror. Then this was broken into many pieces. Someone picked up one piece, and claimed that to be the mirror. Others did the same thing. But each piece of mirror was only one part of the whole."

Michael said, "Yes, we belong to different races and religions, but we have no problem with believing that there is after all only one God. We just have different paths to this Supreme Lord. But in our village, there is always the temptation to drop in to a rum shop instead of a church."

Nazir said, "Look, we Guyanese know how to hedge our bets. We seek out the help of the Lord when we go to our Churches, Mandirs and Mosques, and, just in case we do not get our answers, we cannot resist dropping in to the other places where the Yang spirits dwell."

Michael smiled, and said, "That may be true, but you and your Muslim brothers are not supposed to drink alcohol, or even smoke cigarettes."

Carlos said, "I look at it in this way. We turn to smoking, alcohol and drugs to find some kind of solace for our problems. But these three things make up the word SAD, and they will never make us happy."

Michael smiled, and said, "I like your reasoning, but we do not smoke, drink or take drugs when we are sad. We do this to help relieve some stress. The problem is that we do not do this in moderation, and we over-indulge. We should seek to imbibe the love that our Lord gives us for free, at all times instead of paying for the other spirits."

Nazir said, "Now I understand this diversity thing. We should really indulge in the variety we have here in Guyana, in our foods, festivals, and of course, our women!"

Michael said, "Ah! Our women are the best thing going for us Guyanese men. I am really proud of being married to the most beautiful and intelligent woman in the world!"

Nazir said, "You are only saying this because you live in real fear of your Doreen!"

Carlos said, "Man, Michael needs to get his eyes tested, and change those old glasses."

John said, "Despite our admiration for our women, we still have issues with multi-racial mixing. As a mixed-race person, I know how difficult life has been for my mother and father, and for my brothers and sister."

Michael said, "Mind you, this kind of resistance and intolerance is gradually changing. In fact, here in Guyana, the mixed-race people are the third largest group in our population, after Indians and Africans. These mixed-race people will become a very powerful group in the future. This trend is also happening all over the world."

Arthur said, "Except in China."

Nazir said, "Arthur, I hear that China has several types and tribes of Chinese peoples, and many religions as well. They may not have Africans and Indians there, but it is a very diverse nation."

Arthur said, "Yes, and you can say the same for India as well."

Afzal continued to study the seven dominoes played on the table, looking closely at the number of Sixes, Fours and Aces used. He held his remaining five dominoes in his left hand, and carefully considered what options he had. Members of his team and supporters told him to take his time, and not to rush into his next move.

The referee turned to them, and said, "Please gentlemen, no coaching!"

Michael continued the conversation with his teammates, and said, "You know, I love everything about our different cultures, but lately I began taking more interest in the Buddhist ways and teachings."

Arthur smiled, and said, "Is this why you have shaven your head completely?"

Michael said, "You don't have to be completely shaven to become a Buddhist. It's about adopting a simple life, and pursuing knowledge and wisdom."

John said, "The last thing we want in our villages, is to see a bald-headed Michael in his monk's outfit, wandering around the place like a madman!"

Nazir said, "Michael, if you carry on like this your Doreen will certainly leave you."

Arthur said, "Michael, you are only interested in the simple life because you are damn lazy, don't want to help your wife with the shopping, and you just wish to stand here to talk nonsense. You are not into Buddhism, but into Layaboutism!"

Everyone who overheard Arthur laughed out loudly.

Michael sighed, and said, "You see the domino with Four points at the end on the table? This reminds me of the four kinds of people who worship God. Those who are sad and distressed with lots of problems, and who go to the Mosque, or Hindu Temple, or Christian Church, to beg God for help, to relieve them of all their pains and suffering. But God cannot help in this way, because we bring these problems unto ourselves."

Nazir said, "Look Michael, people get fed up with all this praying, and that is why they go to the rum shop where they can find some Yang. Some real enlightenment!"

John said, "I think I will rename my bush rum as Yang Spirit!"

Michael frowned, and said, "The second kind of worshipper is one who always seeks knowledge and understanding of their religion, life, and everything around them."

Arthur said, "Michael that must be you."

Michael said, "No, I do not just seek knowledge. I try to use this. It is like John here. He has his knowledge, and he is passing it on through teaching."

Nazir said, "Aha! Islam teaches all to pursue knowledge, and to use this for the betterment of all people."

Carlos said, "And what about all those people who use their knowledge to make more money? Surely they are the best!"

Arthur said, "Not quite Carlos. I may have a business, and may appear to be doing fairly well, but this does not mean that me and my family are content, and feel blessed by God. I may be here with you, but I am thinking about my business all the time. It is constantly on my mind."

Michael said, "So, going to God firstly for relief of distress, secondly for more knowledge, and thirdly for better fortune, will never be enough. The fourth type of person is the one who acquires wisdom. This person becomes closer to God."

John said, "This is really deep man. I think that my Amerindian peoples must be the closest to God, because they live very simply, respect their surroundings by only using what they need, and try to pass on their centuries old wisdom to their children and grandchildren. This must be the secret of our survival over thousands of years, despite all the disasters thrown at us."

Carlos said, "The only time I can remember when every Guyanese sought out our God, was the night in the 1960s when a heavy earth tremor passed through the coastlands. It was a very strange feeling as without warning, all the dogs, donkeys, cows, and other animals started to wail in a very frightful way. Then, within seconds of waking up in our beds, the heavy and very scary rumbling of an earthquake shook everything. I remember my father staggering towards us trying to tell us not to move or worry. Then all around him things began to rattle on the table, and all the pictures fell from the walls."

Michael said, "Oh yes, I remember this very well. Thank God there was no eruption, and the tremor passed through in only about thirty seconds, which seemed like forever. It went on to hit parts of Venezuela, and caused some severe damage in that country. But, my God, everybody turned up in their churches the next morning. There was a lot of praying that day!"

Carlos said, "Yes man, everybody prayed. But like true Guyanese, no sooner than some people came out of the churches, they found the nearest rum shop to taste the other spirits on offer, just in case the Holy Spirit fell short of answering their prayers."

Michael said, "Man, I would not blame them. The priest at the Anna Catherina Anglican Church was a tall and huge man whose cries of "Holy!" shook the building from the ground to the roof! Man, I felt like the earthquake had come back!"

Nazir said, "Allah O Akbar! Thank you very much gentlemen. I have learnt more about myself here today. All I wanted was to come here to witness a good game of Dominoes. But you have given me much food for thought. Now, all I am thinking about is food to keep the Yin and Yang in my stomach very happy, so that I can retain my balance and great happiness. Come on now Afzal, get cooking!"

* * *

When Ramesh reached his nineteenth birthday in May 1985, Vishnu and Parvati decided to ask him as to whether he had any plans for his future. Ramesh was surprised, and had not given this much thought.

Vishnu said, "Well my son, you have now completed your High School studies, and done very well in your examinations. I hope that you wish to continue higher studies, and take up a good profession."

Ramesh said, "Paa, some of my friends are going on to the University of Guyana, and some are trying to get to England, or Canada, or America."

Parvati placed her right palm to her forehead, and said, "*Baap re Baap!* Where do you want to go? If you go away, I will miss you so much!"

Vishnu said, "Parvati, let Ramesh tell us what he would like to study, and then we can talk about where he should go to do this."

Ramesh said, "Maa and Paa, I am very confused at the moment. I have had very good exam results in both Science and Arts subjects. I could do Medicine, or Law, or Engineering. I just cannot make up my mind."

Vishnu said, "Well, I think that any of these will be useful to you. But in Guyana right now, we need more Doctors and Engineers. We already have too many Lawyers and Accountants here."

Parvati said, "But Vishnu, if the boy goes for Medicine or Engineering, he will have to do this abroad. And, we do not have the money to pay for this. Even if Ramesh gets a scholarship we will still have to find the money to send to him."

Ramesh said, "Maa, if I get a scholarship, then everything will be paid for. You and Paa do not need to worry about the money."

Vishnu said, "Well, I have also been approached by a very rich businessman from Georgetown who has asked for you to marry his only daughter."

Parvati said, "Vishnu, why did you not tell me about this?"

Ramesh said, "Paa, and why did you not tell me about this? I need to know about these things. I am old enough to make these decisions for myself. And, furthermore, I do not like these offers based on money. I am not a product for sale to anyone. I don't even know the girl. And, what about her feelings?"

Vishnu said, "I am sorry. The offer was that the businessman would pay for your education abroad, and give you and his daughter your own house here in Guyana."

Parvati said, "Vishnu, I hope that you did not agree to this and promised the man anything, before talking to me and Ramesh!"

Vishnu said, "No! That is why I am asking you both about Ramesh's plans!"

Ramesh said, "Maa and Paa, at the moment, I am not sure what I want to do. I wish to stay here and think about this some more. Paa, please tell that businessman friend of yours that I will never agree to such an offer, and please do let me and Maa know when people approach you about these things."

8.

The spirits of darkness and light

Afzal wasted no time in studying Vishnu's move. He quickly opted to play his Four Five, thus *cutting* the end with the Four, and presenting Peter with a Five at that end, and an Ace or One at the other.

The Four Five domino that was just played, prompted Michael to start a new conversation with his teammates.

He said, "1945 was the year that the Second World War ended. It is now nearly forty years since the defeat of the Nazis."

Carlos looked at Michael, and asked, "What do you mean by the nasties?"

Nazir said, "Not nasties you fool! The Nazis were the German people who were led by Adolf Hitler, to believe that their blond haired white race was superior to all others. I think that they even called themselves the Master Race. I read about this in my war comics, and saw this in the movies about the Second World War. Carlos, how come you did not learn about these things?"

Carlos said, "I can remember this, now that you mentioned the war comics and war films."

John said, "I heard that this Master Race was based on an Indian race called the Aryans. But the Germans' whole idea was completely mad, and misguided. The Aryan people did not go about invading other countries, and killing people they did not like. And, worse still, the Aryan symbol on which the Nazis based their Swastica was also wrongly copied."

Michael said, "Yes John, this idea of a German Master Race must have hurt the English people who spent hundreds of years trying to conquer, and rule over people in all parts of the world."

Carlos said, "I agree, but it was not just the English who did this. It was done by the Spanish, Portuguese, Dutch, and French who also fought each other to achieve supremacy. Do not forget that the English thought that the Indians of India were heathens who should be converted to Christianity. So, for Aryan Indian philosophy to be used to challenge them must have hurt their pride!"

Nazir said, "The worst thing about that war was the Germans' destruction of about six million Jews in Europe. That was the most barbaric thing that any human race has ever done to another. I also cannot understand why white Christian people did that to white Jewish people."

John said, "We must never forget that the Americans destroyed most of their Native American Indians, and the English and others wiped out millions of our Native Amerindians, particularly from the Carib tribe across the islands of the Caribbean."

Michael said, "And don't ever forget who slaughtered millions of innocent Africans through forced slavery, and brutality over hundreds of years."

Carlos said, "So, all these major nations took turns to kill other human beings. The two Atomic bombs that the Americans dropped in Japan are still killing the people there, even after forty years! You have to believe the Hindus who say that we are now in the dark age of *Kaliyug* which will last for over one hundred thousand years!"

Michael said, "Hallelujah! No wonder that even more wars have followed on since 1945. In fact, I do not think that there has ever been a day of complete peace in the world at any time over the last two thousand years. Mankind has to suffer much more, and for much longer, well after we have all gone to meet our Maker!"

Nazir said, "Only Allah knows what is in store for us all. And by the way Michael, here comes your beloved Doreen to take you away, and to dish out more pain, and suffering onto you!"

Doreen stood by the entrance door of the hall, and presented a fearsome figure as the light created a dark silhouette of her within the frame. She shouted, "Michael! If you do not come home right now, you will find the door locked in your face!"

Michael mustered up some courage, and said firmly, "Do what the hell you wish! I need to see this game through at all costs! So, you can go home, and please don't come back here to bother me!"

Doreen snapped back, "How dare you speak to me like that? I have a damn right to come here, and to drag your damn ass home!"

Carlos said, "Doreen, please spare him this time. It's only one final game, and win or lose, we will make sure that Michael goes home straight away."

Doreen turned to Carlos, and said, "You are the last person to advise me. Your wife Maria, is also coming over here to sort you out as well!"

John said, "Now, now Doreen. Please give us this one more chance. We will certainly take both Carlos and Michael home, as soon as the game is over."

Doreen said, "I do not believe a word of what you just said. I am going back home now, and I will bring all the wives here to stop this stupid game, and drag you all to your homes."

She turned and stormed out of the hall in a fury.

Michael smiled nervously, and said, "You see how loving, but powerful our women are? She really misses me so much, but she can't express this deep love she has for me in any other way. Her bark is much bigger than her bite!"

John said, "Michael, you are lucky to have such a faithful wife. Do you remember the story about the man who ended up killing his wife for cheating on him?"

Nazir said, "Yes, he was a very quiet, hardworking young man who hardly said a word to anyone. He would get up early every morning, and go off to the sugar factory in Leonora, do his long shift, and eventually return home at six o'clock on the dot. He was never known to be late."

Carlos said, "And then he and his lovely wife would start bickering, and quarrelling. Nobody would intervene. Then everything would quieten down for the rest of the evening."

John said, "The problem really started when the man's wife began a love affair with a young man called Joey. The lovers would meet at the house everyday shortly after the husband left for his work, and then Joey would leave just before six o'clock in the evening."

Carlos said, "This went on for quite a while, and everyone in the villages knew about the affair, except the husband."

Nazir said, "Yes man. Nothing is kept secret in the villages for too long. Our lovely wives are great at talking name, and spreading rumour all over the place."

John said, "Finally, one night, the husband returned home just a little bit earlier than usual. But luckily, Joey did manage to slip away without being noticed or caught."

Nazir said, "Aha! Unnoticed except for one very reliable witness to the love affair!"

Michael said, "The husband had bought a young parrot, and trained the bird to speak. The parrot soon learned simple words like hello, pretty polly, and then more short sentences."

Carlos said, "The parrot had learned to say "Go Joey go! Six o'clock ah come!"."."

John said, "That was the message that the parrot learned to say only when the wife started to usher her lover out of the house. This worked very well for the lovers."

Nazir said, "Eventually, the husband heard the parrot repeating "Go Joey go!", and he kept his suspicion without apparently asking his wife about Joey. He left his work on one pay day, and for the first time, he stopped to have a few drinks in a rum shop before he went home. Man, I heard that when he got the parrot's message, he got into a rage and committed the most brutal killing by chopping his wife's..."

Michael put his hands up, and said, "OK Nazir, we all know what happened to that young lady."

Nazir said, "I still cannot understand why he did not get the death penalty for such a brutal murder which he confessed to."

Carlos said, "Yes, the parrot which soon became known as "six o'clock", was not allowed to give evidence at the trial, but the defendant's lawyer managed to convince the court that his client was being provoked by the infidelity of his wife over a very long time."

John said, "I think that they call this a crime of passion, and the murderer was given ten years jail, instead of capital punishment."

Nazir said, "So, if I get vex and kill my wife, I can only get a few years?"

Michael said, "No Nazir, it does not mean that anyone can go around and kill people due to such anger. Anyway, my friends, it is not surprising that whilst we are all here watching this epic game, our feathered friends are looking after our interests at home."

They all laughed heartily. Even the referee could not resist a chuckle.

Carlos said, "Michael, if I were you, I would check out what your own pet parrot says when you get home. Especially since I heard that your parrot keeps saying "Doreen good girl! Doreen good girl!"."

Michael stopped smiling, and shook his head.

John said, "That is why we should all have a chat with our pet parrots when we get home today."

Carlos said, "No, there is no need for this. Our wives are very faithful, and so are we."

Nazir said, "You know, I have to listen to my parrot a bit more carefully. I am never sure that when he says "Allah O Akbar", he is not saying "I love you Akbar"."

The referee smiled after over-hearing the last conversation. He seemed to accept that he could not stop the spectators from having their discussions whilst the game was being played.

Michael said, "You know, I also keep champion birds, and this reminds me that as soon as this game is over, I have to go home to check that they are fed properly, and their cages are clean. My Doreen and the children are not allowed anywhere near to my birds."

Carlos said, "Michael that reminds me about our bird competition for next Sunday morning. My finches are ready for battle, and you will not stand a chance."

Nazir said, "You guys are really cruel. I do not like how you set your traps on the barbed wire fences, and catch those poor birds when they land on the sticky gum. I also do not like when you just pick out the birds you like, and destroy the others such as the *kiskadees* and the *blue sakis*."

John said, "We Amerindians believe that the birds are the spirits of our ancestors, and we should respect them."

Michael said, "I am not so sure about this. Are the carrion crows which eat up all the discarded birds, respectable spirits as well?"

John said, "Yes, even the carrion crows are only performing their duties to the dead."

Carlos asked, "So your peoples believe in reincarnation like our Hindu friends?"

John said, "No, our ancestors' spirits will always be here to watch over us, to guide us, and to protect us."

Michael said, "I am sorry to offend you and your peoples. But we bird lovers do not bring harm to the birds we keep. We protect them, feed them, and respect them."

Nazir said, "You see Michael, on the one hand you preach to us about Buddhism and wisdom, and on the other hand you imprison those innocent and harmless birds. You take away their free spirits. They should not be tortured in this way."

Carlos said, "Well, this is the first time I am hearing about your feelings towards our bird catching, and bird keeping. But you also have a parrot which cannot fly away because you have clipped its wings. Is that not the same thing you are accusing us of?"

Nazir said, "I agree with you Carlos. I think that we all need to look at how we treat animals and birds, as we all indulge in the practice of keeping guard dogs under leash, and in cages. Some of us even have pet *saki winkie* monkeys, and other animals. But this does not alter the fact about my dislike for your bird keeping, and bird fights."

Carlos said, "Nazir, the birds do not actually fight each other as cockerels do. They spar with their wings when each bird is shown another in a cage. They whistle, and the one that shows more aggression towards the other, wins the fight. That is all there is to it."

Nazir said, "I fully accept what you say about my parrot, but I do not agree with this sport, as you all place those little creatures under a lot of unnecessary stress. Worse still, you cover the cages in black cloth, and keep them in almost solitary confinement. So, you can go to your bird fights. I will just keep well away from them. In fact, I promise to ensure that my parrot is able to grow back its wings, and I will release him back into the wild."

Michael said, "So be it Nazir. But I fear even more for the future of your parrot, simply because it will not know how to survive in the wild. It only knows how to live in captivity. My advice to you is to hand it over to one of us so that it will live out its remaining life as safely as possible. It may even learn some proper curse words!"

Carlos said, "Michael, if you take over Nazir's parrot, you will have to listen to its Islamic chant of "Allah O Akbar", day and night. It may even cause you to convert to Islam!"

John said, "No matter how you all look at this, and whatever you do with your pet birds, please look after them properly. Their spirits will not die and will remain with us forever."

Michael said, "John, thank you for your understanding. I think that all of us, when we were much younger, used to indulge in making *slingshots* with strong forked stems, good pieces of rubber, and with leather to cradle the *gola* that we made with hardened balls of dried mud. We were very accurate, and specialised in shooting at birds."

Carlos said, "If I had known what John has just told us, I would never have killed those innocent birds."

John said, "Now that you all know, you can at least tell your children to stop killing our beautiful kiskadees, blue sakis, *yellow plantains*, doves, and even the parrots that come out in large flocks at around Easter time. There are so many birds that swarm around the *gamma* trees for those sweet sticky fruits."

Michael said, "I now agree that we should encourage our youngsters to leave the wild birds alone. But Easter will always be a special time for us all. Our kites are all handmade, and we even use them in our own kite competitions at the seaside."

Nazir said, "You know, I thought that we all shot at the parrots in the gamma trees because we wanted to scare them away so that we could use the sticky gamma as the glue for the paper on the wooden kite frames."

Carlos said, "I thought so too. But my kites were the best. I made my kites sing, and fly side by side with the tail full of razor blades that cut loose any other kite that was being used to compete with mine."

Michael said, "That is great fun to watch especially as your kites cut loose those that were almost static over hundreds of feet high. When they were cut loose, they would sail away for what seemed like miles!"

Nazir said, "It is always funny to watch the owners trying to run after their giant kites. I have never seen any of them returning with their kites. Then they had the problem of slowly reeling in the hundreds of feet of string left below their lost kites. Some of those youngsters were left in tears for the rest of their Easter. We just laughed at them."

Michael said, "The biggest and most celebrated kite flying day in the two week season was the Easter Monday. The skies all around the villages, and especially over the seawall and beach areas, were ablaze with brightly coloured and buzzing kites fluttering in the warm Atlantic breeze. But do any of you know why kite flying on Easter Monday is so important?"

Carlos said, "Yes, this is the third day after the death of our Lord Jesus, and when he ascended to heaven. Actually, the kites are supposed to represent his rise from his tomb."

Nazir said, "I never knew this. But it makes good sense to me. Maybe Carlos's kites cutting others, was to allow them to fly further up towards heaven!"

Carlos said, "No, I just do this to have some fun."

Michael said, "But Carlos, you do not like it when others start to attack your kites. We all learnt how to use the razor blades on the tails of our kites, and we also began to give you a good fight."

Carlos said, "It is great for all of us to come together as one, and to celebrate those two weeks, making kites, flying them, and just having great fun. Let us not complicate this with too much meaning, and just enjoy our festivals. The only thing I do not like about Easter is to sit up for midnight mass."

Nazir said, "We Guyanese know exactly how to celebrate each other's festivals. They are bright times that come by to light up our lives for at least a short while, and we all love this."

Michael said, "Yes, you Muslims do all the hard work of fasting for twenty eight days through *Ramadan*, then as soon as the new moon is spotted to signal *Eid ul Fitr*, you go off to the Mosque, and all of us Non-Muslims just wait for the celebrations, and the feasts afterwards!"

Nazir said, "We love to celebrate Eid ul Fitr and also the sacrificial *Eid ul Adha*, with prayers, and by sharing our delicious vermicelli sweet, mutton and chicken curries, and other treats, with everyone. We also hand out money to the poor people who would sit in lines outside the Mosque waiting patiently in the hot sun."

Carlos said, "Nazir, I love going over to your home to enjoy the amazing food. Your wife and mother are wonderful women. They would always make sure that their guests would also take away some food along with parcels of other gifts."

Nazir said, "Thank you. Nothing is to be thrown away. These are always times for giving."

Michael said, "I love that. They are not only times for giving, but for forgiveness."

Michael said, "Brightness comes and goes in so many forms, as in times like Easter and Eid, but darkness just hangs around, and never seems to go away. I hope and pray that more brightness stays in our hearts to push out darkness and evil."

Carlos said, "Michael, this is a great wish, but it seems that in this age of Kaliyug, we and very many others after us, will have to do much more to dispel evil, fear and darkness. These are like moving targets, and require sustained attacks. One strike will never be enough."

Michael looked over at Vishnu, and smiled.

* * *

The driver of the car, and two of his friends who had lifted and taken Raana from the seawall, carefully laid him on the back seat. They hurriedly jumped into the front seats, slammed the doors shut, and sped away from the village over the nine miles eastwards of Cornelia Ida, to Georgetown. The driver had taken the empty bottle that was found beside Raana.

The Public Hospital in Georgetown was teeming with very ill patients in the Emergency area. Raana was promptly examined by a team of doctors and nurses, who proceeded to resuscitate him, and to pump the poison out of his stomach, as soon as they established that he had taken potash.

Raana's survival from the overdose was quite surprising, but was of great relief to his parents, relations and friends. Sati was also very pleased to learn that Raana had survived the ordeal, and that he was returning home after a few weeks of rehabilitation. However, her parents and her father Peter Ramdin in particular, began to impose an even stricter restriction on her movements. She was not allowed out of the house, unless she was being accompanied by someone from her family.

Raana was also kept under close observation by his relations. His parents removed all potentially poisonous liquids from their home, and he was watched even when he was allowed out to go with other family members to the local village Mosque.

The *Imaam* of the Cornelia Ida Mosque took a special interest in Raana, as part of the young man's recuperation. He offered Raana more counselling time than usual, and acted as a special mentor and tutor to him.

Raana soon became more immersed in his religion, and took to reading the Holy Qur'an, the *Hadith*, and singing *Nasheeds* and *Qaseedas*. He was also encouraged by the Imaam to do short talks on Islam, particularly on Friday afternoons, after the *Jumah Namaaz*. This transformation provided Raana's family with the confidence that he would forget his longing for Sati, and eventually settle down into a relationship with someone from his own religion.

9.

Of Bahais and Bhais

Peter "Smokey" Ramdin smiled as he looked around to see the Cornelia Ida COBRAS supporters sighing with great relief. He observed both ends of the dominoes played on the table, and thought of resting his Double Ace at one end, or, whether he should pass his Double Five at the other.

He tried to weigh up the risk of foregoing this first opportunity to get rid of the Double Five which carried a total points score of ten, should the game reach a point where there was no outright winner, and no one could play their remaining dominoes. He also held the Double Ace, which was his lowest potential residual of two points. Should he ignore the chance to pass his Double Five and thus give Afzal and Vishnu the impression that he did not have this double? Or, should he cut the Ace, and check to see who had more Fives or Aces?

When Peter finally played his Double Five, some of his supporters shouted a resounding "Yes!". The referee turned around to face them, and warned them to stop showing such obvious signs of approval. The supporters of all three teams angrily advised the referee that there was nothing wrong with applauding a play. After all, this was why they were there.

Michael, in one of his coaching sessions with the ACES, held in the pavilion of the Leonora Cricket Club Ground at Edinburgh which was situated between Leonora and Anna Catherina, opened the discussion after a round of practice games of Dominoes.

He said, "Gentlemen, the Doubles in Dominoes are very important tickets. Vishnu, our captain, knows how very important the Double Six is. When a player starts a game with the Double Six, he or she immediately has one less domino to worry about. Instead, this play adds pressure on the next player who has only one option to play; the Six. So, the chances of having a domino in hand to play are reduced by about fifty percent."

Nazir sipped some of his mauby drink, and said, "So, this is why our captain Double Six tries to grab this domino as soon the shuffle ends, and thus put him into a position of great strength, right at the start of the game. The next player has only one option, and if he does not have a Six, he has to rap."

Carlos said, "We all know about this, but if that next player has actually drawn a few Sixes, then the pressure is much reduced. So, it is possible that this player can claim the early advantage in the game. In other words, this is one way that Vishnu's ploy to be the first to play the Double Six, could backfire on him."

John said, "You can talk as much as you like, but this game is not so difficult, and a lot depends on the luck of the draw. It's the same with card games. In our local game of *trup chaal*, if a player is dealt with more of one of the four suites of clubs, diamonds, spades, or hearts, then he or she will always have the upper hand."

Michael said, "Aha! But you still have to be able to read the game, and use this advantage properly. Otherwise, you could end up losing the game. Skills have to combine with luck, and the opponent's incompetence, to improve the odds of winning."

Carlos said, "I can only agree with this to some extent. Sometimes you have to bluff your opponents to make them think in one way whilst you do something completely different. Some Domino players are very predictable. They would always try to play their biggest numbers, and keep the dominoes with the least points, so that when the game comes to a dead-end, they declare the least total points held to win the game. Some players go to great lengths to hang on to the Double Blank or Ace Blank, or even the Double Ace or Two Blank. I often try to draw these dominoes out from those types of players."

Nazir said, "When I first started to play Dominoes, I would do just that. But now, I try to win the game without having to rely on a less points situation. Sometimes this may mean that I avoid passing my Double Fives or Double Fours at the first opportunity, just to add some doubt in my opponents' minds."

Michael said, "Nazir, no wonder we call you "Snake Eyes". You are always full of tricks, and trying to outsmart everyone. Right now, I do not believe a word you just said. I have observed your play, and you do not play as you just said. You may be too clever for your own good, and many times you end up losing games you should have easily won."

John said, "If that is true, I have to admire Nazir. He would be very stupid to tell anyone about his real tactics, even though we are his teammates!"

Carlos said, "I agree with John that this game is very simple. You all try to complicate things too much, and can forget what your plans are during the heat of the moment. I play a safe and steady game, and put pressure on when I need to, and ease off when the time is right. Then sometimes it's all out attack. No one can work out my approach or tactics."

Michael said, "Well, you have just told us something very interesting. We are all guilty of doing what Nazir has just said. We do not really give away our real plans, and true tactics."

Vishnu said, "To me, Dominoes can reflect life itself. It is a simple game. We make it sound as if it is so complex. I agree with Carlos that you just have to adjust your tactics, and play as you go along. Contrary to what you all think I do not just rely on drawing the Double Six to start every game."

Nazir laughed, and said, "Well Mister Double Six, you can try and pull that one again!"

Michael said, "Gentlemen, there is something I wish to share with you."

Nazir said, "Oh, at long last this man will buy us all a round of drinks!"

John said, "Yes man, history is about to be created by our Histry Maan!"

Carlos said, "No way! I think he wants to pass on some more new found wisdom to us."

Michael said, "The Double Five is something that reflects much about us as human beings. We all have five fingers on each hand, five toes on each foot, and so much of what we do depends on these digits."

Nazir said, "Never mind about our digits. Can you use one of yours, and take out some money from your zipped up pockets, and buy us some refreshments for a change?"

Michael ignored Nazir, and said, "For example, if we lose one of our big toes, we will find it very difficult to climb up the stairs. We also have five senses, and we live in a world with five main elements on five large continents. Right here in Guyana we have five main races of people, and five main religions."

Carlos asked, "Is that why you chose to have five children?"

Michael said, "No, I just love, along with my beautiful Doreen, the fact that God in his wisdom blessed us with five beautiful children."

Carlos said, "They may be beautiful, but thank the Lord that he chose to make them resemble their mother, and not you!"

Michael smiled, and said, "So, speaking about the relevance of five and fifty five, I wish to tell you all about a faith that we should all take notice of, and embrace. I told you about my respect for Buddhism, but I really do admire the Bahai Faith."

Nazir asked, "The what faith? The *Bhai* faith? We are all Bhais or brothers. I have never heard of this being a religion."

Michael said, "Not bhai as we say *jahaji bhai*, but Bahai!"

Carlos said, "Michael, do carry on, and try to ignore Nazir. You are our Histry Maan, so let us hear what you wish to share with us. And, to ease your pain, I will buy the round of drinks."

Nazir said, "Michael is becoming more of a Mystery Maan than Histry Maan! He can never stop coming out with these strange ideas."

John said, "Michael, so what is this Bahai Faith? I have never heard of this. Is it some kind of secret movement? Is it to do with the supernatural? Like *Obeah*?"

Michael shrugged his shoulders, and said, "Look my friends, the Bahai Faith was founded by a man called Baha'ullah, in Persia. In fact, before Baha'ullah, there was a great soul called the "Baab" who declared that there is only One God who is the source of all creation. He also recognised that all religions came from this One God, and that all humans have been created as equals, and should respect each other."

Nazir said, "Wait a minute Michael. This is exactly the same as in Islam. We Muslims are taught to submit ourselves to the One God that we call Allah. We respect all other religions provided they have this One God as their focus. And despite what people say, we do respect men and women as equals."

Carlos said, "Well, from the little I know of my Catholic Faith, this is also our belief."

John said, "And what about our Amerindian traditional tribal worship and practices? We also believe in One God, and this is so as we also worship the spirits of our departed ancestors. This is because we believe that God is within all of us, and in everything he created in this world and beyond."

Vishnu, who was not particularly religious, said, "As a Hindu, our sources of learning about God and Faith are several. We have the *Upanishads*, the *Ramayan*, and the *Bhagwad Gita*, which are all epic poems. These teachings, and our practices, go back much further than Judaism, Christianity, and Islam."

Michael said, "The Bahais believe that all religions have had divine messengers who have come into the world, and delivered their messages based on the situation they found. Thus I regard Lord Raam and Lord Krishna as divine Prophets from God. This is the same for Abraham, Moses, Jesus, and Mohamed."

Nazir said, "May the peace and blessings of Allah be with them."

Vishnu said, "Michael, I think that my fellow Hindus will dispute your idea that Lord Raam and Lord Krishna are Prophets of God. We believe that they are human manifestations of God."

Carlos said, "Well my friends, this is all news to me, and sounds too damn complicated. I just wish that we all do our own worship, and try to get along with everyone else."

Michael said, "Aha! This is on the right track! The Bahais believe in this, and want us to go even further. They encourage us to do our own prayers, reflect on who we are, why we are here, and to give selfless service to humanity. They want to achieve peace, unity, and freedom for all peoples across the planet."

Vishnu said, "But Michael, all the main religions teach this. Hindus do selfless service for the community, and we call this *sewa*. Muslims are expected to give generously to the poor and less well off through *zakaat*, and Christians have charity in everything that they do."

John said, "Please do not forget our Amerindian peoples try to live in peace, share their knowledge passed down by generations, and help each other in their villages, settlements, and tribes. Our people also show great respect for the environment."

Michael sighed, and said,"Well, the main difference here is that the Bahais want world peace, and to see the eradication of poverty through education. All of the major wars we know of have been as a result of one religion trying to impose itself over another. And we, that is humankind, have pursued this with extreme brutality. Even the Devil must be proud of us! In fact, when the Baab declared his mission on the 23rd of May in 1844, he and his followers were persecuted by the

Persians who were mainly *Shiite* Muslims. He was executed in a place called Tabriz in Persia, in the year 1850."

Vishnu said, "Man, to think that all of this was happening around the time that my ancestors were leaving India to come to Guyana and the other colonies, to work as indentured labourers on the sugar plantations."

Nazir said, "Vishnu, please don't forget my ancestors too!"

Michael then took out a neatly folded piece of paper from his right side trouser pocket, and looked at it before saying, "Then Baha'ullah became the torchbearer for the new message, and in the forty years to 1892, the faith developed despite many followers continuing to be persecuted and executed, until Baha'ullah's death. Then Abdul Baha became the leader of the faith until 1921. Shoghi Effendi became the Guardian of the Bahai Faith in 1921, until he died in England, in 1957."

Nazir said, "Michael, you continue to amaze me with all this knowledge! You just seem to pick this up, and reel it out to us. And how the hell do you remember the dates? Man, you should be trained to become a Professor in History!"

Carlos said, "I do not know whether Michael could have studied for a long time, and then pass all the examinations to reach this kind of level. He was too damn busy fathering children, and wasting our time to pass on these facts."

Michael said, "Look, I love to speak to people all the time, and I learn from them. This is the way I have educated myself. I also love to go to the Public Library in Georgetown to read a little, whenever I happen to be in the City. I also like to hear what you all think about these things, and hopefully we can all improve our knowledge. This is what the Bahais suggest."

Vishnu said, "OK, we understand this. But why are the Bahais important to us here in Guyana?"

Michael said, "I believe that the Bahais, by insisting on not becoming involved in politics wherever they are, is a big difference from the main faiths. I read that the first Bahai who came to live in Guyana, was a Dr Malcolm King from Jamaica. In 1955, the first Bahai Local Spiritual Assembly was elected by the members in Guyana. People from all our main races and religions have joined the Bahai Faith. And John, I have something that will be of great interest to you."

John looked up with a frown on his face, and said, "You are not going to tell me that my Amerindian people have also joined the Bahai Faith?"

Vishnu said, "Michael, you know full well that we Guyanese are keen to be involved in politics. This is so important for all the people to understand. Our democracy will grow stronger by this."

Michael said, "Let me deal with John first. I have read that by the late 1970s, many Amerindian people from tribes such as the *Wai Wai*, joined the Bahai Faith. Maybe this is something that you should check out for yourself. The important thing is that they were never forced to join, and they did so because they could see that the Bahais just wanted to help their communities with their education, and their provisions. Your people are very intelligent, and know when to trust others, after years of suffering at the hands of colonists, and certain missionaries."

Carlos said, "Man, this is all beginning to make sense to me now. But I am just happy with my Catholic Faith, and I see no reason to change."

Michael said, "Aha! The Bahai Faith does encourage us all to remain Catholics, Muslims, or Hindus, and we can all join in their gatherings to discuss our Faiths, and so on. They have nothing to gain by wasting time to try to convert you from your religion. Everyone who joins does so voluntarily, as have the Amerindians. The Bahais respect our religions, our customs, and our values. All they want is for world peace, the betterment of humanity through education, and the removal of poverty."

Nazir said, "Michael, this is very interesting to know. So, what else do the Bahais do? Do they pray five times per day, fast for twenty-eight days, and so on?"

Michael said, "They do not have a Bible or Qur'an as such, and they just contemplate God with respect as they gather to discuss religion, and other issues. But strangely, they have nineteen months in their calendar, and perform fasting for nineteen days from the first of March to the twentieth of March. Then they celebrate their New Year on the twenty-first of March."

Nazir said, "The twenty-first of March is the first day of Spring. In Guyana, we do not have the four seasons of Winter, Spring, Summer and Autumn. We have dry seasons and rainy seasons. So, celebrating a New Year will feel strange in March. I will never do that, and prefer to stick to our Ole Years and New Years as we do."

Carlos said, "You see, this is the problem with all religions. The teachings are great, but the festivals can cause a lot of confusion."

Nazir said, "Well, I have no problems with religious celebrations like Easter, Eid, Pagwa, Diwali, Christmas, and so on. But a Bahai New Year will confuse things. Then we also have to take note of the Chinese New Year. Furthermore, I will never change my religion which tells me that the Prophet Mohamed, On Whom Be Peace, is the last and final Divine Messenger of Allah!"

John said, "That is a big issue for everyone who is not a Muslim. Great people have come into this world since Prophet Mohamed, On Whom Be Peace, and any claim that they were divine in any way, will always be opposed by Muslims all over the world. Then the Jews say that they are awaiting the final Messenger, and the Christians are awaiting the return of the Lord Jesus to save mankind, and so on."

Michael shrugged his shoulders, and said, "Yes John, and whilst we await the arrival of the Messiah, we get a lot of cranks like the Reverend Jim Jones from America, who led his followers who were mostly poor black Americans, to the worst mass suicide in this country in 1978."

Carlos said, "I still want to know how the hell these people managed to get into our country, take up land in the interior, and even barred ordinary Guyanese from going there."

Nazir said, "This is not difficult man. Anything can happen here when money changes hands."

Michael said, "I still can't believe that over nine hundred people could be fooled into taking their lives by drinking poison. Maybe we do need to see the return of the Messiah to save us all from madmen like Reverend Jones."

Arthur, who just arrived late for the session, said, "Michael, I do not mind who comes along to save us, because the world is in so much mess at the moment."

Vishnu said, "Yes Arthur, we Hindus know that we are in this long and dark age of Kaliyug, and nothing will change for mankind unless we all change our attitude towards each other, do our prayers properly, serve our communities selflessly, and cleanse our minds of evil. We should all seek God within ourselves, and within others, and everything. We are all one in the sight of God. I would even go so far as to say that I believe that we are all God!"

Michael said, "Amen to that my brother! Amen to that!"

Nazir said, "I like the idea that we should regard each other as Bhais, or brothers, and in this way we will not need to become Bahais. Likewise, our women should be treated as Behens, or sisters."

Carlos said, "I like that! But what about all the people who do not believe in religions, and God?"

Michael said, "Man, that is a whole new conversation!"

Nazir said, "Well, we have to learn to love and accept all of God's creation!"

Michael looked at Nazir, Arthur, Carlos, John, and then turned to face Vishnu.

He said, "When all is said and done, we have to remember to keep our focus on the one most important target. We must never let that out of our sight. We must take careful aim and direct everything to hit the bulls-eye of the target, for we may never get another chance."

Vishnu nodded.

* * *

Ramesh finally took the opportunity to meet with, and speak to Sati during her visit to the Monarch Cinema to see the latest Indian blockbuster movie of 1985, titled Raam Teri Ganga Maili. She slipped away from her two companions, and took a seat next to Ramesh in the balcony of the old cinema.

They both briefly acknowledged each other, and did not speak for a while, until the three hour long epic movie started. The audience cheered and whistled until the opening scenes caused others seated in the Stalls or "Pit" to shout at the hecklers to stop, and to watch the movie.

The music, dancing, and spectacular views of the beautiful upper reaches of the source of the sacred Ganges River in India, drew compelling attention from the full house. Fifteen minutes into the movie, Ramesh nervously reached out with his right hand, and held Sati's soft and smooth left hand. They looked at each other briefly, and then continued to stare at the action on the screen. They both, as with most of the audience, could not understand Hindi, but eagerly followed the dialogues through reading the English sub-titles appearing at the bottom of the screen.

Indian films with a patriotic or religious title or story drew special attraction to the Indian community in Guyana. Films such as Mother India, Raam aur Shyaam, Ganga Jamuna, Mughal-e-Azam, and Satyam Shivam Sundaram, provided the people with opportunities to connect with the land of their ancestors.

As the romance of the two main characters of Raam Teri Ganga Maili developed on the screen, against the spectacular backdrop of the mighty Himalayas Mountains, and the rapidly tumbling white water of the Ganges, Sati and Ramesh would exchange loving and coy glances.

Ramesh leaned over, and whispered into Sati's left ear, "I want to spend the rest of my life with you."

Sati blushed, and asked, "So, what is stopping you?"

Ramesh said, "My parents want me to continue my studies, and I may have to go abroad."

Sati sat back, and looking straight ahead at the screen, said, "So, will you go away?"

Ramesh said, "Sati, I am confused. A part of me says I must go away, and take up Medicine or Engineering. But another part says I should stay here, and do a degree at the University of Guyana, and then settle down. What should I do, Sati?"

Sati paused as she was attracted to another interesting moment in the movie.

Ramesh said, "Please Sati, do not ignore me. Tell me what to do."

Sati turned to face Ramesh, and said, "I do not want to see you go away. But you must listen to your parents, and do as they say. We are both very young, and maybe you can come back for me when you have done your studies. I will wait for you."

Ramesh noticed that tears were welling up in her eyes as she spoke.

He said, "That is my problem. I know that if I go away, it will be for at least three years. I cannot imagine how I will live alone, and concentrate on my studies, whilst thinking about you all the time."

Sati wiped away her tears, and asked, "So, how have you managed to go away, and stay in Georgetown, and still study even though I have been here?"

Ramesh said, "This is different. We both know that we can meet and talk to each other at least once every week. But being thousands of miles away in England or Canada alone, and without you, will be impossible for me to bear."

Some of the patrons sitting near to Ramesh and Sati overheard their conversation, and pleaded for them to be quiet. Others just threw empty wrappers, and other paper missiles towards the couple, hissing and swearing to emphasise their disquiet.

10.

The power of one

Vishnu relished the great opportunity to apply his most aggressive, and attacking tactic. The Double Five passed by Peter was a reasonably good move. But Vishnu's Five Ace now presented Afzal with the serious challenge of playing to the only choice on the table; an Ace at both ends.

The young fans of the ACES spotted the attack made by Vishnu, and applauded as they shouted, "Up the ACES! Up the ACES! Up the ACES!"

The referee turned around once again to face the fans, and he tried to regain some sense of order.

He said, "Please keep the noise down, and give the players a good chance to concentrate. We don't have long to wait for the end of this game. So, can you be a little more patient?"

Michael and the other ACES players gave Vishnu a thumbs up in full approval of their captain's play.

The Cornelia Ida COBRAS supporters looked on in shock as they began to realise that their applause for Peter passing his Double Five, may have been misplaced.

Michael turned to Nazir, and said, "Ah! Look at how powerful a simple low number One can become. An Ace on its own may be half as strong, but when it is joined by another One, suddenly you can feel the force. This is how we Guyanese must strive even harder to become; One People! One Nation! With One Destiny!"

Nazir said, "Michael, I agree that we have to become One People, One Nation and with One Destiny. This is the right thing for us all. Our President and all of our leaders share this hope. But when it comes to putting this into practice, we just seem to fail, time and time again."

Carlos said, "It is not just about the President or the Government. It is about every single one of us citizens of this beautiful country, pulling our weight. We have to show the way through all the things we do and say."

John said, "I have heard such talk too many times my friends. But our leaders and their stooges somehow manage to get caught up in this oneness. They seem to think one thing for us all, and look after themselves through much bribery, corruption, and "scampishness"!"

Carlos said, "My friends, we have to be very careful with our allegations. Walls have ears you know. Besides, we must deal in facts and evidence to back up what we say. These politicians have access to very good lawyers."

Nazir said, "That is total nonsense man! If anyone of them wishes to sue me, let them take me to court, and prove that they are honest!"

Michael said, "Nazir, you and I know that not all politicians behave in this way. The vast majority of them are honest, and are truly dedicated to the service of all Guyanese, as one people."

Carlos said, "So Michael, why is it that we keep reading in the newspapers about so much corruption in Government?"

Michael said, "You cannot believe everything you read in the newspapers. They try to sensationalise any piece of news, and put out very bold allegations. But hardly any of these are ever proven."

John said, "Man, we Guyanese do not need the newspapers to spread the news. Just tell the wife only half a truth, and in no time the whole village and entire district will know about it."

Arthur said, "But we Chinese believe that by the time the original story gets from one person to another at the end, the whole story is contorted. We call that Chinese whispers!"

Michael said, "Yes, the people call this "small talk", but we do know how quickly this becomes "big talk"!"

John said, "I think that our newspaper journalists do serve a good purpose by making us think about things going on around us. The politicians have to think twice before they get caught with their hands in the tills."

Nazir said, "John, I never thought about it like this. I always felt that the newspaper editors are themselves playing politics, and trying to influence our thinking. But they play too much with the amount of freedom that they have; the so called freedom of the press."

Michael said, "Carlos mentioned a good thing just now. I think that this idea of each one of us working towards our country's development, and not just to rely on the government to do everything for us, came from the late John F Kennedy in his inaugural speech when he became President of America. This was back in the early 1960s."

Carlos said, "Yes, do not ask what your government can do for you; ask what you can do for your government, or something like that. It was very inspirational for me as a young person in High School, and it still holds true today."

Michael said, "Aha! Nations are built out of the efforts of their people, their citizens working for each other, and serving their country."

Arthur said, "But sometimes this gets too far when the whole population is forced to do this in a way dictated by the government. This is what happened in China with Mao and his damn red book!"

Michael said, "Yes, and there will come a time when China will use this power of the people to build up their country, and become a very successful economy."

Nazir said, "That may be so, but all I work for is to feed my family, and pay my damn taxes to those crooks. Michael, you should have been a politician. You know so much history, philosophy, and economics. And, above all, I think that you are a very honest man."

Michael adjusted his spectacles to sit just on the tip of his long nose, and smiled.

Carlos said, "Michael a politician? You must be mad! He just appears to know the things we have never heard of. For all we know, he just makes these things up, and then passes them on to us. He cannot even organise a drink up in a distillery!"

John said, "Look, to be a politician you have to have the ability to speak fluently to the public, to know what you are talking about, and to have some experience of helping to change peoples' lives for the better."

Nazir said, "Yes John. I love the way our leader of the opposition, Doctor Cheddi Jagan speaks to the ordinary people when he comes to our villages. He speaks like the common man in our broken English so that we all believe everything that he says. He is also the most honest politician that I have ever known. He is a true man of the people. I mean every kind of person whether we are African, Chinese, Indian or Amerindian. I think that our Michael here is a person like Doctor Jagan."

Carlos said, "Nazir, I just cannot agree with comparing Michael to such a great man. Michael passes the speech element, even though he really does not know what he is talking about. But most importantly, he has never run anything."

Nazir said, "I think that you are being too harsh on our coach here. If this man never comes here, and shares all this information with us, we would be left in the dark. Don't forget that it is Michael who tries to advise us in our Domino Team. We may not listen to him all the time, but without him we may never win a game."

Carlos said, "Nazir that does not make him suitable to be a politician. He needs to be more convincing, and be able to inspire people to do things his way."

Michael lifted his spectacles, and rested it over his forehead, and said, "My friends, you are all wrong about me. I love my world. I love to read widely about all kinds of things. And, I love to share my knowledge with everyone. I do not like politics and politicians, so I can never be one."

Nazir said, "Michael I think that we all really appreciate you. But this is typical of us Guyanese. When a man or a woman tries to lift themselves up, we always try to pull him or her down. We behave like live crabs in a barrel. We climb over each other, and not one of us gets to the top."

Carlos said, "The problem with the crabs is that none of them wish to be left at the bottom of the barrel because the ones which manage to escape will never turn back to those left behind."

Michael said, "The real difference between our people and those crabs is that most of our people who have left to better themselves abroad, have turned back to support their family or relatives to survive in, or get out of Guyana."

John said, "Do not believe that those people who left Guyana over the last thirty and more years, either to work or study in England, Canada and America, have had it all on a plate. They have had to face up to blatant racism, prejudice, and discrimination in every step in their journey to better themselves. My father told me that in England, during the 1950s and 1960s, some of our people, and those from the Caribbean Islands, were faced with signs at houses offering rooms to rent, that read "No Irish, No Dogs, and No Blacks". In other words, Black people were treated as inferior to dogs."

Michael said, "I was told about how the immigrants were regularly picked on, spat at, sworn at, and attacked by racists, young and old.

But our people put all their effort into working hard, sometimes in two jobs, to save some money, and send some help to their family and other relations back home."

Carlos said, "How can the English people forget that so many millions of people from the Commonwealth sacrificed so much in the two World Wars, and yet treat them with such nasty contempt, and hatred. I for one would have packed up, and get the hell back to Guyana."

Nazir said, "I agree with you Carlos. One negative thing about this business of receiving handouts from relatives abroad is how much it has created a culture of dependency here in Guyana. The free goods and money have made us so damn lazy. We need to get up off our asses and work even harder to build our own country, and not go abroad to build theirs."

Michael said, "We are a very strong people. We know how to survive, and to build. We still have a lot of very bright people here. But we can do with some more additional experience which Guyanese living abroad have accumulated, in many fields and over many years."

John said, "We can still recover from this, and our government should try harder to encourage such Guyanese from abroad, to come back, and help us build this country together."

Michael said, "All very good. But firstly, we have to make the conditions in this country safer for everyone. The criminals and crime are doing this country great harm. We have to find ways to end this and control such tendencies. Then we have to re-build the things we have lost. Like, for example, renovate and modernise our factories, transport, schools, and hospitals."

Nazir said, "Michael, now you are talking like a real politician! We must also have regular supplies of clean drinking water, and cheaper electricity. Even the rich countries like America, Canada and England always try to develop these things further. We just seem to allow everything to be run down, and left abandoned. You cannot build a country in this way."

Carlos said, "We do try to spend on these important things, and end up borrowing more and more from the World Bank, and still we cannot have these developments that you and Michael mentioned. Just look at that stupid floating bridge across the Demerara River! It was a great idea to build a crossing there to help speed up our travelling, and for transporting goods to and from Georgetown. But it looks so damn cheap, unstable, and always seems to need repair."

Michael said, "Carlos, you have to be a bit more realistic. The Demerara Bridge could never be a massive expensive construction that you see in the rich countries. If it was ever built like a great suspension bridge, we will never ever be able to pay for it, let alone maintain it."

Arthur, who was constantly looking through the windows of the hall to check on whether the wives were on their way back, turned around and said, "The problem with a cheaply built bridge like ours, is the need to always have some kind of repair work going on. Every time there is some repair to be done, there is a massive traffic jam. Then we have to learn the timetable as to when it would be opened and closed to allow large vessels to pass through the middle section. But we all have to agree that it is a far better option than the very slow ferry system. Sometimes we have to give the government some credit."

Nazir said, "I can't argue with that. The ferry system was a much better and safer option than crossing the river in those small boats. But the ferry was too damn slow. Maybe we should have had two ferries working in tandem, and that would have speeded things up."

John said, "I loved the ferry, and especially at the time when we were all travelling to go to our High Schools in Georgetown. I loved talking to the lovely young ladies who used to huddle together in small groups in their brightly coloured uniforms, like different types of birds."

Nazir smiled, and said, "Yes, the girls seemed to flock together according to their High Schools, and the uniforms were very bright greens, or yellows."

Carlos said, "Yes John and Nazir. You two did think that you were some kind of Romeos!"

Michael said, "I don't think that we could trust any ferry captain to avoid crashing their ferry into the other. You know how reckless we Guyanese drivers are. Mind you, that idea could work in the larger and wider Essequibo River, and the Berbice River."

Arthur said, "All very good ideas my friends, but Guyana has one major problem. If we develop these things too quickly, they may never become economic and pay for themselves. You see, simply because our country's very small population of only three quarters of a million people, we do not have enough consumers of our own, to support large scale production."

Nazir said, "Arthur, you are right to some extent. I am not the economics scholar here, but our country's growth can only improve if we produce things that people outside of Guyana really want. This is what we should be doing with our sugar, rice, bauxite, gold, and diamonds. We have to become greater exporters."

Michael said, "Well said Nazir. But we do such exporting, and still we seem to struggle!"

Nazir said, "Well, the answer is very simple. There are many other much larger countries that produce sugar and rice in much larger quantities, and at much lower price than us. We just cannot compete with them. We need to find other things to produce, and to develop good markets for them."

Carlos said, "You may be right Nazir. Look at tiny Trinidad and Tobago. They have oil and asphalt which they export to all over the Caribbean and Guyana."

Nazir said, "This is a very interesting point. None of us can ever understand why Guyana, being so close to Trinidad and our close neighbours Venezuela, do not seem to have oil in Essequibo, or even off that Coast. This is a real mystery to me."

Michael said, "Yes, all attempts to find oil in Guyana seem to fail. We have been trying to unlock this mystery for a long time, and with no luck."

John said, "Man, I think that the Venezuelans know why they continue to claim the whole of the Essequibo. They have a damn good idea of where all the oil and other minerals are."

Carlos giggled, and said, "Maybe we should allow Venezuela to invade Essequibo, wait until they find the oil, and then let America and Britain kick them out!"

Michael said, "That is just such a stupid idea!"

Nazir said, "Yes Michael, they will never be allowed to invade Guyana, and take away almost half of our country. America and Britain will not stand aside and let this happen. Just look at how Britain fought for the Falklands Islands, and kicked out the Argentineans who dared to invade them."

Michael said, "Those small Islands only have a few thousand people and sheep on them, and yet Mrs Thatcher, the British Prime Minister, sent the Navy, Army and Air Force thousands of miles to reclaim them. Venezuela will not stand a chance if they invaded Guyana."

John said, "When all is said and done, if and when oil is found and starts to develop, we will see a lot of Guyanese overseas rushing back to get some of the action."

Michael said, "Nice to have such dreams, but I think that people who are running this country will be first in the queue, and soon the shutters will be put up."

Arthur turned to his friends, and whispered, "Shh! Keep quiet now. Just pay attention to the game, and stay as still as possible."

Michael asked, "Why? What's the matter?"

Arthur said, "Well, Doreen and at least three of our wives are marching towards the hall. And, to make things worse, they are all armed with broomsticks! I think that this invasion will be very painful for some of us!"

Nazir said, "Oh Allah! I can see my wife Neesha is also with them. She has a leather belt in one hand, and a broomstick in the other! I think that we should run like hell from this place!"

Michael stood up proudly, and said, "Come on man. Don't be a coward. Stand up like a man! The moment you show any signs of panic, and try to evade them, you will be in bigger trouble."

John said, "Michael is right. Let us all walk quietly away through the back door, and leave him here to take the blows!"

Carlos said, "Yes, I agree. Since Michael knows the power of one so much, he can face up to the women, all by himself."

Arthur said, "John, Carlos and Nazir, shame on you all! You are all strong grown men. Surely you can stand here and help Michael."

John, Carlos and Nazir together asked, "And what will you do?"

Arthur inched away, and said, "Well, I will run for it!"

He made a dash for the back door, and as soon as he opened it, he was confronted by Vishnu's wife, Parvati, and Carlos's wife, Maria. He stopped abruptly, and ran back towards his friends who were standing beside the Domino table. All the other spectators were in fits of laughter at the commotion.

Doreen, Neesha, and Muriel, who was John's wife, appeared through the front entrance, and took up their positions directly in front of Michael, Nazir and John.

Vishnu, Afzal and Peter, along with the referee, stood around the table, in preparation to protect the dominoes played in the game so far, and the seven lying face down.

Doreen led the attack by threatening to strike Michael as he stepped forward with his hands held up as if in surrender.

He said shakily, "Buttercup, please don't do this to us. Look at how everyone is laughing at us. Please let us finish this one last game. And, we will do anything you ask."

Doreen raised her broomstick aloft, and was restrained by Neesha who said, "They have all pushed their luck too far! Stop the game right now, and everything will be fine!"

Nazir said feebly, "Neesh! Please don't hit me in front of all these people here! What will they think of us?

Parvati, who was a very imposing woman, banged the base of her broomstick on the wooden floor, and shouted, "Vishnu! Come home right now!"

Vishnu was about to quietly obey Parvati's order, and as he began to walk towards her, the referee intervened.

He said, "Please good ladies! There is no need for this fight. The game will be over soon, and I will personally make sure that they all return to their homes."

Just then, Ruff eased himself off his chair, and stepped forward to face the ladies.

He said, "Now now girls. You should not break the law here. Or else..."

Muriel stood in front of Ruff, and said, "Or else what! You can't do anything to us! You are not a policeman anymore. So just sit down, and keep well out of this!"

The LIONS and COBRAS supporters shouted instructions to Ruff, to arrest her, to take them all away, and to "Ruff" them up!"

The women quickly gathered around Ruff, and vented all their anger and frustrations towards him. He quietly backed away towards the exit. They then marched behind him, and continued to shout abuse at him as he left.

The room was restored to order, and as everyone settled down to continue with the game, Michael said, "Good old Ruff. He's done it again, and rescued us. God bless him!"

The referee announced the resumption of the game, and everyone began to anticipate the next move. Afzal looked at the Aces at both ends of the string of dominoes on the table, and finally decided on his action.

* * *

Ramesh looked at his watch, and said, "Sati, this movie will go on for another two hours. Please come with me, and we can talk some more."

Sati looked across to where her two chaperons were sitting, and signalled to them that she and Ramesh will go out. They nodded back their approval, and Sati left the cinema with Ramesh.

Ramesh mounted his motorcycle, and encouraged Sati to sit behind him. She was very nervous about the motorcycle, and about being seen by anyone who would recognise her. She covered her face with her scarf, and held on to Ramesh's shoulders.

The motorcycle ride was smooth and pleasant on the newly tarmacked road from Anna Catherina westwards to Parika, which was on the edge of the Essequibo River.

They found a secluded area a short distance away from the seafront, and Ramesh spread out a small blanket beneath the shelter of a large mango tree. They sat down, leaned against the thick trunk, and stretched their legs outwards.

Ramesh said, "Sati, I really need to know from you, how you feel about me going abroad, and leaving you here. I am worried that in three to four years time, you may meet someone like Raana, and you will not wait for me to return."

Sati said, "I wish that you do not mention Raana to me ever again. We are finished, and there is no way that we will ever be together."

Ramesh said, "But Sati, I have heard that Raana has become more religious, and he wants to get married before he goes off to Saudi Arabia to study his religion."

Sati said, "What? This is news to me!"

Ramesh said, "Well, that is what I have heard, and I am not lying to you."

Sati said, "There is no way that Raana's parents will ask for me, as a Hindu girl, if their son is going to become an Imaam. So, there is your answer Ramesh."

Ramesh said, "But there will be other people who will ask for you when I am not here."

Sati said, "The truth is that I love you more than life itself, and I will refuse every approach until you come back."

II.

El Dorado

When Afzal clenched his right fist and hit the table, saying *rap*, all the ACES and COBRAS supporters cheered wildly. Some of them jumped up and down so vigorously that the wooden floor of the hall bounced, and creaked under the new pressure.

Everyone now knew that Afzal did not hold any Aces, and he and his team were thus in the worst position with four dominoes left in his hand. When a player is forced to rap or pass, the opponents could begin to make assumptions about which numbers he has, and thus adjust their tactics in such a way as to deny him further opportunities to play his remaining dominoes.

Both Vishnu and Peter now knew that they held a distinct advantage over Afzal. They studied the dominoes that were played on the table, assessed whether or not their remaining dominoes held greater power, and they smiled at each other.

Vishnu and the ACES supporters knew that the greater advantage in the game was with them, as the pressure to make a good move was now transferred to Peter.

Michael said, "Well, well, well! The tide has really turned our way. But before we get too carried away, one brilliant move can take this advantage right out of our hands."

The referee looked at Michael, and put his right index finger to his pursed lips in an effort to stop him from openly commenting on the game.

Carlos said, "Michael, sometimes when you have to make choices, and you are not completely sure about which one to take, you can end up losing a lot."

This comment once again prompted Michael to pass on some more of his acquired wisdom to his friends.

He said, "Yes, when Sir Walter Raleigh came to Guyana in 1595, he was looking for this city called El Dorado. He and his crew reached the mouth of the river that he thought would lead them directly to this amazing place. But one wrong move, and he never found El Dorado here."

Nazir asked, "Is this Raleigh person the same as the one who made the bicycles?"

John said, "Nazir, sometimes you ask the most stupid questions. The Raleigh bicycles were invented long after Sir Walter Raleigh lost his way, and his head."

Arthur said, "Man, my experiences of trying to ride one of those bicycles always put me in danger because I couldn't control the steering handle."

Michael continued, "Yes, Sir Walter Raleigh, the great explorer, was executed back in London. I think that he paid the ultimate price for his mistakes in not finding the elusive El Dorado, the city that was supposed to be paved with gold. We are told though, that he was a great author, and wrote a popular book about Guyana being a great and beautiful land, with lots of riches."

Arthur said, "Sadly for him, we now know that Guyana has a lot of good quality gold; the same gold that he and the other so called explorers could not find here."

Carlos said, "But we still find that our local jewellers always mixing our pure gold with copper, and passing this off as good pieces. That is why I prefer to buy my jewellery in Georgetown."

Nazir said, "It is a great shame that we have to risk being robbed in broad daylight in the streets of Georgetown, by the expert *choke and robbers* whom the police can never catch."

Carlos said, "Nazir, people from the countryside are so stupid. Why do the women wear all their finest necklaces, bangles and rings when they go to Georgetown to do their business? They just invite trouble."

Michael said, "No Carlos, people now know not to wear the real stuff. They put on their fake jewellery, and know that if they get robbed, they would not lose much."

John said, "Do you really think that the criminals do not know about this trick? They now threaten some of the women, and force them to go to the jewel stores to buy the real gold, and then take them away. Why don't we all do as my people? Simply wear our colourful beads, and no one wastes their time to rob us."

Michael shook his head, and said, "This kind of street crime is now too petty. The robberies have now grown too violent with criminals from Georgetown raiding homes and businesses here in the villages, with heavy arms. They even shoot some of their victims who refuse to open up their safes. This terror has been allowed to spread all over our country, and no one seems to be able to stop it."

Nazir said, "Sadly, the targets are mostly the richer Indian people who think that keeping large amounts of money and jewellery in safes in their homes is better than in banks."

Carlos said, "Our family and friends from abroad also come over here, and just seem to feed this crime wave. As soon as they land at the airport, the criminals can see who the Guyanese tourists are. They follow them from the airport, and find out exactly which homes they stay at."

Michael said, "I heard that there are people who work at the airport, who can see what is declared by the visitors, with the addresses they plan to stay at, and then sell this information to the criminals."

Nazir said, "I think that sounds very clever. So, how come none of these airport workers have been caught?"

John said, "Look, it's all down to people being stupid. Why do our family and friends from abroad come here on their holidays, and wear clothes which make them stand out, and become the obvious targets? They walk around with their large expensive cameras round their necks, and step out in their oversized hats, and squeaky clean trainers. It's like they are saying "Look at me. Come over and rob me!""

Nazir said, "We all laugh at our own relatives when they come over from America, Canada, and England, and start to speak like true Americans or English people. They sound so ridiculous!"

Michael said, "Do you remember the time when people were rushing out of Guyana to New York, and many of them would be held up at the airport, and after a couple of days, get deported back to Guyana?"

Carlos said, "Yes, I remember one of my friends from CI who was away for only two to three days, and when he returned in shame, he locked himself up in his parent's home for weeks. Then when he finally appeared, he started to speak in this bad American accent. We all could not stop laughing at him."

Nazir said, "That guy even said that he locked himself away so that he could preserve his new complexion!"

They all laughed heartily, and the referee gestured at them to be quiet.

Peter, ever the slow, deliberate thinker, seemed to realise that Vishnu had switched his attack from Sixes, to Aces, and with Afzal not having any Aces, he needed to work out which Aces Vishnu held, if any.

He could see that Vishnu had played a Four Ace, a Six Ace, and a Five Ace. Then Afzal had played his only Ace; the Three Ace. Peter held the Two or Deuce Ace, and Double Ace. Therefore, Vishnu either had the remaining Ace Blank, or, he had tried to bluff, or pretend that he actually held more Aces. Or, the Ace Blank was part of the seven dominoes remaining face down on the table.

Peter felt that if he rested his Double Ace, and forced Vishnu to either play his Ace Blank, or rap, then he may not get Afzal to play a Four, and thus allow him to *pass* his Double Four. Or, should he *cut* one of the Aces with his Deuce Ace, and put pressure back onto Vishnu?

The spectators of the three teams all seemed to be attuned to the challenge facing Peter, and they whispered amongst themselves.

Michael realised that Peter's next play could turn the game round towards the COBRAS.

He turned to Carlos and said, "Coming back to Sir Walter Raleigh, do you know that even after he and his crew failed to find El Dorado up the Orinoco River, he took back some rocks to England, and tried to convince his Queen Elizabeth the First, that he knew where Guyana's gold was? And, in no time, England's great rival, the Dutch, sent their first expedition to explore Guyana."

Carlos said, "You are going to tell us that even the Dutch failed to find the gold."

Michael said, "Yes, not only the Dutch, but sadly for Raleigh, he returned in the year 1617, and failed yet again. This time, when he returned to England, he ended up being executed."

Nazir said, "Man that is the kind of punishment we should have here in Guyana, to help put a stop to all this armed robbery and violence. If the police cannot catch these criminals, then we should take the law into our own hands, and hunt them down."

John said, "Nazir, you are talking like those Western cowboy movies you see. As soon as a bank is robbed in those American frontier towns, the Sheriff gathers up a posse of men to ride out to look for the outlaws. When the suspects are caught, the Sheriff quickly gets the local Judge to do a trial, and pass the death penalty. The Sheriff and his posse and all the town folk would gather round the execution site, and one by one the condemned outlaws would be hanged. We do not want that kind of cowboy operation here in these modern times."

Michael said, "You are talking about the kind of justice that happened over one hundred years ago. We cannot go around rounding up people we suspect, and have them executed."

John said, "No, the best thing to do is to catch them, and give them a good hiding before handing them over to the police."

Nazir said, "Yes, I agree. Perhaps we need to change our laws into an Islamic *Sharia* system where people who are found guilty of stealing get their hands chopped off. This still happens in Saudi Arabia."

Michael said, "I have been told that Sharia Law is very good for resolving family disputes, and so on. But I think that such brutal punishments are too barbaric for these modern times."

Carlos said, "But I also heard that you can walk with all your expensive jewellery in Arabia quite freely. Thieves and stealing are very rare."

Nazir said, "Yes, very rare because anyone without hands cannot pick pockets!"

Michael said, "Was it not Mahatma Gandhi who said that if you have a system with "An eye for an eye", you will end up with the whole world becoming blind?"

Carlos said, "Maybe we are all blind right now, and cannot see why these things are happening to us here, and in almost every other village and town. As Gandhi was saying, if the robberies go on unstopped, then there will come a time when we will all have nothing to be robbed of."

Nazir said, "Then the gangs of robbers will start fighting each other until only one survives."

Carlos said, "Aha! This is like the Mafia movies you have seen where the gangs end up in gang wars, and massacre each other."

Michael said, "No my friends, the Mafia in America and Italy are very different compared to our jackasses. They are much more clever and sophisticated to be compared to our low lives. Our gangs are just clumsy, brutal, and are completely lacking in intelligence. Someday, someone will step up, and sort them all out."

John said, "Michael that is the problem with us Guyanese. When we have a problem, we just sit back, and hope that some "Lone Ranger" will come along, and sort things out for us. We just do not have that fighting spirit that our ancestors had. They would not stand back and let this nonsense take over their lives. They would get up, stand up and fight for their rights. We have become so cowardly, and all we can do is stand here and talk about the problems."

Nazir said, "Well, right now in Guyana we do not have such a person, and we just have to wait and see. Unless Michael, you have some plans to sort all of this out."

Michael coughed slightly, and said, "The root of the problem is all about some people believing that it is a waste of their time to work honestly, and hard, for a living. So, the easiest thing for them to do is to rob others who are prepared to put in such effort for their families. These gangsters do not understand responsibility and respect for others, and their property. They truly believe that armed robbery is their job and career."

Carlos said, "Yes, all well and good for them as long as they get away with their robberies and murders. But I believe that when they are caught, it should be the end of their career, and life."

Nazir said, "Yes Carlos we should "Hang em High!""

* * *

Ramesh and Sati continued to talk about what they would each do when they were thousands of miles apart.

Ramesh said, "I heard that the winter months in England, Canada and America are dark and very cold. The nearest we feel such coldness is when we take a shower first thing in the mornings, from our overhead water tanks."

Sati said, "Well, all you have to do is think of me, and you will feel warm. I will also think of you, and send you warm thoughts."

Ramesh smiled, and asked, "Is this possible?"

Sati blushed, and said, "Well, they say that when two people are so close together, anything is possible."

Ramesh said, "I worry that this will not happen."

Sati said, "Well, you will have to put all your energy, and concentration into your studies."

They clung to each other more tightly as they continued to express their fears and hopes for the future.

As time rolled on, and as the film began to move towards the climax of the story, Sati's two chaperons began to look around with increasing concern. One of the girls stood up, looked towards the doorways that led from the balcony, and was promptly heckled by other patrons, to sit down.

A few more anxious minutes passed, and the chaperons became very relieved to see the return of Ramesh and Sati, only just before the end of the movie.

Sati took up her seat beside her two companions, and they began to whisper to each other. They would then look up in the direction where Ramesh sat, and giggle.

When the movie ended, the three girlfriends stopped to buy some snacks from the vendor whose stall was near the entrance to the cinema, and below one of the two large poster boards advertising the current shows and the next attractions.

They tried to ignore the teasing by a group of young men who seemed to be on the lookout for prospective girlfriends. Sati led the rebuff by arrogantly dismissing their flimsy efforts at making conversation, and telling them to get lost.

The young men ignored Sati's threats and instructions, and moved closer to the three girls. They continued to ask for further details as to their names, and where they lived. The girls tried to ignore the advances, and began to walk away as briskly as they could. Unfortunately, they found increasing difficulty with their stiff new high-heeled shoes. They quickly gave up trying to walk faster in them, and took them off. Then, despite the relative discomfort of walking bare feet on the tarmac road, they finally hastened away. The young men stopped their pursuit, and settled for whistling and shouting at the girls.

Ramesh walked up to the young men whom he knew from the village, and warned them to behave themselves.

12.

The Lusignan Strike

Peter smiled as he decided to opt for his risky play. Instead of resting his Double Ace, and thus push some pressure back onto Vishnu, he opted to play the Ace Two.

The COBRAS supporters clearly did not agree with Peter's move, and showed their contempt for this by flinging their arms in the air, and kissing their teeth. Some of them swore several abuses to emphasise how angry they were. The referee stepped over to the supporters, and pleaded for calm. Once again he threatened to ask them to leave the hall if they continued with such bad language, and abuse. To emphasise that he really meant what he said, he picked out one particularly vocal young man, and escorted him to the exit door.

Ruff, the retired policeman, wearily plodded back into the hall. He was bearing scratch marks on his face, and arms. He appeared very tired, and worn out. He must have had a very difficult time with the wives as he tried to calm them down.

Michael asked for someone to give Ruff a cool drink to soothe him, as he slowly eased himself onto his chair which was placed just a few feet from the table where the game was being played.

Ruff took his seat quietly, and began to sip his ice cold soda cautiously, wincing with each mouthful. A young spectator offered him a dampened handkerchief to place on the bruises on his face.

Michael said, with some concern, "Ruff, thank you for helping to protect us from our very angry wives. I hope that we can get on with this final game, and sort out which team will be this year's champions."

Ruff nodded, and settled into his position to observe the game at close quarter.

Carlos noted the One Two domino played by Peter, and asked Michael, "I suppose that you have something to tell us about the One Two, or the number twelve?"

Michael smiled, and said, "Now that you have asked, I do have something to tell you all about the year 1912."

Carlos said, "I hope that it is something much more sophisticated, such as the story behind the 1912 overture."

Nazir said, "The 1912 what?"

John said, "I think that Carlos means the classical composition by Tchaikovsky, the Russian music composer. But that was the 1812 overture, not 1912."

Nazir said, "Since when Guyanese have become so interested in western classical music? I can tell you all something about our Indian Classical music which we see in the Indian films, and hear on the Radio."

Michael said, "No Nazir, we have always been listening to Western Classical music in our churches and the Hollywood films with the great Mario Lanza. You just happen to prefer to listen to your own kind of traditional music. John, I did not know that you were so familiar with this music?"

John said, "Yes, I am very informed, and I also love the Western Classical music. You see, one of the English priests who lived on our settlement up the Pomeroon River, was a great fan of this music, and he played this all the time on his gramophone. And, all the settlers soon became very familiar with Mozart, Bach, Tchaikovsky, as well as all the hymns we learnt."

Nazir said, "I must say that I am truly impressed. So, even our Amerindian people know more about Western Classical music than us."

John said, "Not all of us. Just some people."

Michael said, "The 1912 I was about to mention, is the year that we had the Lusignan Strike here in Guyana."

Carlos said, "Michael is there no end to your knowledge? Man, I have to say that I am so glad that I came to witness this great game of Dominoes. I have already learnt so much more in this one session than the sum total of all my schooling!"

Nazir said, "Well, we are about to receive another important lesson from our great Histry Maan!"

Michael said, "You all know that Lusignan is an estate on the East Coast of Demerara, and in the year 1912, the Indian Indentured labourers were still being transported to Guyana. You see, these newer immigrants were more willing to speak up for themselves, and were prepared to demand more pay from their Sugar Estate Manager."

Nazir said, "I don't quite agree with you here Michael. Every labourer, from the African Slaves, to Portuguese, to Indian and Chinese workers was always prepared to demand their rights. In fact, our women were very vocal, and they pushed the men to stand up to the Estate Managers and Drivers."

Michael said, "Yes Nazir, I agree. But in this case, the shovel gang at Lusignan decided to go on strike because of the very low wages for digging trenches and drains. With more workers coming into the country, some basic foodstuff, utensils, and clothing were becoming more expensive. The cost of living for the workers and their families was rising rapidly, and the people found that they could not keep up with the price rises and so on. And, as Nazir has said, the wives began to insist upon a demand for more money to help pay for these goods."

Carlos said, "Man, my wife does this all the time, even in these days!"

Arthur, who was still on the lookout for the return of their wives, said, "Yes, the ladies do make these demands, and I normally have no choice but to agree with them."

Michael said, "Well, many more of the workers on the Estate joined with the angry shovel gang, and they marched up to the Manager's quarters to challenge him. But soon it became like a small siege, and the Manager, his Deputy Manager, and a few other workers thus armed themselves with rifles, and aimed them at the growing mob."

Nazir said, "Do you mean to say that they were willing to shoot those people who had only their shovels, spades, forks and cutlasses to defend themselves?"

Carlos said, "Man, if I see a large and angry mob of people coming towards me and my home with shovels and so on, I would be very nervous, and want to defend myself. Especially if there was nowhere for me to run to save my life!"

Michael said, "I do not know what made the people so angry. I guess that if they were not happy with a refusal to their request for more pay for their hard work, then they had every right to give vent to their feelings. Nowadays we have Unions which would enter into tough negotiations, and hopefully come away with reasonable settlements."

John said, "But even nowadays our Unions seem to always go for strikes, just like in Lusignan."

Nazir said, "In those days, the management just said no to everything, and expected people to shut up, and get on with their work."

John said, "So, those people were right to make their demands, and when ignored, they also had the right to raise their voices and arms in protest."

Michael said, "In the decades before 1912, the workers would be told no, were beaten, and then forced to get on with their work. Anyway, despite being warned by the Manager not to cross over into the compound, the strikers tried to do so. The Manager and his Deputy started shooting, and one worker by the name of Nankoo, was hit. This caused absolute panic and mayhem. The strikers picked him up and took him away from the scene."

Carlos said, "That was terrible. It just goes to show how the English masters just did not give a damn about our people. To them, once you signed or put your thumb print to their so-called labour contract, it gave them this right to bully people, and take full advantage of them."

Nazir said, "And to shoot them as well!"

Michael said, "Despite this shooting incident, an even larger number of Indian workers marched for over twelve miles from Lusignan to Georgetown to speak to the Governor of Guyana. They even took the very sick Nankoo with them. Just imagine how brave those people were! Can you see how amazing they were to walk for such a long distance in such hot conditions? Many of them were bare-footed, and they suffered serious blisters and cuts to their soles."

Nazir said, "My heart bleeds for them. But we all know how strong and tough our people are. We would go to the ends of the earth to get what we deserve."

Carlos said, "So what happened when they reached the Governor's house?"

Michael paused for a moment, and then said, "Well, when they finally reached the Governor's house, they were prevented from entering the compound by some armed police. So, they started to chant their demands for more money, and for justice. The Immigration Agent for Guyana met with a few of the protesters, and then they were allowed to go in to meet the Governor."

Nazir said, "I cannot imagine what it must have been like for those people who would not have been able to explain their demands in good English to the Governor. So, I would not hold out much hope for them."

John said, "At least there seemed to be some common sense from the higher ups. The Lusignan Estate Manager and his Deputy should have sat down and discussed the problem with the workers. But I can see how they would behave so arrogantly towards the workers. This was the way they all knew, and there could be no room for negotiation."

Nazir said, "So, if you are not prepared to talk with people, the way to deal with them was to shoot them?"

Michael said, "Sadly, the injured Nankoo died from his wound, and the Manager of Lusignan Estate was actually arrested, charged, and brought to trial."

Arthur said, "What trial? There was no justice for the workers in those days!"

John said, "I agree Arthur. There is still no justice for our peoples. When you go to the jails, you will not see justice, you will see just US!"

Michael said, "Not only did the Manager get off because he pleaded self-defence, twenty four strikers were charged with causing a riot or disturbance. Then, to add more salt into their wounds, the Manager decided to get rid of many of the protesters, by sending them to other Sugar Estates."

Nazir said, "I bet that if the strikers had managed to harm the Manager in any way, they would not have gotten off on the grounds of self-defence!"

Michael said, "Our peoples have suffered greatly over many decades. I do hope that we can all learn from the past. Knowing about these injustices is really important to us all."

John said, "Yes, the knowledge is good to have, but this becomes very powerful if we can use it in the right way. Even today many of our so-called Managers exhibit the same bullying, and racist attitudes towards the people who work for them. And, our Managers are not Englishmen!"

Nazir said, "I agree wholeheartedly with what you have just said. We seem to have learnt to copy the English Colonialists. We hear stories about our own Guyanese businessmen in Georgetown taking advantage of the young female workers. This is so disgusting that if this ever happens to any of my daughters or relations, I will personally go to Georgetown, and beat the shit out of those bastards."

Michael said, "We have to continue to free ourselves from such hatred, and be more forgiving. We should have more control of our emotions, and have more faith and trust in God."

Carlos said, "All very well and good. But the people who rule over us also claim to have the same God, and yet they do exactly the opposite of what you just said."

Michael said, "Still, we have the one choice; not two, but one. We need to always focus our attention on the One!"

Vishnu continued to scan the dominoes played on the table, and tried his best to give the impression that he had more choices in playing at either end. Afzal looked across at Peter who just continued to mime at the hit Indian song being played on the radio across the road.

* * *

The Cornelia Ida Mosque was full to capacity for the once weekly special *Jumah Namaaz* prayers. At the end of the worship, the congregation stood up and embraced each other in the customary manner. This simple act of brotherliness of the men, young and old, was a constant reminder that they were together, and mutually respectful of each other, regardless of their status.

They all sat down and crossed their legs, facing the pulpit to listen to the special sermon. The Imaam spoke passionately about the need for Muslims to continue to support each other, and the wider community in the village. Then he introduced his avid student Raana, who stood up to deliver his talk.

Raana began by quoting verses from the Holy Qur'an and the Hadith. His Arabic was impressive, and immediately drew his audience's attention in rapt silence. He then translated the verses into English, and this caused members in the audience to stir, and murmur phrases of great appreciation, and some surprise at the young man's new knowledge.

He spoke about suicide, and why this act was deemed to be a terrible sin for Muslims, with immediate condemnation of any individual taking his or her own life in this way.

Raana continued to speak in English, and asked for forgiveness for his own act of attempting to commit suicide. He wished to dedicate the rest of his life to the service of the Mosque, and the wider community.

Members of the audience asked him very personal and intimate questions as to why he tried to kill himself. He responded by suggesting that his passion for Sati was overwhelming. It was not an overnight occurrence, but one that grew with time over a few years of their very close friendship. He had no control of his feelings, and was blinded by the desire to spend the rest of his life with her.

An older man whose neatly brushed grey beard and strong voice caused others to stop speaking and to listen, stood up. He asked for greater understanding and respect to be shown towards Raana.

He praised Raana for his boldness to speak so openly about the issue, and his personal experience. Then he turned to the congregation, and asked for everyone to show more compassion for the young man, and to accept that he was willing to change for the better.

The Imaam concluded the session by making a final *dua* in which he asked for greater understanding and support for Raana. He also warned against the growing tendency of young people to seek to take their own lives without caring about the harm to themselves, their families, and to the community.

13.

God's creations

Vishnu took out his Ace Blank domino, and slammed it down at the only end he could actually play. The show of arrogance and confidence was intended to give his opponents the impression that he could play at either end. This move presented Afzal with a real opportunity to get back into the game, and to attack Peter with another Six.

A great commotion erupted just in front of the hall. It was a massive "dog war" between several snarling, barking, and biting stray dogs of the village. Many of the spectators of the Domino game looked out through the shutters of the front windows, and seemed to momentarily lose interest in the titanic struggle between the ACES, LIONS and COBRAS.

A group of children who were on their way back from their school in Anna Catherina, stopped, and gazed at the warring dogs, from a safe distance. The dog war took a nasty turn when all the dogs began to attack one helpless mongrel. Ruff stood up to witness the furore, and soon realised that the dog that was being mauled by the pack, was his own.

He shouted, "Oh Bruno! Get away!"

He picked up his walking stick, and hurried out of the hall as quickly as he could, waving the stick frantically.

The attacking dogs were increasing the pressure on Bruno who was now pinned into the dusty bank beside the main road. The vehicular traffic slowed down to almost a halt.

Ruff finally reached the scene of the vicious assault, and lashed out wildly, hitting a few of the attacking dogs so hard that they yelped in great pain as they scampered off in different directions. Ruff continued his one man attack, and soon the other dogs also ran off. He stooped down, and gently cradled the badly beaten, bitten, and bloodied Bruno who was yelping in great pain, and was struggling to breathe.

The children also realised the extent of the tragedy unfolding before their eyes, and the spectators of the Domino game looked on with sadness and shock on their faces. Ruff spoke to Bruno as a father to a child, and no amount of comforting could save his best friend, and companion.

Arthur said, "We have to do something about those damn wild dogs just out there roaming the streets. They are such filthy, mangy, and useless creatures."

Michael said, "No Arthur, it is not the fault of the animals. This is to do with the owners who just do not care about their dogs, and just allow them to roam around as strays."

Nazir said, "It is not only about these dogs, but all the donkeys and horses which are allowed to roam free. They cause so much disruption to traffic, and to everyone going about their business in the villages."

John said, "I think that we have to be careful not to offend people who believe that all these animals should be left alone as they are sacred, and are God's creatures. I hear that the Hindu people believe that we must look after them all, especially the cattle and the monkeys."

Carlos said, "The monkeys? We do not see too many of these around nowadays. But what is so special about monkeys?"

Michael said, "My friend Vishnu told me that the monkeys are sacred as they represent the army that accompanied Lord Hanuman in his fight to defeat Raavana, the enemy of Lord Raam."

John said, "This is in the story of the Ramayan."

Nazir said, "Yes, I know that cows are also sacred, and should never be harmed. Our Prophet Mohamad, Peace be unto Him, loved cats and kept several of them. This is a tradition in the Arab countries."

Arthur said, "That means we should stop eating cattle meat, as we will be regarded as sinners in the eyes of our Hindu friends."

Michael said, "Well, I know that my Hindu friends do not make a fuss about this. But I agree that we should all respect all creatures as God's creations."

Ruff picked up Bruno, and took him away towards his house further up the main road. Arthur peered through the slats of the shutters, and followed Ruff's movements.

Carlos said, "Arthur, I hope that you are not thinking that poor Bruno could feature on your next menu!"

Michael said, "Come on Carlos that is not fair. Arthur does not use dog meat in his restaurant."

Nazir giggled, and said, "You know very well that our Chinese friends treat dogs as quite special delicacies!"

Arthur turned around, and appeared quite upset by Nazir's and Carlos's assumptions.

He said, "You two should stop talking about Chinese people in this way! This is not funny! We do not use dog meat, or cat meat, ever! Besides, you have never complained about my food!"

Michael said, "Come on guys. This is not fair on Arthur."

Nazir said, "Sorry man. We did not mean to insult you. Sorry!"

Carlos said, "Sorry Arthur. I was only joking!"

John, peering through the shutters, noticed the local butcher driving past with his latest stock in his van.

He said, "There goes Manzoor Khan. I wonder what we will get in our *pepperpot* this Saturday. Donkey and horse meat mixed with beef?"

Everyone in the hall, who overheard John, burst out with laughter. Vishnu, Afzal and Peter looked at each other, and then at the referee.

The referee called for order in the hall, and the spectators resumed their positions to observe the ongoing clash.

Michael said, "Well, we have just witnessed the dog war, and now let us see what will happen in this cat and mouse battle."

Nazir said, "Yes, we have Afzal the Mule, and Peter the Cobra, but we are very lucky to have Vishnu who is the really smart cat!"

Arthur said, "Talking about pepperpot has made me feel very hungry. I love my pepperpot with salted bread. Then, as a side dish, I like boiled *yam*, sweet potatoes, *eddoes*, plantains, and carrots."

Nazir said, "Arthur, apart from the pepperpot, you have just talked about some of the very best vegetarian food we have. I would like to add some fried *breadfruit* to that beautiful mix."

Michael said, "And don't forget to put in some sweet dumplings!"

John said, "I hope that Manzoor still has some of the *cassreep* I brought for him from the Amerindian settlement up the Pomeroon River. That is the best sauce to cook the pepperpot with."

Arthur said, "John, you have hit the nail on its head. We are so very lucky in this country. I know that our relations and friends abroad literally pine for this stuff, and when they come over for their holidays, all they want is the local fresh produce, all the time!"

John said, "Man, you cannot get a better selection of fruits and vegetables than in this beautiful and fertile land of ours. Just think of our fruits like cashews, *granadilla*, *psydium*, *genip*, mangoes, *sapodilla*, *star apple*, *custard apple*, *awaara,* guava, *sumatoo, monkey apple*, *five finger*, bananas, *soursop*, pineapple..."

Nazir said, "Man you sound like a damn fruit seller at Leonora Market!"

John continued, "Tamarind, watermelon, coconut, orange, *jack fruit*, *jamoon*, *whitee*, plantain..."

Michael interrupted, and said, "Wait a minute. Plantain is not a fruit. It is a vegetable."

Nazir said, "Here you go again. These are all fruits. In fact things like the tomato, potato and tobacco were all grown by our Amerindian friends long before other people came here."

John said, "It is amazing to think that whilst our peoples were almost wiped out by the Europeans, they have also managed to kill many millions more through the reckless overuse of tobacco as cigarettes. It is like my ancestors' revenge for what they suffered."

Michael said, "So, we must learn to respect all of God's creations, and only then we will get closer to Him."

Carlos said, "Amen to that! Amen!"

Afzal took one final look at the dominoes in his hand, and prepared to unleash a most fearful attack on Peter.

Nazir said, "Gentlemen, after all this talk about food, I hope that our wives will offer us some great stuff when we get home. I cannot wait to see what surprise my lovely Neesha has for me."

John said, "I only hope that none of us gets home too late, otherwise the surprise might be too painful to bear."

Michael said, "Well, all I can say is let's get this game over and done with, and make a dash for our homes."

* * *

When Ramesh finally met his parents to discuss his decision about his future intentions, he was full of trepidation. Having overcome his own fears and doubts about leaving his true love Sati, with her full blessing, he was not sure as to how his loving mother Parvati would react to the news of separation.

Ramesh and his parents sat down on the wooden veranda of their house which was overlooking the main road in Anna Catherina. They were comfortable in three of the four beautifully designed easy chairs placed safely behind the finely carved wooden barrier which was just above waist level, and strong enough to lean on.

They each had a glass tumbler of freshly squeezed lime juice mixed with vanilla flavouring in water. The drink was chilled by several ice cubes, and served to make the dry heat of the late afternoon more bearable.

Ramesh took a sip, and said, "Well Maa and Paa, I have made up my mind to go to London, or Toronto, or New York to study engineering. I should only be away for three to four years at the most, and I know that this will be very difficult for me, and for you both."

Tears immediately started to flow from Parvati's eyes as soon as she heard the news from Ramesh.

She said, "My son, how can you leave me like this? I love you more than anything else in this whole world. You have always been everything to me. Every breadth I take I feel your presence. It will pain me greatly to see you go so far away, and I do not know if I will still be alive when you return."

Ramesh reached out and held his mother's tender hands in the palms of his, and said, "Maa, please let me go with a cheerful heart, and with your full blessings. I shall never be happy and at ease knowing how you would be grieving for me."

Vishnu looked at his wife and son, and he also began to feel very emotional about the impending separation.

He said, "Parvati, I shall always be by your side. Of course we will both miss Ramesh, and he will miss us too. But I dearly want him to go abroad to study, and to gain a respectable qualification. Then, he can return home, and be with his family."

The family continued to discuss the effects of the separation, and the benefits of Ramesh's chosen career would bring to him, his family, and his country. Eventually, as the evening wore on towards bedtime, they agreed to Parvati's suggestion that they should perform a three day *yajna* as a blessing for Ramesh.

14.

The Golden Arrowhead

Afzal sat upright, pushed his powerfully muscular chest forward as if to emphasise the sheer strength of his move, and slammed down his Two Six domino. A Six used so late in the game, following three already having been played on the table, would normally be seen as quite potent.

Michael breathed in deeply, and exhaled with a great sigh. He said, "Ah! The 26th of May in 1966, will always stir great emotions in all Guyanese wherever they may be."

He raised his right hand, and made a salute towards the Guyana national flag that was pinned up on one of the walls of the hall, beside a large print picture of the President, Mister Linden Forbes Sampson Burnham. Some cynical spectators simply sneered at Michael, whilst the others stood to attention.

He said, "Just look at our flag, which is known as the golden arrowhead. It is so unique and outstanding. It always brings tears to my eyes. And look at that proud smile of our dear President as he watches over us!"

Carlos said, "I think that he is not watching over us, he is looking down at us poor people who have no real hope for the future."

John said, "But, at least we can be very proud of our flag, and what it stands for."

Michael lifted up his spectacles, and wiped some tears from his sullen eyes. He said, "Yes John, our flag has five prominent colours which have their meanings, but to me it is about our main races and cultures living together, and pointing to a future together."

Nazir said, "That is a nice way to look at things. But can you remember what the colours represent?"

Michael said, "Of course my friends. I will never forget that the green is for agriculture, and the main reason why our ancestors were brought here. Green also represents our forests which you can call the lungs of the country. We must thank the Lord for this blessing. Our lands are so fertile, and there is so much beauty in our forests. Our timbers are also the best in the world."

Carlos said, "Nevermind the forests being the lungs of our country. We should be cutting back on chopping down so much of them."

Nazir said, "We love to build wooden houses, with wooden furniture, and we still use too much wood for fuelling our open cookers."

Arthur said, "I will always keep our open mud stove that we call fireside. The food always tastes so much better than when we use a gas cooker."

Nazir said, "Man, every time you mention food, my belly starts to burn with hunger. I wish I could have some *saada roti*, daal, and *coconut choka* right now!"

John said, "Nazir, just bear up a little bit more, and we will all get what we are pining for."

Michael said, "Right, now back to our glorious flag. The white represents our natural and vast sources of water through our magnificent rivers."

John said, "Ah, we call our land Kaywana, the Amerindian name which means land of many waters! I think that we should change the name of this country back to Kaywana."

Nazir frowned, and asked, "Although you say that the water is white, how come everywhere the water in the canals, trenches, and rivers is always so dirty looking?"

Carlos said, "I like the Amerindian names for things, and I agree that we should go back to calling and re-naming our country, Kaywana. This is so beautiful, and unique. It will give us more a sense of belonging to an ancient tradition of the first ever Guyanese peoples."

John said, "I agree with you, but we now have so many races in the country, and each claiming greater importance over the other. This is not an African country, nor an Indian country. But we all make up a kind of diversity which is truly beautiful, and reflects the colours of our toucans, our macaws, and our tropical flowers."

Michael said, "Of course, we should be telling the whole world to come here to see the wonders of our many rivers, and our waterfalls. Our Kaiteur Falls are the most breathtaking to experience, especially in full flow."

Nazir asked, "But Michael, how can we tell the world to come here when none of us have ever seen the Falls?"

John said, "Sadly for you all, the cost of a flight by small aircraft is just too much for the ordinary Guyanese person. But for us Amerindians, and other people who have spent time in the interior, we have trekked through the jungles to go there to pay our respects on behalf of our ancestors. It is a very difficult way, but when you reach the point of hearing the waters roar, it fills you with all kinds of emotions. You feel relieved that you have finally reached so close to the Falls. Then fear at the thought of so much power being generated by the huge rush of millions of gallons of dark rusty river water. Finally, you are filled up with so much joy that you feel a massive urge to run towards the point of the water's edge, and leap over the top down to the white rapids below."

Michael said, "John that must be the best way to capture the whole experience of such a wonder. We hear that the Kaiteur Falls is about five times the height of the Niagara Falls in Canada, and it is the tallest double drop Falls in the world."

Carlos said, "Michael you talked of our fertile land, expansive forests, and Kaiteur Falls. What about our highest mountain Roraima? It is a very high plateau that straddles over a point where Brazil, Venezuela, and Guyana meet. That is also a place of great wonder, mystique and intrigue. Sir Arthur Conan Doyle wrote about this as the lost world where he thought that ancient dinosaurs and undiscovered botany still exist."

Nazir said, "Whilst we are exploring our glorious interior, please do not forget our unique jaguars, and the largest eagle in the world, known as the Harpy Eagle!"

John said, "So much natural beauty and potential! Do you know that if we manage to harness the power of our rivers we could have almost free electricity forever? I do not understand why our government is not acting on such wealth?"

Michael said, "You have to ask our President Burnham and all the other politicians that question. We all know that some attempts have been made, but unfortunately something always seem to block further progress. I suppose that if we were positioned in a very strategic point for the great powers like America, a lot more investment into these things would have been here a long time ago."

Nazir said, "Michael, you may be right. If we had oil like the Arabs, then everyone would be falling over themselves to come here. Certainly, no Guyanese would have wanted to leave this beautiful place to go abroad to make their living."

Michael said, "Talking of natural wealth, the yellow in our flag is about our vast mineral resources. Our bauxite is used to produce aluminium. We have high quality gold, diamonds, manganese, and God only knows what else, lying undiscovered all over Guyana."

Nazir said, "Maybe if we had some kind of Klondike, then real excitement will be generated with massive gold rushes!"

Carlos said, "Despite all you say and hope for, perhaps it is better for us to only have enough for what we need as a country. Too much of a good thing can eventually bring greater harm. People will become much richer too quickly, and excessive greed will take over. The next thing you know will be people reverting to crime, and other activities that cause so much grief in society."

Michael said, "Carlos, that is a bit of a bleak picture. But you may be right. Just look at how the wealthy nations end up attracting people from all over the world, and in no time, large ghettos appear in their cities."

John said, "Yes Michael. And look at all the race riots in England and America."

Nazir said, "Maybe the governments need to impose greater restrictions, and only allow foreigners to stay and work on short term contracts, and then return to their countries. This is what they do in Saudi Arabia. It is almost impossible for any non-Arab to become a citizen in those Arab countries."

John said, "What a circle! Nazir that was the very colonial idea that brought Portuguese, Indian and Chinese workers here! People will move from place to place in search of their betterment, and will eventually settle down. Can you imagine a Guyana with forty to fifty million people?"

Arthur said, "No way! Just leave Guyana with the number we have. We can hardly cope with living in harmony amongst only three quarters of a million people. What chances will we have if our population vastly increases very quickly?"

Michael said, "There is a lot of potential for us to become happier, and at peace with ourselves. The black colour in our great flag signifies our endurance. Our peoples have come through decades of struggles for our freedom, our rights to better wages, our drive to educate ourselves, and our desire to build a new nation."

Carlos said, "Michael you sound like our heroic ancestors, and the leaders of our short history who have all wanted betterment for us all. Are you sure that you do not hold any desire or ambition to go into politics, and to put your knowledge to better use?"

Michael blushed as he smiled. He said, "You are very kind to me. And as I have said so many times before, I do not have a political bone in my body. I can never be a politician where I end up compromising my own principles and beliefs just because of a desire to achieve, and stay in power. I will not be able to betray my brothers and sisters, and grab power for myself. I long for the day when all Guyanese will wake up, and push for a much greater united stand to properly exploit our freedom."

Carlos said, "There you are. You sound exactly like every politician when they start out. They have very noble intentions, and win over people's support, only to change when the desire to hang on to power takes over."

John said, "Michael, I hope and pray that the time will come when all the peoples of Guyana will be free of mistrust, and any hatred for each other. We must unite for the good of this country now, and for our future generations."

Nazir said, "I do not know what you all ate today, but you sound very drunk with so much dreaming. Right now, I cannot see such a future. You are all dreamers, and if we do not get up off our lazy asses, and do something, nothing will change here."

Michael said, "The red in our flag portrays our zeal and dynamism. Quite like Nazir's call for more action. In order for us to achieve real happiness, we have to awaken from our slumber, and take action."

Carlos said, "Michael, are you sure you are not trying to start up some kind of revolutionary movement here in our small easygoing village?"

Someone broke wind, and all the spectators responded with howls of sheer disgust, pointing at the person next to them.

Nazir said, "There is your answer! Someone here is a damn walking sewerage! This is the only movement we can make!"

When the commotion died down, and the foul smell passed, everyone settled down to witness the next move in the great game.

Michael said, "The Two Six that Afzal played, reminds me of the 26th of May 1966" Carlos said, "Yes! Michael you mentioned this before. This is the date of our Independence. It is a day for true rejoicing, of real freedom, and a new beginning for all Guyanese!"

Nazir said, "There you go again. How many times do we have to talk of freedom? Freedom from what? We have African Emancipation Day to celebrate the end to African Slavery. All the Indentured labourers became free when their contracts ended, and they made their choice between going back to their country and staying here. Then, this Independence Day, followed by Republic Day. And yet we are not free."

John said, "We Amerindians have never felt the need to celebrate any of these freedom days simply because they do not apply to us. We are still entrapped by everyone who has come here, and taken what they want from this land of ours."

Michael said, "You are right. These freedoms are only limited to certain situations, conditions, and times in our history. But we must celebrate such freedom from Slavery and foreign rule."

Carlos said, "I agree with Michael here. These times of significant change must be celebrated. Otherwise things like Slavery will never go away. I hear and read of Slavery still existing in many countries and societies all over the world. It continues to be man's worst form of inhumanity to his fellow man."

Arthur said, "There is still a lot of Slavery in child labour and entrapment in places like India and China. And, worst still, the rights of women are still being fought for all over the world. Even in the countries which have called themselves civilised!"

Nazir said, "Yes Arthur. This is what I was trying to say. Freedom is something that people will always have to keep fighting for. Then when we get it, we find that it is not quite what we expected. So we fight on."

Michael said, "Nazir, this is the essence of our existence in this world. We must not allow ourselves to be lazy, to close our eyes to what is going on around us. We must wake up to injustice and suppression in whatever form it takes, and do something about it."

Arthur said, "You know I heard that the British were made almost bankrupt by the end of the Second World War, and the Americans and Russians told them that they should not hold on to their colonies. That is why India got Independence in 1947. Then other colonies got their freedom as time went on. Can you remember how we all celebrated when Ghana became Independent?"

Michael said, "Yes, Ghana is one place where my ancestors came from as slaves. Guyana and Ghana should always remain very close, as we are with India and so on."

Nazir said, "I think that the British were very wrong in allowing India to be split to form East and West Pakistan. That was a disaster. How can you have a country called East and West Pakistan with the massive Himalayas dividing it? The British have the worst record of dividing peoples, as they have done to us here in Guyana."

Carlos said, "And, ruling them. Divide and rule has always been the British way."

Nazir said, "Well, I am sure that I speak for most Indians here in Guyana when I say that as far as we are concerned, we will always be Indian, and I personally cannot see any sense in a country called Pakistan, or for that matter, Bangladesh, which was once East Pakistan."

Carlos said, "Nazir it is much too late to even think of going back to one India. We as Portuguese have also lost much of our links to Madeira. We have lost much of our Portuguese language, and do not connect with Madeira or Portugal as you do with India. We tend to be more closely connected to Brazil."

Michael said, "All of this means that we, as Guyanese, with all our different backgrounds, heritage, culture, and religions, should find more ways to celebrate this diversity."

Arthur said, "Well, that is why we have Mashramani!"

John said, "Aha! That is also an Amerindian word used as a festival to celebrate any great event in our tribes or societies. It is like a Carnival, but our Guyanese Mashramani is to celebrate when we became a Republic on the 23rd of February in 1970."

Carlos said, "I like the idea of Mashramani, but it is too much dominated by our African brothers and sisters with all the entertainment linked to this culture, such as calypso singing, masquerades and so on."

Arthur said, "So what is wrong with this? We are all Guyanese, and nobody ever stops other people from going to the parades, and taking part in all the activities. This is an attitude problem we have here in Guyana. This Republic is for all of us, and we should all be proud of it, and always celebrate together."

Nazir said, "I agree with all of what you just said. But this Mashramani thing started up in Linden or Mackenzie back in 1970, and I think that people immediately associated it with African Guyanese culture. But I agree that we should open Mashramani much more, and give everyone a fair crack at the festival, starting with our Amerindian people right at the front of the parade."

Michael said, "Well, I am sure that the organisers actually want for all Guyanese to love and embrace Mashramani, just like the Trinidadians do for their Carnival, the Brazilians do in Rio, and even the British do at the Notting Hill Carnival in London."

Arthur said, "Before we all get too carried away with the celebrations, I think that we will now see Peter start to play some music with his bare knuckles!"

* * *

The hastily arranged three-day Yajna was held at Vishnu and Parvati's residence with an open invitation for all to attend on each of the three evenings. The main readings or *katha* were conducted by the most prominent local Pandit who was accompanied by members of the congregation of the Anna Catherina Hindu Temple. The members provided all the music and renditions of appropriate *Bhajan* and *Kirtan*.

The texts or *Chaupai* chosen by the Pandit for the three nights were from the Ramayan. They told the story of the impending banishment of Lord Raam and his consort Sita, to the forest from Ayodhya, the grief of King Dasarath, Lord Raam's father, and the utter despair of Queen Kausilya, Lord Raam's mother, at the unbearable loss of her son, for fourteen years.

Ramesh and his parents listened to the beautifully crafted poetry of Sant Tulsidas, the clear English translations, and the Pandit's skilful adaptation of the episode, to their own dilemma.

Parvati sought and obtained great consolation through the Pandit's exposition of the Ramayan, and by the end of the Yajna, she became more assured that Ramesh's departure abroad was the right thing for him to do, and that the time away was much shorter than the fourteen years of Lord Raam and Sita's experiences.

She was able to reflect on the battles that Ramesh would have to overcome as a young man in such a large city as London with a population that was over eight times that of the whole of Guyana. How would such an inexperienced boy cope amongst so many people? How would he manage on the busy streets with hundreds of cars, vans, buses and trucks? What about the trains that run below the ground? And the cold winters when darkness come as early as four o'clock in the afternoons?

Parvati realised that her wait could never compare with Kausilya's, and that Ramesh's challenges were not comparable to Lord Raam's fight with his formidable enemy, Raavana. She told Vishnu that she approved of Ramesh's trip.

Vishnu and Ramesh were very pleased with the acceptance given by Parvati, and they all set about making the preparations for Ramesh's departure.

15.

Emancipation

Peter briefly scanned both ends of the dominoes laid out on the table. He clenched the fist of his right hand, and pursed his lips.

The ACES and LIONS supporters were alive to the situation, and started to shout in unison. "Rap Peter rap!"

Peter reluctantly hit the table with the knuckle of his right fist, and almost whispered "Rap".

The ACES and LIONS supporters cheered very loudly as if the game had finally ended in their favour. The COBRAS supporters could just look on sullenly. To have to rap at this stage of any Domino game was critical, and significantly reduced a player's chances of winning the game outright. Although, if other players also struggled to play at any end, the game could be shut, and the player with the least points on their remaining dominoes will win.

Vishnu, and the ACES supporters knew that the advantage in this critical final game was now firmly within his grasp. But he had to make the right move in his next play. Or else, this advantage could easily pass onto Afzal.

He carefully surveyed his final two dominoes which he held in his left hand, and tried his best to conceal them from everyone.

Michael assumed his role as the main commentator, and said, "You know my friends, that whilst we talk so freely about our struggles, and the fight for various freedoms, we must never forget the greatest of our heroes; the mighty Kofi!"

Carlos said, "How come Cuffy was our greatest hero? He was a criminal in the 1960s who terrorised everyone until he was shot and killed by the police after a massive manhunt."

Afzal said, "Man, that Cuffy was very scary. He used to hide and live in the bush, and would only come out at night time, sometimes dressed as a woman. He would demand food, and other things from people. He was truly fearsome, and managed to keep on the run, and not get captured for a long time."

John said, "Oh yes, I remember feeling very scared to sleep at night, and people got more nervous as all kinds of rumours were spread about him."

Michael said, "No, this is not about the criminal Cuffy, but Kofi who led the Berbice Slave Rebellion in 1763."

John said, "1763? Man that was a hell of a long time ago! How can this be so important to us nowadays?"

Carlos said, "Michael must have a very good reason to choose to talk about 1763 at this moment in time. Let the man continue."

Michael said, "Thank you Carlos. It was on the 23rd of February in the year 1763, that the Berbice Slave Rebellion started against the Dutch Plantation owners. By the way, you will notice the date of the 23rd of February."

Nazir said, "Aha! This date is the same as our Republic Day which was in 1970!"

John smiled, and said, "Nazir, I am becoming more and more impressed with you, and how you are learning. If only you had paid the same sort of attention in school, heaven knows how far you would have reached!"

Michael said, "Well done Nazir! This date is very important for all Guyanese. The Berbice Slave Rebellion was a major event in our history. In fact, the African slaves were being very badly treated by their Dutch masters. Their living conditions were deplorable. They never received decent foodstuff, and their suffering was compounded by lack of good treatment for the dreaded malaria. Whenever they protested against their treatment, and the poor conditions as well as the overwhelming demands on their weakening bodies, they were badly beaten. Their punishment was meted out in front of their families and others, as a way of instilling greater fear all around them. They were expected to take their punishment, and just continue to labour without resistance."

Michael paused to adjust his spectacles, and wipe away the tears streaming down his face. Nazir reached out to hold his arms in an effort to console his friend. Those in the audience, who overheard Michael, switched their attention away from the game, and turned towards him.

Carlos said, "Those were very hard and sad times. The Dutch had a reputation for being very cruel towards their slaves."

John asked, "You mean that the Dutch were even more cruel than the English?"

Arthur said, "John, your people were also used by both the Dutch and the English to capture any runaway African slaves, and bring them back to the plantations. Perhaps your people may be able to judge which set of masters was the more brutal."

John said, "No Arthur. Only our African brothers and sisters can tell us this. The fact remains that all the Slave masters were cruel to even enter into this vile trade in the first place."

Michael recovered his composure, and said, "Well, all the disruptions which took place in Canje as far back as 1733, were just building up to the biggest rebellion in 1763, led by Kofi."

Arthur said, "Those poor people continued to suffer so much for another thirty years!"

Michael nodded, and continued, "Nazir, you will be proud to know that Kofi was a Muslim from the Akau tribe of Ghana. Also, Kofi means Friday or *Jummah* in Arabic and which represents the holiest day of the week for Muslims. This is the day that you go for Jummah *Namaaz*."

Nazir said, "Allah ho Akbar! May Allah always bless and keep him until the Day of *Qayaamat*!"

Michael smiled, and continued, "Kofi's main collaborators and followers were also of his Akau tribe, and were also Muslim. Their names were Akara, Atta and Quabi. Kofi and his Muslim and Non Muslim army was about three thousand strong. Although they were never trained to fight as a military force, they battled fiercely, and managed to push out the Dutch supporters from many of the plantations in the South of Berbice. Kofi was a remarkably brave man, and he even took as his wife, the sister of one of the plantation owners!"

Nazir said, "Man, if that was true, Kofi was really amazing! This action would have been more than hurtful to the Dutch."

Arthur said, "The rebels must have been really strong fighters to kill, and defeat so many Dutch people who would have been better armed."

Michael said, "Kofi was a very intelligent man who was actually brought up on his plantation as a house slave. He was even trained as a cooper."

Nazir asked, "What is a cooper?"

John said, "I think that this is someone who was trained in making barrels with the metal bands round the wooden frame."

Michael continued, "Kofi then tried to annex the South of Berbice for his followers, and even declared himself as the Governor of Berbice!"

Arthur said, "What? Governor of Berbice? Man I am getting to love this Kofi!"

Nazir said, "Praise be to Allah! Kofi was such a brave man! What happened next?"

Michael said, "You can well imagine that the Dutch would not just give in to such arrogance from any slave. They did not take their losses lightly, and in a matter of just a few months, they re-captured their land from Kofi and his army. When they finally caught the rebels they dished out some of the most barbaric punishments ever witnessed in the colony."

John said, "Oh my good God! What more could they have done that was worse than beating and starving their slaves?"

Michael said, "You know, when I say barbaric, we can only begin to imagine what this meant. Some of the rebels were burnt alive, and others were beheaded to show just how far the Dutch were prepared to go to scare others who would even think of rebelling or disobeying their masters from then onwards."

Carlos said, "That means if the Dutch were prepared to brutalise and kill their slaves in this way, they were planning to replace them with even more slaves. Therefore the rebellion was bound to fail in the end."

Michael said, "No Carlos, the rebellion was a great success! It was one way to teach the Dutch that they would never get away with their ill-treatment of the very people they depended on for their wealth and living. Kofi and his companions must always be honoured and remembered by all peoples who have had to endure such disgusting and unforgiveable dominance over other human beings."

The supporters in the audience demonstrated their agreement and solidarity by clapping and shouting, "Long live Kofi! Long live Kofi!"

Nazir said, "There you are Michael. You have succeeded in getting your wonderful message across to everyone here. So, what happened to Kofi and his army?"

Michael said, "You know that we talked about winning freedoms, and then finding that we still have to struggle to enjoy the fruits of these freedoms? Well, Kofi tried to convince the Dutch Governor that he and the other rebels did not want to fight wars with the Dutch whom he referred to as Christians. But the Governor stalled with his answers whilst waiting for re-enforcements from Demerara, Surinam and as far away as his home country, Holland."

Carlos said, "You see, we should never trust a white man who is only interested in exploiting people for his own gain."

John said, "Spoken as a true Portuguese white man!"

Nazir said, "No John, he is not a white man. He is red, and that is why we will always call him "Reds"!"

Arthur said, "The problem with this kind of freedom fighting is that you think that you have won the battle, and then you suddenly realise that there is still a whole war to fight. The Dutch knew this, and despite Kofi's attempts to negotiate a kind of peace, they would never give up their plantations so easily."

Michael said, "Arthur that is very correct. The Dutch inflicted one defeat on Kofi, and within a very short time, the rebels began to quarrel amongst themselves, and this division spelled the beginning of the end for them."

John said, "This is what history teaches us. Disunity is still a problem for all of us. Unity is strength. Divisions only serve to weaken us. This was a common thing amongst our Amerindian peoples. There was always something which would cause trouble, or someone who would stir up some grievance, and the next thing you know is that it became a full scale tribal war."

Michael said, "Yes, the slaves were not just from different tribes and with different customs. They were behaving differently towards each other because of their different positions on the estates. The older and more wizened slaves, who had been in the colony for a long time, were also suspicious of new arrivals. The Dutch were military experts, and knew that with some stalling and other tactics they would eventually cause some dissent amongst the ranks of Kofi's army."

Nazir said, "Man this sounds like the same divide and rule tactics of the English!"

Arthur said, "Aha, this is the lesson we fail to learn, and understand. We as Guyanese need to wake up, and fight harder for unity, and then anything and everything will be possible."

Michael said, "Kofi was a great and inspirational leader, but it seems that others from within his own circle were after their own greater position and power. This kind of thing has happened here in Guyana amongst the political leaders of our country. If only they could learn from our history we would all be working as one people, and building one nation."

John said, "To me, this is really the lesson from the Berbice Slave Rebellion, and all other uprisings and rebellions which have taken place here, and in other countries around the world."

Nazir said, "I think I am getting to understand what you are saying. Look at India and the struggles that the great Mahatma Gandhi and his followers went through against the British rulers. Everyone wanted to see the end of British occupation and rule in India, and fighting for that main goal was therefore easier to organise. But, as the goal became closer and closer within their grasp, they started to see how they could divide up the benefits. This is what caused the call for the partition of that beautiful country. Independence was won, but the price was a division which was really hurtful to millions of people affected by it, and this division will be very difficult to repair."

John said, "Nazir, you sound just like Michael! I can see where you are coming from. When we win the prize we must look at ways to make everyone share in this, and we must not divide ourselves."

Michael said, "These lessons are playing out right before our eyes, and yet we seem to be incapable of learning from them."

Arthur said, "Gentlemen, the Berbice Slave Rebellion was the greatest of the fights for the end of African Slavery here in Guyana. We all owe a great deal to Kofi and every single one of his companions who woke up to fight for their rights, for their freedom against the Dutch, and, the others who fought for the same against the English."

John said, "Well, it took almost another seventy five years for African Slavery to end here in Guyana. This emancipation was a very hard fought for release from bondage and hundreds of years of untold suffering of countless innocent human beings. I can only pray that they are at peace with themselves and God. This is the ultimate freedom; the realisation of the supreme spirit."

Michael said, "Hail the Lord! John, I am very proud to know that you are so well up on your history, and have seen what the true fight is for."

John said, "Well, that is only because I have been listening to you for many years, and you may not know this, but you do tend to make sense, even though you also have a habit of repeating yourself from time to time. Besides, I catch up on this kind of stuff by reading our newspapers like the Chronicle, watching the movies, and picking up books from our Public Library in Georgetown."

Carlos said, "And, you also used to borrow my comic books when we were young boys, and you would even rent them out to your other friends as if you were the owner."

John said, "Carlos, that was a very long time ago, and I am willing to pay you back for what I owe you."

Carlos said, "No need for that. I used to borrow the comics from Mr Rayman Ali's store here in Anna Catherina. I used to run into trouble by eventually returning my books much later than expected. Mr Rayman used to tell me off for this, but he never imposed any fines on me. He was a wonderful man who was very well known and loved by the people here in the village and all over the West Coast, West Bank, and East Bank Demerara."

Nazir said, "So many good business people like him and their families who helped us all over many years."

Arthur said, "Those people were amazing. Guyana will never be the same without so many wonderful people who have passed away, were forced to leave due to the political situation here, or simply sought to better themselves and their families in England, America, and Canada. Such a great loss!"

Michael said, "That is so true. But we are here now to try to re-build our beloved country. We have a long history of start and stop. The Dutch built up a lot of the sea defences and water systems that we can still see today. It was on the 20th of November 1815 that they handed Guiana to the British. Then it was on the 21st of July in 1831 that Berbice, Demerara and Essequibo were united by the British, as one colony called British Guiana."

John said, "Michael, you never fail to amaze me with all these dates and events. How the hell do you remember these things man?"

Carlos said, "Man, I am just amazed how one power just seemed to hand over countries to another!"

Nazir said, "Wow! That means we became united as a country for over one hundred and fifty years! And yet we say that we are not free?"

John said, "Well done on the sums there Nazir! I had no idea that you can count!"

Michael said, "Nazir, we are still a very young nation whichever way you look at it. Countries such as the UK, USA and Russia have all been much older than this, and still they are trying to improve and develop further. They all have their problems, although they are very much bigger problems than ours."

Carlos asked, "Michael, how and when did African Slavery end?"

Michael took a deep breath, and glanced over to the table where the Domino match was at a standstill as Vishnu studied which end he should make his penultimate and most decisive move.

Michael then turned to his friends, and said, "You know that I talked about 1763, and Kofi and his companions. But as John said, African slaves continued to suffer at the hands of the Dutch and then the British who took-over all the plantations left by their rivals. Interestingly, the plantation names used by the Dutch still remain with us to this day. Names such as Anna Catherina, Leonora, Cornelia Ida, Hague, Vreed en Hoop, Zeeburg, Uitvlught, Meten Meer Zorg, Den Amstel...."

Nazir interrupted, and said, "Stewartville!"

Carlos laughed, and said, "No, you fool! Stewartville was, and is an English name!"

Nazir said, "Well smart ass, how about Parika then!"

John said, "I think Parika is more an Amerindian name."

Michael said, "OK, you get the picture. The British really inherited some well planned and set out plantations with amazing irrigation systems such as the canals, aqueducts, and *kokers*. These things were so strongly built that they have survived so well even without very much maintenance. There must come a time when they will have to be replaced with more modern systems."

Arthur said, "Don't forget the sea defences and seawalls all along the coastline."

John asked, "Did the British also take over the African slaves as well?"

Michael said, "Yes, and they made sure that the African slaves were all converted to Christianity, especially the Muslim slaves who were always seen as the trouble makers, and the ones who were always willing to pick up arms against their masters. The new African Christians became more willing to accept their masters who at first seemed to be calmer, and more tolerant than the brutal Dutch."

John said, "Yes, the British had a way of making people believe that they were there to look after them, and not to torture hard-working people. They started to provide better housing, medical care and provisions. So, the slaves began to feel better than they were under the Dutch."

Nazir said, "John that is a whole load of rubbish! I do not believe this. The colonists were all evil bastards who raped women at will, and beat people with their cat-o-nine-tails, and showed the slaves utter contempt. They counted slaves as if they were stocks in their account books. Slaves were never treated as human beings, even though they were now Christians. The British continued to behave like this even after the end of slavery, and the introduction of Indian and other workers."

Michael cleared his throat, and said, "Nazir, much of what you said is true. But you must appreciate that it was the English Christians such as the Reverend John Smith who used the power of words and argument alongside the words of our Holy Bible, to fight against African Slavery. There was a great anti-slavery movement in England, and many members of the British Parliament made speeches against this evil inhumanity to man."

Carlos said, "Michael, you told us some time ago that there was a big misunderstanding which caused the Demerara Slave Uprising in eighteen twenty something. What was that all about?"

Michael raised his right hand to his right temple, and scratched it gently as he pondered upon his response. Then he said, "I think that you mean 1823. Yes, you could well imagine how anxious our brothers and sisters were as they prayed for their freedom. So, any bit of information that suggested slavery will end, was treated with great joy. They heard that something was passed in London, and felt that the local Plantation Manager on the East Coast of Demerara was holding back from telling everyone about the good news."

Nazir kissed his teeth, and said, "You see what I mean about not trusting the English? They were devious people back then, and I get really angry when I hear our people say that they wished that the white man was still running Guyana."

John said, "Nazir, we all know that there was not much to choose between the Spanish, French, Dutch and English. They were all fighting each other for the wealth that they saw in all of their colonies all over the world."

Michael said, "We can say what we like about the Colonial rulers, but we now have our own equivalent treating our people with the same contempt. We have to do something about this."

Carlos said, "Never mind your call for revolution, what happened next?"

Michael said, "The Demerara Slave Uprising was a brutal event with thousands of African slaves taking action against their masters on many plantations across the East Coast of Demerara, starting with Plantation Success. The Reverend John Smith tried to calm down the rebels, and to work with the Governor to restore order. Many white people were killed by the rebels, but when the rebels were finally defeated after having lost many more fighters, the English executed the main ring-leaders, decapitated them, and paraded their heads on poles along the main road for all to see."

Nazir said, "Truly uncivilised behaviour! Barbaric! They showed no mercy, no forgiveness, and no respect for the dead. So much for their Christian upbringing. This is what I mean by the evil practised by the colonial masters. This is the true history that must be taught in our schools. We have nothing to thank either the Dutch or the English for."

Carlos said, "Nazir, you have to remember that those times were different. It must have been terrifying for the white people when so many thousands of rebel slaves were on the rampage."

Nazir said, "I do not agree with you at all. If the English wanted peace, then they should never have indulged in enslaving human beings, and mistreating them. The real shame was converting those innocent people to Christianity, and then beat the hell out of them for hardly any so-called misdemeanour. Then they would all go to Church on Sundays, to pray at the head of the altar, and have the slaves sitting or standing at the back. Some were clearly more equal than others before God."

Michael said, "We all know that it is not the religion of people that is bad, but the way people abused it for their own purpose. This is still a problem all over the world today."

Nazir said, "Never mind what you say Michael. I wish that the Muslim African slaves did not convert to Christianity as we Muslims treat people equally. We all pray side by side, whether we are rich or poor, one race or the other, and so on."

Carlos said, "I understand what you are saying Nazir, but why do you not let Muslim women and girls pray beside you in the mosques?"

Nazir said, "Actually, women and girls are allowed in the mosque, but I understand that given the way we bow down and prostrate, it would be improper for men to be distracted by the bodies of women next to, and in front of them. But apart from this, all women and men are treated equally in Islam."

Michael said, "There is good in all religions, and amongst peoples. In fact, the Demerara Slave Uprising had two real martyrs, one Quamina, and the other, the Reverend John Smith, who both wanted peace, and not war."

Carlos said, "Michael, I heard you say before now that Quamina was with many other great men such as John Gladstone. In fact you said that Quamina was actually shot by Amerindians working for the plantation owners. His body was then hung up on a post beside the public road for all to see. This was typical of the way the English used to punish their criminals such as the highway robbers, back in England."

Nazir said, "Oh yes! I have seen this in the English films where the robbers would be hung, and then their bodies would be displayed in metal cages for all the citizens to see. And, more importantly, to let anyone who was a criminal know what will happen to them when they were caught. These so-called masters were really barbarians posing as civilised people."

Michael said, "But Nazir, there were very decent, caring, and God-fearing English people like the Reverend John Smith who was wrongfully accused of inciting the slave rebellion, and for not controlling Quamina, or stopping the rebellion. He was sentenced to hang, and he made an appeal against this. Unfortunately, whilst he awaited the answer of his appeal, he died in prison. His pardon did eventually arrive after he was buried, and the African people began to refer to him as the Demerara Martyr."

Nazir said, "Well of course there will always be good people amongst the bad."

Michael said, "Back in England, there were very many English people of high standing who risked their own freedom to protest against African Slavery. The most famous of these was William Wilberforce, and his many followers. Reverend Smith's treatment and death in Guyana sparked a lot of speeches in the English Parliament, and reports in the newspapers. But it still took another ten years before African Slavery came to an end."

John said, "My friends, please allow me to say sorry for all that my Amerindian ancestors who worked for the plantation owners, did in hunting down and capturing any slaves who ran away, or those who took part in the rebellions you have been talking about. I do not know why they sided with the Dutch and English in this way."

Nazir said, "Maybe they felt that it was a way for them to be protected from enslavement after having suffered so badly at the hands of the Spanish, Dutch and English colonists who stole their lands."

Carlos said, "John, it is not for you to apologise for your peoples. Those who should be apologising are the Dutch and the English. I am glad that they do not rule over us any longer."

Arthur said, "I agree with you. But the power and influence that the Dutch held over our ancestors must have been so frightening that even up to now we are told not to go near to, or deface their tombs."

Nazir said, "Oh, we have all grown up in our villages, and were always told not to touch or tamper with the Dutch tombs wherever they are. Do you remember the story about the Sugar Estate Manager who ordered that an old Dutch cemetery in Cornelia Ida must be bulldozed to make way for a new sugarcane filed?"

Michael said, "Yes, I think that the Drivers warned the Estate Manager against destroying the cemetery, and after he refused, people became very ill. Eventually, when the Manager himself felt unwell, the operation had to stop, and all the tombs that were broken had to be repaired."

Nazir said, "My father told me that one day, as he was rounding up their sheep from the grazing areas near and in the Anna Catherina cemetery, he saw a Dutch tomb slightly broken. He put his hand through the large crack in the tomb, and grabbed a lot of silver coins, and some jewellery. He took them home, and was warned by my grandparents to take everything back and replace them where he found them. He did this, and later that night he suffered his worst nightmare, and woke up sweating and shaking like a madman. My grandparents immediately called the local *Imaam*, and they read certain chapters from the *Holy Qur'an*, and then my father recovered."

Carlos said, "No wonder none of us, or anyone else have dared to rob those tombs. I know of the one that is in the yard of the Hindu

Temple in Leonora. The devotees regularly keep it clean, and whitewashed."

Michael said, "Man, we Guyanese are too worried about these fears of the dead. I prefer to keep praying, and I am never worried about these things. The dead body is just a perishable thing. There is no such thing as an evil spirit, but just our undying soul."

Carlos said, "Michael, you are such a great liar! I remember the night times when we were all young boys coming back together from the Roxy Cinema in Leonora after watching the movies. As soon we got close to the area of the Anna Catherina cemetery, and we saw our long shadows dance in front of us, we started to walk faster and faster, talking more loudly, and then as soon as anyone said "Look out there is a *Jumbie*!" we ran for our lives. You were right at the front, and would disappear faster than an Olympic sprinter!"

Everyone in the room broke out in mocking laughter. Vishnu looked up at Michael and smiled.

Michael said, "No! I just liked to run to keep fit! I was never scared of what I could not see! My friends, this is all about six of one and half a dozen of the other. There is no truth in what you just heard."

Vishnu winked at Michael, and then prepared to make his move, with a broad smile on his face.

* * *

Ramesh's application to read Engineering at a University in London was successful, and Vishnu managed to secure a scholarship to cover his three years degree course, from the Ministry of Education in Georgetown. Contacts were secured with family relations in London to allow Ramesh to rent a room with a close relative, at a nominal rate per month. This was agreed so that Ramesh would not have to spend the first year at his University campus accommodation, and more importantly, to give him a better chance to avoid homesickness.

The family kept their plans in secrecy until they were assured that everything was in place before announcing Ramesh's departure, set for early September 1985.

Ramesh continued his courtship with Sati without disclosing their relationship to his parents. Due to Sati's inability to free herself from her family's house arrest, Ramesh decided to write about his plans in letters to her. This approach seemed to work very well for both Ramesh and Sati, and they corresponded almost daily.

It was in one of Sati's more recent letters that she wrote about how she was missing him so much that it was causing her to feel quite uncomfortable and unwell every morning. His responses were always intended to help her to keep her spirits up, and not to worry about him, and their relationship.

16.

Dreams of change

Vishnu's long-awaited play of his Six Three gave Afzal the option to consider playing at the end with the Three or, at the other, with Blank. The ACES supporters greeted this move with great joy, and loud cheering. Vishnu was now left with one domino, and both of his opponents with three each. This placed him in a position of very significant advantage. He clenched his final domino in his left hand to make doubly sure that neither of his opponents could see it.

Michael caught Vishnu's eyes, and gave him a re-assuring smile. They nodded to each other. Then Michael turned to his friends, and said, "You know, this Six Three domino that Vishnu just played reminds me of the Berbice Slave Rebellion in 1763 that I just talked about. It also towers like the impressive monument of Kofi that we have in the area called the Square of the Revolution, in Brickdam, Georgetown."

Carlos said, "That statue of the great National Hero Kofi is a massive reminder of the stature of the man. But they could have carved out a more normal looking figure of the man, rather than that ugly piece."

John said, "No Carlos, I think that it is very difficult for anyone to imagine what people looked like so long ago. I think that it is a beautiful and powerful reminder of such an important episode in our history."

Nazir said, "Look, let's not beat about the bush and talk as if we know anything about art and sculpture. It is a very ugly statue, and we should have done something much better. Just look at the beautiful bronze statue of the great Mahatma Gandhi in the Promenade Gardens in Georgetown. And don't tell me about not knowing what Kofi looked like. They could have looked at a figure such as our friend Michael here, to represent the great Kofi."

Carlos said, "Now you are really stretching your imagination too far! Michael is a skinny, weak, and ugly specimen. He could not even lift up a cutlass, let alone fight like a true warrior."

Nazir said, "I think that you know what I really mean. I suppose we have to accept that the Kofi statue is there to remind us about his might and power, and the cause that he and his army fought, and died for. I do respect the fact that he was one of my Muslim brothers alongside all the others who stood by him."

Carlos said, "Michael, can you tell us a bit more about the Emancipation Act of 1833? I heard you say that the slaves were not aware that they were not really free to do as they liked."

Michael said, "Whilst the Emancipation Act of 1833 was to free the African slaves across all the British colonies, it contained clauses which were designed to introduce an Apprentice System for all slaves over the age of six. The slaves who worked in the fields had to serve for six years, and all the others, for four years."

Arthur said, "Now that is typical of the British. They give with one hand, and take away with the other."

Nazir chuckled, and said, "Well, at least we can say that Guyanese learnt through the times, the importance of using both hands. Even our beggars do not put out one hand to receive whatever is given to them, but use both with the hope of doubling up on their rewards."

Carlos said, "Even beggars have to be optimistic, otherwise they will walk away with nothing."

John said, "I heard that the ex-slaves who took on the apprenticeship with some small pay, were very surprised when they eventually realised that they were still bound to their plantation owners."

Nazir said, "This idea of an apprenticeship is so ridiculous! How can you spend so many years of your life working so hard and mastering whatever you have to do, and then still become an apprentice when you become free?"

Michael nodded in agreement, and said, "It's like rubbing salt in wounds."

Nazir said, "I am very proud of our African brothers and sisters who stood up against such bare-faced exploitation. The apprentice idea had to fail, and that is why John Gladstone who was the owner of some of the plantations on the West Coast asked his son William Gladstone, the British Prime Minister, for some other labourers to come to Guyana."

Carlos said, "Wow Nazir! You continue to impress me with your knowledge man!"

John said, "How could John Gladstone ask for English labourers? They would never be able to stand the heat and do the hard labour here, unless they tried out their criminals in their prisons."

Nazir said, "You are right. The people who came were some Portuguese from Madeira who did not like the work, and then my ancestors from India came. Later on they were followed by some Chinese from a place called Macao."

John said, "Nazir, there you go again. You seem to know much more than we give you credit for. The newly freed slaves were very angry about the apprentice system, and soon disturbances broke out in the East Coast and right here in West Coast Demerara. Most of the men and women who protested were badly beaten up on their plantations."

Carlos said, "So the British were still happy to beat these poor people who thought that they were free. I also heard that the plantation owners were given a lot of money to compensate them for the loss of their slaves. Worse still, apart from the small payments for toiling six days a week as apprentices, not one slave was given any compensation for all their years of this torture, and suffering."

Nazir said, "Man, this is something all of the people who had ancestors who were in slavery all over the British, French and other so called Empires, should fight hard for."

John said, "I agree my brother. But if all the countries have to pay back compensation, they will become bankrupt!"

Nazir frowned, and said, "I do not give a damn about that. Our ancestors paid with their blood, sweat and tears to make these countries rich. So, they should all pay up!"

Many of the spectators who overheard the conversation groaned to show their disgust.

Michael said, "Such arrogance and deceit by the British are not the Christian way that some of their own people like the Reverend John Smith were preaching."

Nazir said, "You know when the devil is used to sucking the blood out of people it is very hard to stop him. There is no other way to defeat him than by force and violence."

Michael said, "Nazir, I have to disagree with you there. You said that you admired the fearless and non-violent movement led by the great Mahatma Gandhi. This great soul and his companions used the non-violent protests despite being beaten by the Indian police who were serving the British rulers, and being put in jail for no real reason. They finally succeeded when India won its Independence."

John said, "This non-violent way was admired and used by the late Reverend Martin Luther King and the hundreds of thousands who marched from all over America to Washington in 1963."

Arthur said, "The Reverend was a truly brilliant person, and very inspirational to people all over the world."

Michael smiled, and said, "Oh what a great time for all poor African and White Americans to join hands together, and to fight for their freedom, and for jobs. King's "I have a Dream" speech was one of the most powerful in all of man's history. He said that even after one hundred years of Abraham Lincoln's Emancipation Proclamation, African Americans were still not free."

Nazir said, "Oh, Doctor King was following in the same path of all our Prophets, the great Mahatma Gandhi, and all those who prefer to protest against injustice in a non-violent manner."

Carlos said, "Man you continue to surprise us Nazir. On the one hand you would be the first to lift up arms against your enemy, and here you are in praise of non-violence."

Nazir said, "I call for a fight when someone hits me or my friends. I treat this as self defence. But when the State and those in power continue to punish us, and show us real lack of compassion, then I agree that the non-violent protests work."

John said, "The best weapon we have against such tyranny is at the ballot box. If the people dislike a government, then they simply vote against it."

Michael said, "No John, we are not talking about governments here. It is the system of racial hatred, prejudice, suppression and so on. You have to get into the heart of the system, and then try to remove these conditions."

Arthur said, "That is a much harder fight. We all know that despite people like Doctor King, John Kennedy and others, there is still widespread racialism in America, and all the big countries around the world."

Nazir said, "Man, we have to include that great fighter Nelson Mandela and his companions from South Africa. This man has been imprisoned for donkey's years along with other supporters, for their protests against South African apartheid. In fact, Mahatma Gandhi saw the racial injustices when he was a young lawyer in South Africa, before he returned to India to start his campaign against British rule in his country."

Carlos said, "Apartheid! What a truly nasty system of suppression of Black people, Indians, and mixed race people in South Africa!"

John said, "Not surprising since the most influential whites, the Afrikaans, have their roots in Holland! The other whites were mostly British and German. So, the two major oppressors were right in the middle of this vile crime."

Michael said, "But it must be said that people in Britain have been protesting against this injustice by causing the ban on playing sport against South Africans and their teams, and other sanctions against their government. Thank God for right-minded peoples who see injustice, and are prepared to take action, whether by violence or by non-violence."

Arthur said, "The time will surely come when all of these nasty systems will be destroyed by the very peoples who are being suppressed all over the world."

Michael said, "That is why people say that our Messiah will return to save the world."

Carlos said, "Well, you are free to dream on about this. Meanwhile the reality has to be dealt with here and now."

John said, "That is right. Let us not indulge in too much day dreaming. Look at our reality. We continue to suffer at the hands of our own people who are in power despite not having any experience of even running a small business, or farm or industry. They might be lawyers and accountants, but they do not have any experience of planning and running things. Worse still, they do not seem to have basic compassion in their hearts and minds when they dream up their misguided policies, and force them down our throats. We have to find ways to change this. And that is a reasonable dream to have."

Nazir said, "Well, we have to really think much more about your kind of revolution. And, looking around us here and now, I do not see any inspiration. Even our three geniuses and masters of Dominoes cannot seem to play out a simple game of Dominoes without spending such a long time on every single move. Afzal, stop pretending that you know what you are doing, and get on with the damn game! I am getting really hungry man!"

Arthur said, "Nazir, if you are hungry, I can send one of these boys here to get us some snacks. What would you like to eat?"

Before Nazir could respond to the promise of a treat, Michael shouted, "Get us some *baara*, *pulauri*, *googri*, and *mauby*! Oh, and some *bling bling achaar*!"

Arthur said, "Here young man, go over to the lady selling all those things that Michael mentioned. She should be at her stall in front of the Monarch cinema just up the road, and keep the change."

The young man did not hesitate, and after grabbing the crisp twenty dollar note, he ran off to his errand, followed by his three friends."

Michael turned to Arthur, and said, "Thank you Arthur. We must keep some snacks for our captain Vishnu."

Arthur said, "Yes, but only if he wins the damn game!"

Carlos said, "That will be something to celebrate. You should have sent for more snacks and drinks."

Nazir said, "Hmm! Let's hope that the young man brings back the snacks, and do not do a disappearing act on us."

Arthur said, "No chance of that happening. I know him and his friends very well. He will do as he was asked. Otherwise his father will deal with him. I hope that he doesn't keep too much change, and just buy us a little food."

Michael said, "Arthur, I am very grateful for your kindness. But, I don't think that twenty Guyana dollars will go too far!"

Nazir said, "Yes, you of all people should know better! Our Guyanese money is not worth much these days, and should be re-valued."

Arthur said, "Now, that's another story!"

* * *

When Sati complained of acute chest and stomach pain, her father Peter Ramdin and her mother Lakshmi drove her directly to a private clinic in Georgetown, for immediate attention.

After a series of diagnostic tests were completed, Sati was admitted overnight to allow for further observation to be undertaken by the clinical team.

A very tired Peter and utterly distressed Lakshmi returned to their family home later that evening, and could not eat their late meal. They sat down in their modest lounge, and began to discuss as to why their only daughter became so stricken.

Peter said, "I hope that Sati is not still hankering after that Raana. Is this why she made herself so ill?"

Lakshmi said, "No, Raana is living his own new life now after his illness. He does not come here to try to see Sati anymore. At least, not to my knowledge!"

Peter said, "Maybe we should stop restricting her movements, and allow her to get back to being as normal as she used to be."

Lakshmi took a sip of ice cold water, and said, "She does go out when she wants to. She is not kept as if she is in a prison."

Peter said, "I know that. But she must be hurt by this treatment, and we should stop this nonsense."

Lakshmi said, "Well, she is your pride and joy, so you can do as you wish. But first, let us hope and pray that Sati is alright."

Peter sighed heavily, and said, "We will have to ask her what she wants to do with her life. We just cannot continue to keep her penned up here. If she does not want to go to school anymore, I can try to get her a job at my workplace in Georgetown."

Lakshmi said, "That is all well and good, but first we need to know what has happened to her. Then we can start to make plans with her."

Peter nodded, and said, "I'm going to bed now. Its late, and I feel very tired."

17.

Giving and receiving

Afzal licked his lips, and studied the two numbers presented to him at both ends of the Domino game. The Three was only the third one played on the table, and with so few dominoes held by the three players, he felt that Vishnu or Peter must have one or more of the others, unless of course, they were within the seven dominoes in the set covered on the table.

At this stage of a Domino game, the players were more able to predict, or make good guesses as to where the missing numbers were being held. Afzal could work out that the end with the Blank was probably commanded by Vishnu as he did not have any Blank himself, and Peter had rapped at a Six and Blank.

All the supporters looked at the dominoes played on the table, and many began to whisper to their friends about their own thoughts on what may or may not happen as the game proceeded to its conclusion.

The music from the radio across the road continued, and Peter kept up with his slight body movements swaying from side to side on his chair, as he mimed with the song. He looked at his three remaining dominoes in his left hand, and smiled confidently.

A blind man carefully stepped into the hall carrying an aluminium cup in his left hand, and tapping a white walking stick held in his right hand, on the floor ahead of him. A young man deliberately stepped in front of the elderly man as if to test whether or not he was really blind. The man lifted his white stick gently, and tapped it on the floor just in front of the young man's feet. Then he stopped momentarily.

The young man stepped aside, and mumbled an apology. Michael noticed the actions of the young man, and spoke to him directly.

He said, "Hey you! We all know that Mr Lazarus is blind. Why did you have to behave so disrespectfully towards him? God help you if and when you or any of your loved ones ever became disabled in any way! What is there to mock someone that is obviously less fortunate than you? I know who your parents are, and I am going to let them know what you have been up to."

The young man said quietly, "I am very sorry Mr Brown. I am very sorry Mr Lazarus. I wouldn't do it again."

The young man then rushed out of the hall as quickly as he could, and the others just laughed at him.

Carlos said, "Michael, I am so glad that you pulled him up. In our younger days back in the 1960s, whenever we did something wrong in public, an older person would not only tell us off, but also give us a slap or two!"

Nazir said, "That was wrong then, but we soon learned to be most respectful to our elders, or to anyone in public, and in private. But, we were not all saints. We had our moments, and run-ins with our elders."

Carlos poked Nazir at his chest, and said, "And some of us did so with the Law!"

John said, "Every generation throws up a new pattern of bad behaviour, and bad manners amongst the youths."

Michael said, "But if these behaviours are not nipped in the bud at home or at school or in public, then they can become seriously uncontrollable."

Arthur said, "Yes, just look at how all these different gangs have come and gone, not only here but in countries like America and England."

Nazir said, "I liked the movies with the Hell's Angels and Skinheads. Those guys were really wicked."

Michael said, "I am only too glad that we never saw such types here in Guyana. They were not only violent against other gangs, but they were very racist, and beat up a lot of immigrants in those countries. I know that some of my relations in England were beaten up in the 1960s by such hooligans."

Arthur said, "Yes, I heard about this from my relations in London during that time. But thankfully our youngsters cannot afford those flashy and powerful motorbikes used by the Hell's Angels, or even the scooters used by the Skinheads. Our youngsters could hardly afford decent bicycles!"

Nazir said, "Aha, we used to have our specially cleaned and "souped up" bicycles with fancy fittings and bells. All we used them for was to ride off to the other villages to pose, show off, and tackle the girls."

Carlos said, "Yes, we even had the chrome so shinny, and we developed a ticking sound in the gears as we rode our bikes."

Michael said, "All of you looked like stupid clowns riding off to see the girls, and coming back with your tails between your legs, and no romance to talk about."

John said, "Our friend Vishnu over there had great success with his fancy bicycle trips all the way to Parika. That is where he first saw, and courted his beautiful wife, Parvati. Mind you, by the time he got back from his Sunday afternoon rides over the ten miles of rugged, dusty, and muddy roads to Parika, his bike was a complete mess, and so was his trousers, and the back of his sweat stained shirt."

Michael said, "I don't think you guys courted anybody. You tackled them!"

Nazir said, "And Vishnu's mother used to clip him round his ears because she ended up having to wash all his dirty clothes."

Carlos said, "But that did not kill off our friend's passion for his beloved Parvati!"

Michael said, "At least one of you managed to find a suitable girl through those stupid bicycle courtship or tackling trips. I can never forget the time when we all went to Parika as part of Vishnu's *baraat*. We could not afford a hire car, so we went with our well spruced up bicycles, leaving for Parika about an hour before Vishnu's wedding car left our village."

Nazir said, "Oh man! We finally reached the bride-to-be's house just before Vishnu's car arrived, and the hosts were very kind to us as the official baraat. They immediately offered us some refreshment, even before the long Hindu wedding ceremony."

Carlos said, "And, what refreshment that was!"

John said, "I welcomed the ice cold soda which was really refreshing, but the thing that got to us all was the nice hot *daal* with *daal poorie roti*!"

Nazir rubbed his stomach, and said, "Man, I could do with some daal poorie roti right now!"

Michael said, "I warned you all not to eat anything before the wedding ceremony was completed. So, I decided to bear up with my hunger, and waited patiently like all the other guests."

Nazir said, "Michael, you were very lucky. It was not too long after we ate the roti and drank the delicious daal, when we felt this great griping pain in our stomachs."

Carlos grimaced as he recalled the experience, and said, "We all ran off to each one of the outdoor latrines in the neighbourhood. I remember that before I could drop my trousers, my bowels gave way to an explosion of shit that I never experienced before, or since!"

Nazir said, "I jumped over a neighbour's fence, and dashed to their latrine. Then their guard dog came after me with such anger. Luckily just before he could bite a large chunk of my fat ass, I scrambled up to the door, and slammed it firmly behind me. But I could not hold back the shit, and I made a real mess of my trousers and the floor well before I could sit on the latrine seat. I remember sitting there for what seemed like hours, and that mad dog would just bark at me, and not go away!"

Michael smiled, and said, "At least I was able to confront the wretched dog, and distract him away from you so that you could make your escape. But you just stayed in the damn latrine for ages!"

Nazir said, "Michael, my belly was in agony, my trousers were in a mess, there was nothing to clean myself with, and there was a great crowd of the locals just looking on, and laughing at all of us!"

John said, "Man, my belly hurt so much, and my ass was so sore after that experience, that I could hardly walk properly for the next few hours, let alone try to ride back from Parika that evening."

Arthur said, "I travelled in a car behind Vishnu's, and I am truly sorry to say that I could not offer you all a lift that evening."

Nazir said, "No, you didn't dare allow any of us to sit with you, because we smelt like walking latrines, and our trousers were still stinking even though we tried to rinse them in the nearby trench. Man, that evening we could not ride our bikes for any real distance, and had little energy left to even push them. We had to stop by the roadside, and find the nearest bush to hide, and shit. Luckily it was too dark for anyone to see us, or to disturb us."

John said, "But the damn mosquitoes bit our asses so much that it took days for our pains to go away!"

The spectators could not resist laughing at the story being told.

Michael said, "At least you could all thank me for keeping your company all along the way back to our village. But my friends you were all taught a good lesson by those people in Parika."

Nazir said, "It is not surprising that none of us dared to do our bicycle girl watching as far as Parika, ever again."

Carlos said, "What the hell did those people put in our food that day?"

John said, "The special greeting with castor oil in the daal and curries especially prepared for the visiting baraat was a well known thing practised by the islanders of Essequibo. I do not know whether it was a serious attempt by the locals to warn off outsiders from tackling their girls, or it was a genuine source of entertainment for them. But man, it was no fun for us, and at the same time, it was a very effective deterrent."

Michael said, "Whilst you were all trying to deal with your welcoming meal, I heard the Pandit talking about how there are some foods which give people long life, good health, and plenty cheerfulness. Then there are foods which are bitter, hot, and which burn the stomach. And finally, there are foods which are stale, and impure. I think that you all had food which must be in its own category turning your emotions from happiness, to griping stomach pain, and causing you to decorate those latrines."

Arthur said, "Come on, we Guyanese have a great tradition of practical jokes, and our Essequibo friends are no different from all of us. I heard that whenever their baraats came our way, they also got the same latrine experience. In fact I know that we gave them an even harder time by deliberately padlocking all the latrines in the neighbourhood close to the wedding site."

Michael said, "We should not give the impression that our Parika experience was really widespread. We Guyanese are known for our hospitality, and we would try our best to offer our guests the tastiest and most delicious food, fruits and drinks."

Arthur said, "Even the poorest of us would do this for their visitors. We do not even have to make special appointments to visit our friends and relations. We just have to turn up, and we are given such warm welcomes, and offered whatever there is in the homes. We are a very kind and generous people. And when we give, we do not look back for returns."

Mr Lazarus smiled at what he heard, and he took the opportunity to rattle his cup to remind everyone that he was ready to accept their offerings.

Carlos found a couple of coins, and immediately placed them into the cup. Mr Lazarus nodded, and did not say a word.

John said, "Mr Lazarus, at least you could say thank you to my friend here. If you do not, then I don't think that I should give you any charity."

Nazir said, "Mr Lazarus, people like you should not be begging. And the least you can do is to show your gratitude for every little help we give you."

Michael said, "My friends, when we give charity, it should be done with a free will, and we should not look for anything in return. We should never expect thank you or any other benefit. Also, if we give charity with a bad heart, or if we feel contempt, then we should not give."

Carlos said, "Michael, I agree with you. I think that when a man thinks of doing a good deed, he can be regarded as a good person. When he takes that good intention and actually provides the charity or the good, then I think he is a better person. But when a man has thought of a good deed, has seen it done, and then ensures that the person or persons receiving the good has actually benefitted from this, then that giver is the best type of human being."

Nazir said, "Michael, you may be our History Maan, but we now have Carlos as our great philosopher! Carlos, where did you get such wisdom from?"

Carlos smiled, and said, "Well, by being in good company, and listening to my best friends here. If we cannot learn from one another, where else will we learn from?"

Michael said, "Education and lifelong learning are truly great foods. We should never stop learning in this life. Remember what I said about the Bahai Faith?"

Arthur said, "Yes Michael, but all the great philosophies and religions including the Chinese culture, Buddhism, Hinduism, Islam, Christianity, and Judaism tell us that when we give to someone, or to a good cause, we should not look back for benefits, or even gratitude. This is simply because we are already blessed to be in a position to give to others."

Mr Lazarus smiled, and said, "Thank you most kindly my friends. I have come here today not to beg for anything from anyone. I simply wanted to know what is happening in the Domino game. I can only see very little, and even that is blurred. But I can get by. I can live on the little that I have. And, I have always tried to work for the food I get. So please do not feel pity on me. I am very well, and I thank the Lord for allowing me to be amongst you."

He slowly stepped over, and was pleased to accept a seat next to Ruff who closed his pocket sized notebook, and placed it in the left breast pocket of his short-sleeved shirt.

Mr Lazarus smiled, and whispered, "Ruff, I am really sorry to disturb your writing."

Ruff clicked his ballpoint pen, and clipped it securely in his right breast pocket, alongside several other pens and pencils.

He said, "No problem Mr Lazarus, no problem!"

Afzal finally took the Double Three and, unusually for him, he slid it quietly against the only end he could actually play. The LIONS supporters did not applaud much, as they realised that the move was not as contrived as Afzal had tried to infer from his long deliberation. The COBRA supporters looked on with some sadness, as they could also see that Peter will struggle to respond to the Three, and Blank now facing him.

* * *

Lakshmi's discovery of Ramesh's letters to Sati provided her with the real reason for Sati's love-sickness. She did not hesitate to tell Peter about their daughter's relationship with Ramesh. After reading all the letters, she discreetly placed them back to where they were found.

She sat down on the edge of Sati's bed, and tried to reflect on how this had happened without her knowledge. She was disappointed with Sati with whom she had discussed Raana more openly in the past.

Peter and Lakshmi drove back to the clinic first thing the next morning. They were very anxious to learn about Sati's progress. The doctor at the clinic delivered the good news that Sati had rested well, and that she was in good health. Peter and Lakshmi were very relieved to learn of this.

Peter quietly asked, "Can Sati come home with us today?"

The doctor said, "Yes, of course. But I need to let you know something else about Sati."

Lakshmi asked nervously, "Oh please don't tell us that she has some other problem?"

The doctor said, "Well, it is not a problem as such. It is very good news. Sati is actually pregnant."

Lakshmi opened her eyes widely, and asked, "What? This cannot be possible!"

Peter was also taken aback, and was dumbfounded.

The doctor said, "We have run all the tests, and we can confirm that Sati is very well, and the baby is also doing well."

Lakshmi said, "I cannot believe that she would do this to us. I do not know what is wrong with this girl."

Peter said, "Lakshmi, we have to talk about this with Sati when we go home. This is not the right place to discuss this problem."

Lakshmi said, "You call this a problem? This is a disaster! If only you could spend more time at home, instead of playing your stupid Cricket and Dominoes with your layabout friends. None of this would have happened!"

Peter tried to quieten Lakshmi, and whispered, "Please, let us not discuss this here, and wait till we get home. Sorry about this doctor. Can we take Sati home now please?"

18.

Inspirational women

When Afzal played his Double Three domino, he was left with two; the Six Four and the Four Two. His only hope now was that Peter would play a domino that stopped Vishnu from winning the game outright and thus the championship for the ACES.

All the spectators appeared to be aware of the situation. Peter had already rapped on Six and Blank, and his only option was restricted to the end where the Three lay. Peter perused the dominoes on the table, and the remaining three he held in his left palm.

Michael said, "Well my friends, it seems that we have reached the point of no return. You know, we talked a lot about some of our bravest Guyanese heroes of the past. But on the sixth of March this year, we all celebrated the twenty-first year of the memory and outstanding bravery of one of our Guyanese sisters whom we all know as Alice of Leonora."

Nazir said, "Thank you Michael for bringing up the subject of our brave women. In fact, you yourself had mentioned to us how it was the wives and women weeders of Leonora who pushed their husbands and brothers to strike for better pay and conditions, way back at the first strike in 1869. Then seventy years later, we lost another great woman of Leonora, by the name of Sumintra, who was one of at least three people who were killed in the Leonora Disturbance of the 13th of January 1939."

Carlos said sullenly, "Nazir, thank you for reminding us all about those events, and the sacrifices of the women of Leonora, and of course, in other places such as Enmore, and Albion. Michael, I know that it will be hard for you as an African Guyanese, to relate to us what happened to this great sister Kowsilla, who we know as Alice, from Leonora."

Nazir said, "Carlos, in the early 1960s, the racial conflict made a lot of people behave out of the ordinary. People were fighting causes that they believed in, and that is a natural thing. But now, we must be mature, and grown up enough to be able to forgive, and to forget."

John said, "Nazir, you are right about the forgiving bit. But we as Guyanese must never forget those people like Sumintra and Kowsilla who made the ultimate sacrifices with their lives, so that the wrongs done by our masters, whether British or Guyanese, must never be allowed to occur again, ever."

Michael said, "It is difficult for me to say that the African Guyanese whose name was Felix Barr, was a scab who drove the tractor directly, and purposely at the group of Indian women who were protesting on that high bridge in Leonora, on the 6th of March 1964. It was shocking for anyone to even think of doing such a cowardly thing to innocent, and defenceless women. The fact that he was African made it even worse, especially at that dreadful time in our history."

Nazir said, "You do know that people of our two largest races were being used and manipulated by the political powers that ruled. But this does not excuse Felix Barr and all his fellow scabs who took a conscious decision to oppose the protests being made by the Indian sugar workers, and those brave women on the bridge. I think that deep felt issues and resentment between the races were being played out most violently at that time, as if people did not care as to who they were hurting, and why."

Arthur said, "It was a terrible time for us all. But it was not just about Kowsilla whose body was cut in half by that tractor. Spare a moment for Jagdai and Daisy whose backs were broken by the large wheels of the tractor, and Kissoon who was also severely injured. The other women on the bridge just jumped for their lives into the trench below. They could not swim, and had to be rescued by the men."

Nazir wiped some tears from his eyes, and said, "Our beloved Kowsilla was not just any ordinary worker. She was a hard campaigner for women's rights, and the leader of the Leonora branch of the Women's Progressive Organisation, or WPO."

Michael said, "Yes Nazir, the WPO was formed by another great woman, Janet Jagan, the wife of Dr Cheddi Jagan."

John shook his head, and wiped away some tears as he said, "Tragic! That was really tragic. It should never have been allowed to happen!"

Michael said, "We come back to the same thing about not learning from the history lessons of the past. I told you all about the Enmore

Martyrs, the five ordinary Indian sugar workers who were shot and killed by police when they tried to stop scabs from working during their strike. This event did inspire our Dr Cheddi Jagan to promise to dedicate his entire life in the struggle for the working people of Guyana."

Nazir said, "All the sugarcane workers of Enmore Sugar Estate wanted in 1948, was to be treated fairly. Instead of having to cut and load the sugarcane onto the punts, they wanted to cut the sugarcane, and have other workers do the loading. To cut sugarcane has always been a very hard, back-breaking job, and then to lift and carry the large bundles of the cut sugarcane to the punts waiting in the canal beside the sugarcane field was much too unfair."

Arthur frowned as he said, "And all for the same money. That can never be fair!"

Nazir said, "That is the kind of injustice people had to fight against. And, when you are a poor worker, the only real power you have is to withdraw your labour."

Michael said, "Well, the sacrifice of the Enmore Martyrs did eventually help to achieve a lot of improvements for the workers through something called the Venn Commission. This gave the workers some much needed rights, and better conditions. But the most important issue of cut and load, and cut and drop was not fully resolved."

Carlos said, "It must hurt people badly when they make such sacrifices for themselves and others, and then find that the struggle was not complete. No wonder our struggles had to continue."

Michael said, "Yes, the Venn Commission was a significant turning point for sugar plantation workers in this country. The Enmore Martyrs, and all the hundreds of workers involved, must never be forgotten. We must never forget them alongside Kofi, the Reverend John Smith, Sumintra, Kowsilla, and so many more."

Nazir said, "Most importantly of all Michael, is for our younger generation to appreciate these struggles that helped towards the limited freedom we are now enjoying."

Carlos said, "I am not a very religious man, but there is a kind of divinity involved in these struggles and sacrifices. When people lay down tools, and protest against bad treatment, and for their basic rights, we must respect this."

Nazir said, "Carlos, you are right man. But the moment we stand up to champion these people and their causes, we will be targeted, and labelled. Dr Jagan, and his followers were branded as communists by the British and American Governments, simply because they stood up for the working classes."

Michael said, "Yes, the divide and rule tactic pushed us into racial conflict in the 1960s, and it was so divisive, people still carry the mental scars."

Nazir said, "Michael, Carlos, and John, I thank Allah that we have become even closer friends, and can openly share our feelings, and thoughts about these matters. We were all in our early twenties when these events were occurring in 1963 and 1964. I am amazed by the fact that after everything was over, and the killings stopped, we all seemed to just get back together after only a few months time."

John said, "That is true. And, as Michael said, we are still carrying a lot of scars up to now. It will take some time for us all to be completely free from this kind of torture. Giving Sumintra and Kowsilla their full dues as true martyrs, as we have honoured Kofi, is very important for our country, as we strive to re-build our nation."

Carlos said, "It is right for us to seek to become more united than ever before. But both African and Indian Guyanese have left this country for America, Canada and England as well as all over the Caribbean, with a sense of bitterness, and they are not here now to be part of this healing process."

John said, "Well, in a kind of a strange way, Guyanese abroad have had to put aside some of their own prejudices, and face up to the white racists in America, Canada and the United Kingdom. There is a sort of "coming together" of not only the different races of Guyanese, but also people from the other Caribbean Islands. My father told me that some of his best memories of living in London were when he went to the Lord's Cricket Ground to see West Indies play cricket against England. He loved being amongst the noisiest and most entertaining crowd of West Indian supporters from Guyana, Trinidad and Tobago, Barbados, Jamaica, the Windward and Leeward Islands and so on."

Nazir said, "It is a great shame that we do not see that kind of unity when we have our cricket here in Guyana and the Caribbean. We tend to support our own local players in the West Indies team here in Guyana, and so do the others in their islands. I remember one time that we Guyanese booed some of the West Indies cricketers from the other islands. Even the great Sir Garfield Sobers was booed here in Guyana when he was accused of giving away a test match series against England in the 1960s."

Michael said, "I do love my cricket, even though I was never good at the game. I think that the situation has changed a lot now, and we do support our team regardless of where the players come from."

Carlos said, "I can appreciate what John said. It was great to see our various peoples having such a great time cheering our West Indies team in England. The people used that as a way of relief from their daily experiences of racism in all walks of life. The other time they do this is during the best Carnival in Europe. The Notting Hill Carnival!"

Nazir said, "I have read that there is a lot of crime during the Carnival, and most of the arrests are of our young West Indians."

John asked, "What crimes are you talking about?"

Nazir said, "Mostly petty things like pick-pocketing and so on. They call this mugging."

Carlos said, "Yes, but you also see how the British Police stamp on this, and stop bad behaviour in a very aggressive way."

Nazir said, "Sometimes I think that we need such responses right here in Guyana."

Michael said, "Sport such as Cricket and Football do tend to bring peoples together, and I am not ashamed to say that my greatest Guyanese and West Indian batting hero was Rohan Kanhai. I also liked Gary Sobers from Barbados, but I preferred Kanhai because he is a Guyanese. The fact that he is an Indian Guyanese is secondary. I loved the sheer class of that man, from the moment he stepped onto the field at Bourda in Georgetown, with his white kerchief tied round his neck, and his smooth and elegant walk to the wicket, to the way he looked around the field, and then the absolute brilliance of his strokes all round the wicket. As a batsman, he was a true entertainer."

Carlos smiled, and said, "Yes man, one of the true greats of all time!"

John said, "I know that we have not yet produced any decent Amerindian cricketer. But I love the master blasters like Vivian Richards from Antigua, and our own Clive Lloyd. Clive Lloyd was also a great Captain who brought the very best out of some powerful fast bowlers like Michael Holding, Andy Roberts, Joel Garner, and Malcolm Marshall, and the other great players of the best team in the world."

Michael said, "A great example of when unity is strength!"

Nazir said, "Yes Michael, people like Kanhai, Sobers and Lloyd are great role models for us all. We need more of such heroes to pull us together even more strongly. We have to wake up to this sooner rather than later."

Carlos said, "I agree with everything you all have said. But please do not underestimate the deep-rooted prejudices, and suspicions that still linger on, and surface from time to time. We need leaders and role models in this country, to take us out of this quagmire. And then, we have to be prepared for this to take some time before there is complete harmony amongst the people."

Michael said, "That is one hell of a challenge for anyone, including our current President and Opposition leaders. Such a leader has to win over the trust of all the people. He or she has to be seen to be serving everyone with humility, compassion and fairness. That leader has to be completely free of corruption, and with no skeletons in their cupboard! Our opposition leader, the great Dr Cheddi Jagan is the politician I admire the most. He has fought, and continues to fight for the betterment of all Guyanese people."

Nazir said, "Michael, let's be realistic here. We all know full well that we cannot trust any politician in this country, with only one or two exceptions. Besides, we are being constantly watched by the greater powers in America and Britain. Therefore that person will have to convince the Americans and British that they could be trusted with Guyana. Never mind our republican status and so on, America and Britain can step in as soon as they see things are not going the way that they approve of. So, where do we start?"

John said, "Is there such a person in Guyana? Will there ever be such an honest, and inspirational person?"

Michael said, "We all know that we have some very experienced and bright political leaders in our midst, including our President who was an outstanding scholar in London, and, our Dr Jagan, the leader of the main opposition."

Nazir said, "Yes, we have had some great people who tried to bring workers together in the various Unions, and it is a great pity that inspirational leaders like the late Hubert Critchlow, whose bronze statue is in the grounds of the Parliament Building in Georgetown, did not become leaders of the political parties."

Michael said, "Trade Union leaders and activists tend to become so absorbed in their struggles for their members rights, that they stay loyal to their cause, right up to the end."

Carlos said, "The people who are our political leaders, are now getting on in age, and must be battle-worn. We need some new, fresh blood, with modern ideas."

Michael said, "The older leaders, and in particular, President Burnham, should step aside, and allow a younger man or woman to come forward. But I am afraid that these old men will not go unless they are pushed."

John said, "Maybe we need someone from our Amerindian peoples!"

Nazir said, "Yes John, and why the hell not? Amerindian people are the first true Guyanese, and they are very tough and intelligent."

Mr Lazarus, who was sitting next to Ruff, tapped his white cane on the floor to signal some attention to what he was about to say. Everyone turned their gaze towards the old man.

He coughed slightly, and said, "First of all gentlemen, we really need a good woman to lead us. We need to improve our education system, and to exploit all the brains we have here, and those Guyanese living abroad. We have a lot of very talented and experienced Guyanese living abroad, and we should encourage them to return to help re-build our country. But will we be able to embrace them? To trust them?"

Ruff broke his silence, and encouraged to speak by Mr Lazarus's intervention, said, "And, thirdly we have to have more discipline, law and order, and a real crack down on drugs, alcohol, and fraud."

Some of the spectators laughed at the suggestions of the two elderly gentlemen.

Michael turned to them, and said, "There you are. You laugh at people offering sensible solutions to Guyana's problems. What chance will anyone have with people like you showing just how ignorant you are?"

Nazir said, "Come now Michael, people have a right to express themselves just as we have been doing all through this game. If we stop this, then we will continue to just roll along, and our country will get nowhere."

Carlos said, "Guyana will continue to struggle especially in business, as a lot of good business people whether they were Chinese,

Portuguese, African or Indian have left this place, and may never return."

Arthur said, "I do agree with some of that, but I have to say that we also have some very ambitious, and talented business people who have stepped up to exploit the gaps left by the others. Just look at the new establishments beginning to appear, and the magnificent modern houses people are putting up all over the country."

John said, "True, but we are building these houses because we cannot take our Guyana dollars out of this country, because our currency is not recognised or legal abroad."

Nazir said, "Business is about confidence and the ability to see an opportunity, and in taking risks in going for it. But we have so much national debt that I have heard for every ten Guyana dollars we earn, we owe nine dollars to foreign banks. This is an impossible situation to be in. Whoever takes over the running of this country in the future, will have to get these debts written off. Then, hopefully we can start again."

John said, "Nazir, you are turning out to be not only a good historian, but also a sensible economist! You have hit the nail on its head. The money that has poured into this country over many years, has done nothing for us. I also agree with our friends Mr Lazarus and Mr Ruff that we need to re-build from the basics. But have we got the time, and the will?"

Michael said, "Of course we can do this. We need the leadership that can really make our One People and One Nation truly push much harder for the vision of One Destiny."

John said, "I salute to that! Our leader should be truthful, hard-working for everyone's benefit, and have the right people to take on all the most important tasks."

Michael said, "Such a person must be capable of serving others before himself or herself. He or she must also be God-fearing, and honest about their actions."

Arthur said, "I think that we need a really good woman to lead us out of this mess, just like our women martyrs who were the first to stand up for our rights!"

Nazir said, "It's a dream, and we need real action."

Carlos said, "Let's hope our friend Peter can wake up, and make his move right now!"

Arthur said, "Come on man, play a domino, or rap!"

Peter looked around the room, and at his opponents before finally hitting the table with his clenched right knuckle, and saying, "Rap!"

Michael could not contain himself any longer, and he raised his hands in the air shouting, "It's all over now! It's all over! Long live the ACES!"

The young supporters of the ACES joined in the chorus shouting, "Long live the ACES! Long live the ACES!"

The referee pointed at Michael and the supporters, and said, "Please control yourselves! The game is not over yet! Please be quiet!"

* * *

When Peter, Lakshmi, and Sati finally arrived at their home, after a tense journey from Georgetown, they sat down together in their lounge, to have some soothing, ice cold homemade ginger beer.

Sati could not bear the silence any longer, and she asked, "Please Maa and Paa, why are you not speaking to me?"

Peter shuffled uneasily in his sedan chair, and said, "Well, I think that your mother wants to talk to you."

Lakshmi stared at Peter, and then turned to Sati. She said, "Your Paa and me are very upset and angry with you."

Sati was surprised, and asked, "But Maa, what have I done now?"

Lakshmi said, "It's not what you have done. It's what that boy Ramesh and you did together."

Sati said, "I still do not understand what you are talking about."

Peter said, "Well, let's be blunt about this. You and Ramesh are lovers, and he has made you pregnant."

Sati said, "No! This is not true!"

Lakshmi said, "Well, I have seen and read his letters to you, and the doctor at the clinic confirmed the real reason for your illness. Now, can you stop lying to us, and show us the respect we deserve?"

Sati broke down in tears, and reached over to embrace Peter and Lakshmi.

She said, "I am so sorry Maa and Paa. I love Ramesh. I want to be with him."

Peter lost his temper, and banged his fist on the glass table, "You must be mad! That boy comes from a very respectable Brahmin family!

They will never agree to a marriage with you! We are low class, and this will never be allowed to happen! Besides, you are pregnant and they will never accept that their son did that!"

Lakshmi reached out to Peter, and said, "Peter, please calm down. That boy's father is one of the people that you play your Dominoes with. He knows you very well, and I am sure that he has some respect for you as a person."

Peter shrugged his shoulders, and said, "Well, playing Cricket and Dominoes with someone doesn't mean that they will accept you when you are a lower class person."

Lakshmi said, "Never mind what you feel, we need to talk to him and his wife."

Sati felt quite helpless, and found great difficulty to sleep that night. She turned and twisted restlessly, thinking what would be the reaction of Ramesh's parents, and what would Ramesh say about her pregnancy. Will Ramesh accept that the baby was his? Will his parents block her parents' request? Will Ramesh now abandon her in this state? How will she face all her friends and relations? Should she go ahead and have the baby? Or, should she abort it?

19.

Domino!

Everyone's attention was distracted by the beautiful rhythm of the *tassa* and *dhol* drums being played by two very well known friends of Anna Catherina. The tassa was beaten by the much larger and thick set Indian player, and the dhol which was strapped tightly round the shoulders of the taller but very slender African player, was being hit in perfect harmony. The dhol's booming base sound could be felt on the chest of anyone passing by at both kerbs of the main road.

The Domino players and spectators in the hall paused to look out through the windows, and kept very quiet to listen to the message to be conveyed by the drummers. This could be either the announcement of a death and funeral of a local, or, the happier news of someone's wedding.

The tassa player stopped alongside his friend at a safe enough part of the kerb, and faced the hall. The messengers always had a good knack of knowing the right place to pause, and deliver their news so that as many people as possible could hear it.

The tassa player took out his hand held megaphone, raised it to his lips, and shouted, "Attention everyone! Attention!"

A young man standing next to the tassa player at the roadside shouted back, "Switch on the damn thing then everyone will hear you!"

The tassa player coughed slightly, and quickly switched on the megaphone to deliver his news. The growing crowd laughed at his error.

He shouted, "Attention everyone! You are all invited to come to the grand wedding of Ramesh, the son of Vishnu "Double Six" Prashad and his wife Parvati, to Sati, the beautiful daughter of Peter "Smokey" Ramdin and his wife Lakshmi, next Sunday at the residences of "Double Six" and "Smokey"!"

He repeated the message twice more before resuming his march, and drumming with his friend to their next stop.

Everyone in the hall was very surprised at the news, and turned to look at Vishnu and Peter sitting at the table. They applauded them with gusto. Vishnu and Peter raised their right hands in appreciation, and then smiled at each other.

Michael stared at Vishnu, and then at Peter, and said, "Well, you two gentlemen kept that as a good secret! Congratulations to you both. So, whatever happens in this game and championship, we all have a damn good reason to celebrate!"

Carlos said, "Well done Vishnu and Peter! This is truly great news. We all need something like this to take away some of our pain we have been talking about today, and every day."

Nazir said, "I knew that one day there would be a big wedding because everyone in Anna Catherina and Cornelia Ida knew about the young couple's courtship, especially when they were seen at the Monarch Cinema, and also in other places in Georgetown."

Arthur said, "Now now Nazir, people should keep quiet about these things. It is a modern world now, and we have all been through such courtships thinking that no one saw us."

Michael said, "Yes, that is what you get when your hormones become so consumed with love and passion."

John said, "Michael, what the hell are you guys talking about? This is a straight forward thing. Boy meets girl, girl plays hard-to-get, boy tries harder, and girl gives in. Simple. It happens all the time, everywhere!"

Michael said, "No wonder Peter was miming all through the game with that stupid smile all over his face! He wasn't concentrating enough on the game. His mind was on a much bigger event!"

Nazir said, "No man. Nobody or anything gets in the way of a Domino game. Especially one that is so crucial to all of us. Peter, Vishnu and Afzal could never be put off by all the actions around them, and the things we were talking about."

Michael looked at Vishnu, and they winked and smiled at each other. Then Michael said, "Nazir, you are so right. I can assure you that our great captain Vishnu "Double Six" Prashad was concentrating very hard all the way through the game. He is a man with nerves of steel. This is what a good leader must possess."

Carlos said, "Vishnu has been cut out to be our captain. Ever since he was a small boy, he used to be the boss over his older brothers and sisters."

Nazir said, "And even his own friends!"

Arthur said, "I really thought that we were here to talk and to disturb the concentrations of Peter and Afzal. But I am now thinking that something else was going on, and I believe that Michael knows more than he is letting on."

John said, "Arthur, please leave the post mortem for later. Let us now prepare for a great moment of ultimate victory. Let us get ready to jump for joy. Let us wake up to the sound of triumph!"

The referee tried yet again to bring about calm before the next play was made.

Michael said, "Ref, it's all over now. There is no point in trying to impose order. Our man Vishnu has got this game all sewn up! If he doesn't win now, then I will shave my head!"

Nazir said, "Michael, you have really lost the plot now. Your head is already clean shaven! Maybe you should offer another sacrifice!"

Carlos said, "Like, to sew up his lips for a long time!"

John laughed, and said, "I think Michael knows that he can offer any sacrifice or bet on the outcome of this game. How can Vishnu lose this game with having only one last domino in his hand, Afzal having two, and Peter having three?"

Arthur said, "Well, I am not too sure about this. I have seen people lose games from such a position, and this game may go the same way."

Everyone's attention was now firmly fixed on Vishnu as he surveyed all the dominoes that had been played on the table. There was nothing more for him to think about, or any tactic to conjure up. All such thinking and planning were now in the hands of his opponents. But their moves could only be put into action if he could not win at this point.

The LIONS spectators saw Vishnu's hesitancy, and felt that he was in some kind of trouble. So they shouted, "Rap! Rap! Rap!"

The ACES supporters felt uneasy, and nervous at this development. They stood quietly with their fingers crossed.

Then, just before the song finished on the radio across the road, the announcer said in a mournful tone, "Dear listeners, we have just learnt that our great leader and President, the Honourable Linden Forbes Sampson Burnham, has sadly passed away...."

Michael suddenly lost his composure, and shouted, "Slam that domino down! Yes! Yes! Slam that Domino down!"

Vishnu raised his right hand, and slammed down his final domino, the Double Blank, and shouted, "Domino!""

The whole hall was stunned, but the ACES supporters suddenly jumped for joy, celebrating their victory.

Michael raised his arms aloft, and said solemnly, "Please everyone, we must show respect, and mourn the end of an era. And then after that, we must also celebrate our victory, and hopefully, the start of a new phase in the freedom of all Guyanese, here and everywhere!"

John, Carlos, and Arthur said, "Amen to that!"

Nazir raised his hands as in the Islamic supplication, and said, "Allah ho Akbar! Allah ho Akbar! Allah ho Akbar!"

Peter shook Vishnu's hands, and said, "Congratulations my brother!"

Afzal put his large hands on Vishnu's and Peter's shoulders, and said, "Let us all celebrate in true Guyanese style!"

Ruff rose steadily from his seat next to the match table, and reached out to hold Michael by his shoulders.

He said calmly, "Michael, I hereby make a citizen's arrest for plotting to kill our President Burnham."

Michael stood back in shock, and removed Ruff's hands from his shoulders.

He said, "Are you mad? What the hell do you think you are doing?"

The spectators and players were stunned into silence, and looked on with great surprise on their faces. The referee raised his right hand, and tried to get between Ruff and Michael.

He said, "Come on now gentlemen, this is no time to play stupid jokes. We have just lost our President, the great Kabaka!"

Mr Lazarus stood up gingerly, and stepped forward, knocking over his white stick.

He stood next to Ruff, and said, "I support my friend Ruff here, and I can assure you that he has good reason to suspect Michael of plotting to kill Mr Burnham."

Vishnu stepped into the fray, and pushed Ruff and Mr Lazarus aside.

He said, "How dare you two old fools come up with this accusation? Ruff, you are just a damn mischief-maker. I know you never liked Michael and all of us who used to tease you when you were a policeman. Besides, Mr Lazarus, you are almost blind, so how the hell can you see anything?"

Mr Lazarus said, "You better watch your words because we are going to arrest you also. And, let me tell all of you here, that I am not blind or partially-blind at all. And, I have been watching your movements, and listening to all your conversations."

Ruff chipped in with, "And, we have made notes about this, and all the clues that you and your friends have been giving to Vishnu in this game. Michael, you think that you are so clever, and kept passing hints about the target all through this game, and even when you were talking in your practice sessions."

Nazir asked, "What target are you talking about?"

Ruff said, "The target is our Late great President!"

Carlos said, "What nonsense! Michael is our coach, and he just loves to talk about Guyana's history. How can this make him a great assassin?"

Nazir said, "Ruff and Mr Lazarus, you just cannot do this to us! Why don't you just take your medicines, and go home to rest?"

Ruff pushed Nazir aside, and said, "Yes we can! In fact, we want to place you all under arrest. But we will lock up Michael and Vishnu first, and the police will come back for you, Carlos, John, and Arthur."

The friends railed up, and shouted at Ruff and Mr Lazarus. They threatened to beat the two old men.

Then the front door of the hall was opened forcibly, and the wives of the accused men marched forward with Doreen at the helm.

She said, "Right now Michael! Look at what trouble you have come into! It serves you right for not listening to me! God only knows how long you, and your stupid team will be locked away in jail!"

Parvati, Vishnu's wife aggressively pointed at his chest, and shouted, "You should know better than to follow these fools! We have a wedding to do, and here you are playing this stupid game! And, what is in your heads to think that you can kill our President?"

Vishnu tried to offer a response, but Nazir intervened with, "No my sister! These old men are trouble-makers! We have finished the game, and we are going home now. I am so damn hungry that I do not need to waste any more time here arguing with you!"

Neesha, Nazir's wife, said, "Only now you want to go home to eat? Well, you can go to jail, and they will feed you there! I warned you enough about wasting your time with these lazy, good-for-nothing friends of yours! And, furthermore, let me tell you that there is no food at home for you!"

Arthur said, "Now, now, now! Let us all be a bit sensible here. The game is over. We all want to go home, and mourn the loss of our President. No one is stupid enough to plot to kill him."

Ruff and Mr Lazarus made another attempt to grab Vishnu and Michael to carry out their arrest. But Nazir, Carlos and John held them in an attempt to prevent the arrests.

Ruff said, "Now, you will all be charged for resisting arrest, and preventing the course of justice!"

John said, "Please everyone, let us all calm down. No crime has actually been committed. Our President fell ill, and died suddenly. He was not shot or stabbed."

Ruff said, "Aha! So how do you know this? No one knows how our great Kabaka passed away! At least we have not heard anything about this!"

Muriel, John's wife, asked, "So why are you making these arrests?"

Maria, Carlos's wife, said, "Come on everyone, you are all getting carried away here. But I agree with my friends that you should all pack up, and go home!"

Michael, John, Vishnu, Nazir and Carlos all moved forward to embrace their wives in an attempt to pacify them. Arthur stood back, and looked on with pride.

The referee turned to Ruff and Mr Lazarus, and said, "Well gentlemen, what are you going to do?"

Ruff smiled broadly, exposing the large gap between his front teeth, and said, "OK! The women asked me to think of something that will scare their husbands to stop playing the game, and to go home. So, when I heard the sad announcement just now, I felt that this was a good threat to make. By the way, I still do not trust Michael and Vishnu!"

Mr Lazarus said, "Hmm, that is interesting! Who knows whether or not people will start to speculate on the sudden passing of our President. By the way, I really do have only partial sight, so can someone please pass me my stick?"

Ruff stooped down wearily, and picked up Mr Lazarus's walking stick. As he started to straighten up, he saw Ramesh and Sati entering the hall. He pointed the stick towards the smiling couple, and said, "And now my friends, here comes the two very happy young people. Give them a good cheer!"

Everyone turned towards Ramesh and Sati, and applauded as the couple stepped forward to greet Vishnu and Peter.

Before the applause could end, the front door of the hall was forcefully pushed open, and Raana appeared with a shotgun, pointing it towards Ramesh and Sati.

He raised the gun and began to take aim, with his right index finger curled around the trigger.

Raana shouted, "Nobody move! Everybody, stay where you are! One slight move, and I will shoot you!"

Vishnu, Peter, Ramesh and Sati quickly put their hands up.

Raana stepped closer towards his targets, and took aim.

Everyone in the hall was stunned into silence, until Ruff spoke.

He raised his hands, and said, "Young man, please put that gun down. Tell me what is your problem. I am sure we can sort something out."

Mr Lazarus, still a little unsteady on his feet, and without his trusted walking stick, said, "Please do as Mr Ruff says, my son. You have your whole life ahead of you. And killing anyone will not solve anything."

Just then, Lakshmi rushed into the hall towards Ramesh and Sati, crying out, "No! Please don't kill my children!"

Raana turned around to see who had spoken, and in a flash, Ruff raised the walking stick, and lashed out at the gunman's hands.

The blow struck the gun, and before it fell from Raana's grip it fired, and as the shot rang out, everyone dived for cover.

Lakshmi and the other wives screamed, and began to wail in sheer terror. Vishnu and Peter grabbed the unarmed Raana, and wrestled him to the floor. Some of the spectators dashed out of the hall as fast as they could. Others, in their panic, stumbled on the Dominoes table causing it to topple over, and scattering the dominoes to the floor.

Ruff lay on the floor holding his stomach with both hands, and groaning with acute pain. Blood was oozing through his dark fingers, and forming a small thick red puddle beside him.

Mr Lazarus shouted, "Quick! Get him to hospital!"

Michael, Arthur, John and Nazir stooped down beside Ruff, and were about to lift him up to take him towards the roadside, when he briefly opened his reddened eyes, and lips.

He murmured, "No..No...too late...let me go..."

Ruff's funeral took place in the beautiful St John's Anglican Church in Edinburgh, and which was opposite the Leonora Cricket Ground. The church hall was packed with sympathisers from all the villages on the coast, and many mourners could not get into the building. They stood outside, and listened to the service, in respectful silence. When the Priest spoke about the depth of gratitude to be shown to Ruff for his service to the community, and his final act of bravery, everyone applauded.

They all seemed to forget losers and victors, sadness and happiness, divisions and unity, struggles and triumphs, and replaced these with tears of joy.

They were One People, in One Nation, and on their way to One Destiny.

END

Glossary

Achaar	Hindi word for pickle. Achaar is normally made of several spices and with fruits such as Mangoes, Limes, or *Bling Bling*. Also called *Chatney* or *Chutney*.
Aloo	Potato.
Aloo choka	Mashed potato with several spices including crushed ginger, cumin, red chilli pepper, turmeric, and salt.
Arabic	The language of the Arabs, and the Holy Qur'an.
Awaara	(*Astrovarium Vulgare*) A fruit from the palm. The orange coloured peel and flesh is sweet, but can leave a stain on the teeth. It is considered to be nutritious, and is a rich source of carotene and vitamins.
Baap re baap	Hindi expression for "Oh my God".
Baara	A Guyanese bake made with flour and split peas. It is normally used with *achaar*.
Badaam lacha	A sweet snack made with flour, ghee, sugar, and vanilla essence.
Bahai or *Baha'i*	The faith founded by Baha'ullah (The Baab) of Persia (Iran) from a declaration on the 23rd of May 1844, in Shiraz, Persia.
Ball (Delivery)	As in cricket. Refers to the cricket ball used in the sport of cricket. It is normally made of cork encased in leather, and weighs 5.5 ounces. A ball also refers to a single delivery to describe when a bowler bowls a ball or delivery at a batsman, as part of an over of six balls.
Banga Mary	(Macrodon Ancylodon): A fresh water fish usually consumed as a curry, or as deep fried fish.
Baraat	Indian wedding procession of the groom and his entourage that travels to the bride-to-be's residence for the marriage ceremony.
Batsman	As in cricket. A person who bats or specialises in batting.
Bat	As in cricket. A cricket bat is normally made of finely carved willow with a smooth face for striking the cricket ball. It has a fixed handle. Cricket bats are not expected to be longer than 38 inches, and should be up to 4.25 inches in width.
Batting	As in cricket. Batting is what a batsman does by hitting the cricket ball.
Batting crease	As in cricket. The batting crease is a measured line from where a batsman usually prepares to face the ball bowled by a bowler.
Bhajan	A Hindu devotional song or hymn.

Bhagwad Gita	Epic account of the Mahabharat battle; a holy text in Hinduism.
Bhai	Hindi for brother.
Bling bling	(*Averrhoa Bilimbi*) The fruit of the Bilimbi tree, used to make pickles or achaar. It is normally sour, and appears throughout the year.
Blue saki	(Tanager songbird) A native of Guyana, with different shades of blue. Its diet is mainly fruit.
Bowl/bowled	As in cricket. To bowl is to deliver a cricket ball for a batsman to play at. If the ball is missed, and hits the wicket, then this is termed being "bowled out".
Bowling crease	As in cricket. A measured line at the end from where a bowler bowls a ball to a batsman. If the bowler crosses the line as deemed by the laws of cricket, then this is called a no ball, and apart from conceding a run to the opposition, it has to be bowled again.
Breadfruit	(*Artocarpus Altilis*) A large football sized fruit with a tough skin. It has soft white flesh which is high in starch. The flesh can be boiled, mashed or fried, and is normally bland in taste. The fruit was brought to the Caribbean from the Pacific Islands, with the intention of providing a staple food for the African slaves on the sugar plantations.
Bumper ball games	As in cricket. Unconventional cricket games played with rubber balls or soft balls, with rules locally agreed upon. The bats are normally handmade from pieces of light wood, or from coconut branches.
Bush rum	A rum made crudely in secret, and away from normal factory premises. It is illegal, and considered more potent in alcohol content.
Cacabelly	A very small tropical fish which likes to live in drains and trenches. Large quantities are deep fried and used as a snack or "cutters" alongside alcohol drinking.
Calypso	A song which originated in Trinidad and Tobago, and comprises local topical lyrics in a Caribbean dialect of English. A Calypsonian is one who sings Calypsoes. The Calypso is believed to be derived from "Kaiso" which was sung by the West African slaves from the 17th Century.
Cassava	(*Manihot Esculenta*) An edible root tuber, also known as Yucca. It is used as boiled chips, fried snacks, or in local soups. Grated cassava is used to make cakes and other sweet snacks. It is also used to make *cassreep*.
Cassreep	A dark thick preservative made from the juice of the *cassava*, and includes cinnamon and sugar. It is normally used in Guyanese pepperpot.
Catch	As in cricket. To dismiss a batsman by catching a ball struck by him, before it touches the ground.
Channa	(*Cicer Arietinum*) A legume which is high in protein. It has been used by man for over 7,500 years in various recipes. When boiled and mixed with spices, it is called *googri*.
Chaupai	A Hindi verse of the Ramayan, about the story of Lord Raam.

Chatney or Chutney See *Achaar.*

Chinaman   As in cricket. A delivery from a left arm spin bowler where instead of turning away from the right handed batsman, turns in towards him. This ball or delivery is accredited to Ellis Achong, the first ever Chinese man to play Test cricket for the West Indies or elsewhere.

Chinese cake   A sweet pastry made of flour, oil, sugar, eggs, milk, and black eyed peas.

Choke an robbers   Term used to describe Guyanese muggers.

Clean bowled   As in cricket. The dismissal of a batsman by a ball or delivery hitting the stumps or bails, dislodging one or both bails, and without touching the batsman, or his bat.

Coconut choka   A spicy dish made of grated coconut, garlic, onion, pepper, and salt to taste. It is normally used with *daal* and rice as a meal.

Cook up rice   A traditional rice based dish including black eyed peas, chicken (optional), onions, garlic, soya sauce, coconut milk, ochro, pepper, and salt to taste. Other meats and vegetables could be added, if preferred.

Crease   As in cricket. An area on the cricket pitch, which is marked out with white chalk. A batsman normally takes his *guard* using the crease, and bowlers are expected to comply with the rules that determine the legality of a delivery. Over-stepping a *popping or bowling crease* is called a *no ball,* which automatically concedes an extra run to the opposition, and has to be bowled again as a legal delivery.

Cricket   A sport invented by the English. It is played by two teams consisting of eleven players. There are a number of formats of the game including Test Matches intended to be played over five consecutive days, and limited over games of fifty overs, or forty overs, or twenty overs per inning.

Custard apple   (*Annona Reticulata*) A tropical fruit which is not an apple, but is green in colour, with white, soft edible flesh.

Cut /Cutting   As in cricket. A batsman *cuts* a ball or delivery by hitting it as it passes on the *offside*. In Dominoes, a player can cut off the prospect of another trying to *pass* a double points ticket, excepting the *Double Six* which is the highest double that starts a game.

Daal   Spicy Indian lentil soup. There are several types of *daal*, including toor, moong, channa, split peas, masoor, kabooli, urud, and green moong. They each provide individual health benefits.

Daal poorie roti   A roti with spiced dry split peas *daal* within the pastry.

Dhol   A large base drum normally hung from around the neck, and beaten with a stick on one side and the hand on the other. The *dhol* usually accompanies the *tassa.*

Domino/Dominoes   The *Domino* is a rectangle shaped tile or ticket, or piece, with a dividing line in the middle, and black spots to indicate the points value from one to six. *Dominoes* is the name of the game using the twenty eight *Domino* pieces or tickets.

Double blank /six	The *Double Blank* and *Double Six* are two of the *Domino Doubles* from blanks through to sixes. The *Double Blank* is worth zero points, and the *Double Six* is worth twelve points.
Dua	An Arabic word for prayer or supplication.
Dumpling	A soft roll made of flour, butter or margarine, baking powder, salt, sugar, and, can include nutmeg. It is usually allowed to cook towards the end of a vegetable soup.
Eddoes	(*Colocasia Esculenta*) A small root vegetable used as an alternative to potatoes, yams, or sweet potatoes.
Eid-ul-Adha	The second most important festival in Islam after *Eid-ul-Fitr*. It commemorates the willingness of Abraham (Ibrahim - Peace be unto Him) to sacrifice his son to God (Allah). God prevented the sacrifice, and Muslims feast on the permitted sacrifice of cows or rams. *Eid-ul-Adha* also concludes the end of Pilgrimage to Mecca.
Eid-ul-Fitr	The festival to celebrate the end of fasting in the Islamic month of Ramadan.
Fast bowler	As in cricket. A bowler who bowls a cricket ball at speeds of up to ninety miles per hour or more.
Fast medium	As in cricket. A bowler who bowls at a speed that is below that of a *fast bowler*.
Fielder/s	As in cricket. A fielder is one of ten others who take to the field of play in support of a bowler. A *fielder's* task is to stop a batsman from scoring, or catches out a batsman, or runs out a batsman.
Five fingers	(*Carambola*) The *five fingers* is a fruit which is golden yellow in colour when ripe, has a shape with five ridges, and is wholly edible. It is also known as *star fruit* or *shamrock*.
Flattie	A quarter bottle of rum.
Four/s	As in cricket. A four is the number of runs for a batsman hitting a ball that bounces at least once before crossing the boundary. *Fours* can be scored without the batsman hitting the ball, as in *byes*, *leg byes*, and *wides*. A *six* is scored when a ball is hit fully over the boundary.
Gail baaka	(*Sciades Herzbergii*) A tropical fish of Guyana used as fried or curried fish.
Gamma	Also known as *gamma cherry*. It is a small fruit with a sticky flesh and which is normally used as a paste for making kites in Guyana.
Genip	Also known as *skinip*, or *Spanish lime*. Genips grow in bunches, and each fruit has a green outer peel which is not edible. The flesh is yellowish, sweet, and normally sucked off one large seed.
Gola	A small round pellet made of clay, and dried in the sun. It is used as the "bullet" for *slingshots*.
Googly	As in cricket. A type of ball or delivery bowled by a right arm leg spinner. A leg break becomes a *googly* when it turns towards a right handed batsman, instead of away from him.
Googri	Boiled *channa* with some pepper and salt.

Granadilla	A tropical fruit from South America. It is about the size of a plum, with an orange skin, and jelly-like pulp with small black seeds which are edible.
Gulaab jamoon	A sweet dessert in the shape of round milky balls soaked in rose-scented syrup.
Gulgula	A sweet dessert made from bananas, flour, baking powder, cinnamon, currants or raisins, vanilla extract, and sugar.
Hadith	The *Hadith* is second only to the *Holy Qur'an*, and comprises the teachings, deeds, and sayings of the Holy Prophet Mohamed (Peace Be Unto Him).
Hassa	(*Hoplosternum Littorale*) A freshwater tropical fish with a hard outer shell. Its habitat includes the bottoms of slow moving trenches, canals and drains.
Hindu	A person of the ancient Indian faith called Hinduism.
Hindi	Indian language derived from the ancient Sanskrit.
Holy Qur'an	The primary book of *Islam*.
Hopscotch	A popular children's game played on the ground where a small object is moved around by hopping on one foot, within rectangle squares.
Houri	An edible freshwater fish.
Imaam	A Muslim priest.
Inning/s	As in cricket. A fixed duration of a game of cricket where one team bats to score runs and the fielding team tries to get the batsmen out. Sometimes an inning could be cut short by the captain declaring it closed before all ten wickets are lost.
Islam/Islamic	The Faith of Muslims.
Jack fruit	Also known as Jaca, and has a large rough skin. The pulp is yellowish, sweet smelling, and succulent. The large seeds are also cooked.
Jahaji	Seafarer. Indian indentured labourers who travelled together by ship from India, referred to each other as *Jahaji bhai* or *Jahaji behen*.
Jalebi	A sweet made by deep frying a wheat flour batter in circular shapes, and soaked in syrup.
Jamoon	A tropical fruit which is oblong, and crimson when ripe. It is sweet, and can leave a purple stain on the tongue.
Jumah	Arabic word for Friday. *Jumah Namaaz* is an important prayer for Muslims.
Jumbie	A name for a mythical spirit or demon or ghost of the dead, and referred to in Caribbean and Guyanese folklore.
Kaliyug	The last of the four ages of *Satyug, Treta, Dwapar, and Kaliyug* that make up the cycle of creation and destruction in Hindu philosophy. *Satyug* was the age of truth. *Treta* was the age when humans lost a quarter of the truth. *Dwapar* where another half of the truth was lost. *Kaliyug* will last for one thousand divine years, or four hundred and thirty two thousand man years. When *Kaliyug* ends, the world will be destroyed, and *Satyug* will re-commence.

179

Kirtan	A Hindu song where a *mantra* or religious text is sung and the audience repeat this, over several times. A *Kirtan* is normally accompanied by Indian drums such as the *dholak*, and other percussion instruments.
Kiskadee	(*Pitangus Sulphuratus*) A beautiful native bird of Guyana with a strong yellow body, and black and white stripes on its head. It specialises in catching flies, and eats various fruits, including mangoes.
Koker	A Dutch built barrier which helps to control the flow of water into and out of canals.
Late cut	As in cricket. A stroke by a batsman, played after the ball or delivery passes on the off side, often after the line of the Cricket stumps.
LBW	As in cricket. Leg Before Wicket is one way by which a batsman could be dismissed, based on the judgement of the umpire.
Left arm spinner	As in cricket. A slow bowler who spins the ball away from the right-handed batsman, or into a left-handed batsman.
Mandir	Hindu place of worship.
Mauby	A local Guyanese drink made from mauby bark, some spices including cinnamon, and sweetened with sugar.
Mithai	A sweetmeat made with flour, margarine, baking powder, and spices including aniseed and cardamom. *Mithai* is also the Hindi word to describe all sweetmeats.
Monkey apple	(*Anona Glabra*) An edible fruit and medicinal plant. When the fruit is ripe it is yellow on the outside, with a soft pulp inside.
Mosque	A place of worship for Muslims.
Namaaz	An Islamic prayer which is normally set for five times each day. The five *Namaaz* are, *Fajr*, *Zuhr*, *Asr*, *Maghrib*, and *Ishaa*.
Nasheed	An Islamic song usually only accompanied by the *daf* hand held drum.
No ball	As in cricket. A *ball* or delivery deemed to be illegal, and indicated so by an umpire during a cricket game. The team batting is given a run, and the bowler is required to bowl again until a legitimate ball is delivered during the *over*.
Obeah	A term used to refer to religious activities practised by descendents of West Africa, in Guyana and the Caribbean. It is used to ward off evil spirits possessing others.
Opening batsman	As in cricket. An opening batsman is one of two who start to bat at the top of an *inning*.
Out	As in cricket. A batsman is deemed to be *out* when dismissed according to the rules of cricket. A *run out* is one form of dismissal.
Over/s	As in cricket. An *over* is a set number of legal deliveries to be bowled before another bowler continues to bowl at the other end of the wicket.
Pass	To *pass* or *rap* in a game of Dominoes occurs when a player cannot match any of the ends of the dominoes played, with a ticket.
Payra	A sweet made of milk, syrup, and sugar.

Patwa	A small tropical fish, normally found in drains and trenches.
Peerha	A small wooden low level bench.
Pepperpot	A stewed meat dish cooked in *cassreep*.
Pine tart	A tart made with pineapple, sugar, cinnamon, and with a triangle shaped pastry.
Pookni gun	A crude, illegal, homemade hand gun made in Guyana.
Pork knocker	A Guyanese small time miner who digs for gold or diamonds. Knocking pork is the term the miners used to refer to pork meals in the mining towns.
Psydium	(*Flacourtia Indica*) The psydium looks like a berry or plum which is purple when ripe. The pulp is fleshy, sweet, and with a few seeds.
Pulauri	A fritter made with a seasoned split peas batter, and fried until golden brown. *Pulauri* is normally eaten with *Achaar*.
Qaseeda	An Arabic poem sung in praise of the Prophet Mohamad (Peace be unto Him), and the faith of Islam.
Qayaamat	The Day of Judgement in Islam.
Qurbani	An Urdu and Persian word meaning sacrifice. In Islam, a *Qurbani* is an act of sacrifice of cattle or sheep to symbolise the faith shown by Abraham who was prepared to sacrifice his son Ishmael, but was prevented to do so by God. *Eid-ul-Adha* commemorates this incident.
Ramadan	The act of fasting for about twenty eight days from the advent of the moon to the next new moon, during the Islamic month of Ramadan. The fasting concludes with the festival of *Eid-ul-Fitr*.
Ramayan	The *Ramayan* is an epic story of Lord Raam, by Valmiki. It was translated into Hindi by Sant Tulsidas. The *Ramayan* consists of twenty three thousand verses, in seven kands or books.
Rap	To *rap* or *pass* in a game of Dominoes occurs when a player cannot match any of the ends of the dominoes played, with a ticket.
Right handed batsman	As in cricket. A batsman who bats right-handed.
Roti	Indian flat bread.
Rum	Alcoholic drink made from sugar cane.
Run/s	As in cricket. A *run* is scored when a ball is bowled and the batsman hits it and runs from his end to the next, successfully crossing with the other batsman. A *run/s* can also be scored as a bye or byes, or awarded for a *no ball* or wide ball called by the umpire.
Run out	As in cricket. See *out*.
Saada roti	A Guyanese *roti* or flat bread which is thicker than other types of *roti* or *chapatti*.
Saki winki	Small sized monkey, of South America.
Salaara	A cake made of flour, yeast, shredded coconut, cinnamon, vanilla essence, sugar, and strawberry food colouring.
Sapodilla	(*Manilkara Zapota*) The fruit has a brown peel with sweet pale yellow or brown flesh and a few black seeds. It is known in India as *chikoo*.

Scotch bonnet   (*Capsicum Chinense*) A very hot chilli pepper which ranges in colour from green to yellow to red. It is commonly used as a pepper sauce or in cooking.

Sewa   A selfless service to the community, by Hindus.

Sharia/Sharia law   Sharia is an Arabic word for the moral and religious laws of Islam.

Shiite/Sunni   Shiite Islam is a sect which contends that Ali, the son-in-law of Prophet Mohamad (Peace be unto Him), was his rightful successor as the leader of Islam. The Shias or Shiites are the second largest denomination of Islam. Sunni is the traditional and largest group of Muslims, and make up about 90 per cent of Muslims.

Single   As in cricket. A *run*.

Six/Sixes   As in cricket. See *Four/s*.

Slingshot   A hand held catapult made of rubber bands secured to a fork shaped wooden frame. The base is normally made of leather attached to the two pieces of rubber. The *slingshot* is fired by placing a *gola* in the base, pulling the rubbers firmly, taking aim through the fork, and releasing.

Slip/s   As in cricket. A position in the field where the fielder is normally behind the wicket where the batsman has taken guard.

Souped up   A specially modified bicycle or car, to increase their appeal and performance.

Soursop   (*Annona Muricata*) A large, spiny, green tropical fruit with a sweet pulse. The pulse is used to make beverages.

Spin bowling   As in cricket. Slow bowling which is used to turn or spin the ball away or into a batsman.

Star apple   (*Chrysophyllum Cainito*) A tropical fruit which looks like an apple and has maroon and white flesh. When cut across, the flesh and seeds appear to be in the shape of a star, hence the common name.

Strokemaker   As in cricket. A batsman with the ability to play his strokes in a stylish manner, and aggressively scoring runs at a fast rate.

Stumps   As in cricket. One of three sticks making up the wicket. Two bails are placed in grooves of the three stumps to complete the wicket.

Sugar cakes   A sweet made of coconut, cinnamon or vanilla essence, and sugar.

Sumatoo   A tropical fruit that grows on vines. It is normally yellow when ripe and contains a white pulp with small seeds.

Tanya bush   A plant which grows wildly in drains and trenches in Guyana.

Tassa   A small Indian kettle drum usually played with two sticks, and hung from the neck. The *Tassa* is normally accompanied by the large *Dhol*.

Test Match   As in cricket. A game of cricket played between two recognised "Test" playing countries, and expected to last five days. The West Indies is considered to be a Test cricket team comprising representatives from Guyana and a number of Islands of the Caribbean, including, Barbados, Jamaica, Trinidad and Tobago, the Windward, and the Leeward Islands. The other

	Test cricket playing teams are, Australia, Bangladesh, England, India, New Zealand, Pakistan, South Africa, Sri Lanka, and Zimbabwe. A *Test Series* is a number of Test Matches agreed to be played by two teams, and are normally two, three, four or five consecutive games.
Tie/Tied Test	As in cricket. A *Tie or Tied Test Match* occurs when a game is ended and both teams have totalled the same aggregate scores over two innings.
Trup Chaal	A Guyanese card game for four players, where the first player dealt with five cards decides which suite will be the trump cards. The remaining cards of the pack are then dealt out evenly to the players. The player calling the trump card must start the game. It is won by the player who claims the most hands.
Umpire	As in cricket. An *Umpire* is one of two who takes decisions on the field of play. Most decisions tend to be made at the bowler's end, and sometimes the umpires consult on some decisions. Modern cricket now has a *Third Umpire* positioned off the field of play, and who is consulted on specific decisions.
Upanishads	The *Upanishads* are a collection of texts in the Sanskrit language. There are more than two hundred *Upanishads* which are associated with knowledge about several subjects including Shaktism, Sanyasa, Vaishnaism and Yoga.
Wai Wai	The name of one of the nine Amerindian tribes of Guyana. They are very skilled at weaving, and very sociable people. The other tribes are, the Macushis, the Patomonas, the Arawaks, the Caribs, the Wapishana, the Arecunas, the Akawaios, and the Warraus. The Ministry of Amerindian Affairs is an integral part of the Guyana Government.
Whitee	A tropical fruit which has white flesh contained within separate pods.
Wicket	As in cricket. The *wicket* is a set of three stumps with two bails placed in grooves at the top. There are normally two sets of *wickets* twenty two yards directly opposite on a cricket pitch.
Wicket keeper	As in cricket. This is a specialist position on the field. The *wicket keeper* normally wears protective gear including pads, helmet and gloves. The main task of the *wicket keeper* is to catch any deliveries which pass the batsman, and thus avoid conceding extra runs.
Wild cane	(*Gynerium Sagittarium*) A tall, tough cane shrub. It is used by Amerindians for making arrows.
Wiri wiri	(*Capsicum Frutescens*) A small round pepper which turns from green, to orange, and red when mature.
Yajna	Hindu prayers led by one or more Pandits, normally over a three day period.
Yam	(*Dioscorea Alata*) A ground provision which may look like, but is not a sweet potato. It is almost white or pale yellow in colour.
Yellow plantain	(*Icterus Nigrogularis*) The name given to a yellow oriole bird.
Yogi	A practitioner of yoga, the Indian practice of meditation.
Zakaat	Annual obligation for Muslims to offer a proportion of their wealth for the benefit of those in need.

A Chronology of Guyana's History

(Courtesy of Hansib Publications)

Unknown	Origin of the Amerindian Peoples of Guyana.
1498	Christopher Columbus, on his third voyage from Spain, lands on the South Coast of Trinidad, in the Caribbean, on the 31st of July 1498. He explores parts of the Orinoco River of Venezuela, which is west of Guyana on the mainland of South America.
1499	Alonso de Ojeda and Juan de la Cosa of Spain, reach the Essequibo River in Guyana, and then travel onwards to Venezuela, Trinidad, and Tobago.
1595	Sir Walter Raleigh, the English explorer and historian, completes his first voyage in search of the legendary El Dorado, the City of Gold, believed to be in Guyana.
1596	Sir Walter Raleigh's book, "The Discoverie of the Large, Rich and Bewtiful Empyre of Guiana", leads to the search by other Europeans for the mythical El Dorado.
1616	The Dutch establish a settlement about ten miles up the Essequibo River.
1617	Sir Walter Raleigh makes his second voyage to Guyana, and fails to find the elusive El Dorado.
1621	The Dutch West India Company takes control over the Essequibo settlement, and imports African slaves to work on the tobacco plantation.
1627	The Dutch West India Company establishes a Colony up the Berbice River.
1664	The first sugar mill is established in Essequibo.
1671	Abary River becomes the agreed boundary between the two existing Dutch Colonies of Berbice and Essequibo.
1689	French privateers attack the Dutch settlement in Berbice.
1708	French privateers plunder the Dutch settlement in Essequibo.
1741	The Dutch settle in Demerara.
1743	The Capital of Essequibo is moved from Kyk-over-al to Fort Island.
1746	English immigrants are encouraged to Demerara, by the Dutch.
1753	Borselen Island, about 15 miles up Demerara River, is made the Capital of Demerara.
1763	Kofi leads the African Slave Rebellion in Berbice. The 23rd of February becomes the symbolic date and month chosen in 1970, for the Declaration of the Republic of Guyana.
1772	The African Slave Rebellion in Essequibo.
1775	The digging of Canal Number One, linking the Demerara River with the Essequibo River.

1781	The British capture Essequibo, Demerara and Berbice. The City of Georgetown, Demerara, is laid out by Governor Kingston. The Colonies change hands between the British, Dutch, and French several times up to 1814.
1814	The British occupy Guyana.
1815	The arrival of Mr J Booker, leads to the founding of the Booker Empire.
1834	African Slavery is abolished, and is followed by a system of Apprenticeship. On the 9th of August 1834, after a strike in Essequibo, Damon is hanged for the rebellion on gallows outside the Parliament Buildings in Georgetown.
1835	The arrival of Portuguese Indentured labourers from Madeira Island which is located in the Atlantic, and owned by Portugal.
1838	The end of Apprenticeships. The arrival of Indian Indentured labourers on the 5th of May 1838.
1839	The formation of the British Guiana Police Force.
1842	The formation of the British Guiana African Association.
1844	Queens College is founded.
1847	St Rose's High School is opened.
1848	The Demerara Railway is opened.
1853	The arrival of Chinese Indentured labourers from Macao.
1858	The Georgetown Cricket Club (GCC) is formed.
1869	The first Indian Indentured labourers' strike in Leonora.
1870	Kaiteur Falls is sighted by Mr C Barrington-Brown.
1872	The Devonshire Castle uprising by Indian Indentured labourers.
1881	The Stabroek Market, Georgetown, is opened.
1887	The Victoria Law Courts, Georgetown, is opened.
1889	Venezuela makes a claim for a significant part of Guyana.
1893	St George's Cathedral, Georgetown, the world's largest wooden building, is opened.
1903	The first Rice exports from Guyana.
1905	The Ruimveldt Riots by stevedores in Georgetown. Friday 1st of December became known as "Black Friday".
1909	The Public Library in Georgetown is opened.
1912	The Lusignan Strike by Indian workers.
1916	The formation of the British Guiana East Indian Association.
1917	The British Guiana Labour Union is established by Mr H N Critchlow, and led by Mr A A Thorne.
1931	The British Guiana Worker's League is established by Mr A A Thorne.
1938	The Man Power Citizens' Association (MPCA), led by Mr A M Edun, is formed.
1946	The Women's Political and Economic Organisation is formed.
1947	The Labour Party, led by Dr J B Singh, wins six of the fourteen seats at the General Election, but support declines rapidly.
1948	The Enmore Sugar Workers' Riots.
1950	The People's Progressive Party (PPP) is founded by Dr C Jagan as leader, and Mr L F S Burnham, as Chairman.
1952	The Georgetown Zoo is opened.

1953	The PPP wins the General Election and Dr Jagan becomes the Chief Minister. Britain suspends the Guyana Constitution, and the PPP is ousted after 133 days in Government.
1955	The PPP is split into two factions; one led by Dr Jagan (PPP-Jagan), and the other by Mr Burnham (PPP-Burnham).
1957	The PPP-Jagan wins the General Election. Mr Burnham forms the People's National Congress (PNC).
1960	The United Force Party (UF), led by Mr P D'Aguiar, is formed.
1961	The PPP wins the General Election, and Dr Jagan becomes Premier.
1962	Friday 16th of February, known as "Black Friday" Riots in Georgetown in protest against the PPP Government.
1964	Racial Disturbance between people of African and Indian origins. Between the 4th of March and 29th of August, 189 people are killed, and 15,000 displaced.
1964	The Leonora Sugar Estate Workers' Strike, in which Kowsilla also known as Alice, is killed on the 6th of March.
1964	A Coalition Government of the PNC and UF Parties is formed on the 23rd of December, with Mr Burnham as Chief Minister.
1966	Guyana becomes Independent on the 26th of May, with Mr Burnham as Prime Minister.
1968	The PNC wins the General Election.
1969	The Rupununi Rebellion led by white settlers, and Amerindians, is put down by Guyana's Army.
1970	Guyana becomes a Cooperative Republic within the Commonwealth, and with Mr R A Chung as the first President.
1974	The formation of the Working People's Alliance (WPA) Party, led by Dr Walter Rodney.
1978	The "Jonestown Massacre", when 913 members of the People's Temple led by the Reverend Jim Jones from the USA, committed mass suicide on a settlement in the hinterland.
1980	A new Constitution is adopted, and Mr Burnham becomes the Executive President. Dr Rodney is killed on the 13th of June.
1985	Mr Burnham dies on the 6th of August, and Mr D Hoyte becomes president.
1987	The Guyana Prize for Literature is established.
1992	The PPP/Civic wins the General Election, and Dr Jagan becomes President.
1997	Dr Jagan dies on the 6th of March, and Mr S Hinds becomes President. After the General Election, Mrs J Jagan, the widow of Dr Jagan, becomes the first female President.
1998	A State of Emergency is declared.
1999	Mrs Jagan resigns as President due to ill health, and Mr B Jagdeo becomes President aged 35, and the world's youngest Head of State at the time.
2000	Guyana's neighbour Surinam evicts an Oil Exploration rig in an area of dispute between the two countries.
2001	The PPP/Civic wins the General Election, and Mr Jagdeo returns as President.
2002	Mr D Hoyte, leader of the PNC, dies on the 22nd of December, and Mr R Corbin becomes leader of the PNC, and Opposition PNC/R.

2003	Mr P Reid, former Prime Minister (1980 to 1984) dies. Mrs V Burnham, widow of the Late Mr Burnham, and the former Vice President and Deputy Prime Minister (1985 to 1991), dies.
2005	During January and February, Guyana experiences its worst natural disaster, with a third of the population affected by devastating floods.
2006	The PPP wins the General Election, and Mr Jagdeo is re-elected President.
2009	Mrs Jagan former President, dies.
2011	The PPP won the single largest number of seats at the General Election, and Mr D Ramotar is elected President. However, the Government was one seat short of a parliamentary majority.
2014	President Ramotar suspends Parliament and a General Election is expected for the 11th May 2015.